THE SURRENDER

Run, escape, urged Kaia's mind. Stay, surrender, countered her body.

There was no time to debate the matter, even if she had had the presence of mind to do so, because Eben chose that moment to spring forward, wrap his arms around her, and bear down into the soft sand.

For a breathless moment they simply stared at one another, tip of nose to tip of nose, and then slowly, very slowly, his mouth settled on hers and took possession.

Other *Love Spell* books by Jennie Klassel:
SHE WHO LAUGHS LAST

GIRL on the RUN

JENNIE KLASSEL

LOVE SPELL NEW YORK CITY

For Ellen Chvany and Posie Dauphine:
good friends and true.

LOVE SPELL ®

June 2004

Published by

Dorchester Publishing Co., Inc.
200 Madison Avenue
New York, NY 10016

ISBN 0-505-52596-8

The name "Leisure Books" and the stylized "L" with design are trademarks of Dorchester Publishing Co., Inc.

Printed in the United States of America.

Visit us on the web at www.dorchesterpub.com.

Prologue

"Will you mawy me?"

"Of course not. You're three years old."

"Oh. Will you mawy me when we gwow up?"

"I'm already grown up," Eben Dhion reminded her. "I'm fourteen."

Kaia Kurinon twisted a blond curl around a grubby finger as she considered this complication.

"You could wait for me. I'll twy to gwow up fast."

Eben watched the other squires head down the hill toward the practice ground. Kaia had a firm hold on the hem of his tunic. Anxious to end the ridiculous conversation and join his friends, Eben tweaked her nose.

"All right. This is what we'll do. You grow up fast, and I'll wait and I'll marry you."

"Pwomise?"

"I promise, little one."

1

Kaia watched him race after his friends and disappear through the gate that led to the outer bailey. She whirled around and skipped toward the great hall of the Ninth House, hopped up the wide stone steps one at time, and danced a wiggly dance when she reached the top.

All was right with Kaia Kurinon's world. Eben had promised to marry her. Now all she had to do was find a way to grow up fast, or he might forget.

She wasn't ever going to let him forget.

After all, a promise was a promise.

Chapter One

Clearly, Mother Superior had come to the end of her tether. With grim countenance she marched eighteen-year-old Lady Kaia across the scrupulously tended flower garden that separated the refectory from the ancient church that served the Sisters of Valiant Virtue. She deposited her upon the prie-dieu before the altar of the Lady Chapel, there to contemplate her many transgressions and receive what measure of grace and forgiveness the Blessed Virgin might obtain for her from the Good Lord.

An optimistic and kindly shepherdess to the neophytes placed in her care by the nobility of the Dominion, Mother had done her very best by Lady Kaia. Doggedly determined, she had dedicated herself to redirect and calm the headstrong nature of the girl which had caused her father to ship her off to the convent in the first place. But now, after four months of stress so unholy that Mother was seriously considering retiring to a hermit's cell, not even the generous endowment Lord Kurinon had settled on the convent, nor the fact that Lady Kaia was first cousin to King Jibril himself, not even that she had grown quite fond of the bright, engaging young woman, was sufficient to bolster Mother's flagging spirits. Kaia's mischievous ways were just too disruptive to the contemplative life of the community, and Mother had regretfully concluded that Kaia must return to her father. To that end, a message would be sent to Lord Kurinon on the morrow suggesting he retrieve the girl at his earliest convenience.

Mother suspected that Lord Kurinon would not take the news well.

Kaia continued to kneel, ostensibly in prayer, as Mother glided about, a graceful shadow in the dim confines of the church, arranging fragrant white roses in an urn here, replacing a sputtering candle there. Finally Mother murmured a few heartfelt Hail Marys herself before softly closing the heavy wooden door behind her.

That Mother Superior had not delivered her usual homily on obedience, humility, and respect for senior members of the community of the Sisters of Valiant Virtue did not bode well. Kaia suspected that yet another night in the chapel would not be the end of it.

This evening's misdemeanor, though not as serious as the mysterious disappearance of the hard-pressed pads of sphagnum moss used by the nuns for their monthly courses, had sent Sister Lazarus—normally a dour, phlegmatic sort of person—shrieking into the night when presented with an apple which Kaia had suggested might be possessed by demons.

It was the old beetle-in-the-apple trick, quite simple really: Cut away a chunk of apple, hollow out core, insert beetle—the uglier the better—replace missing chunk, and find your victim. If everything had gone according to plan, the apple would have jiggled about a bit on the table, propelled by the frantic efforts of the beetle to find a way out. The apple would then have been pronounced possessed, and the demons exorcised.

Kaia had never seen the exorcism of an apple—or a human being, for that matter—and had been looking forward to witnessing one firsthand. In the event, however, Sister Lazarus had dismissed Kaia's suggestion as superstitious nonsense and had taken a healthy bite of the enticing fruit.

Apparently Sister Lazarus did not care for beetle.

"She wasn't supposed to eat it, the gluttonous old bat," Kaia explained to the serene visage of the Virgin.

It was a poor defense at best; more so because it was only the latest in a string of pranks—some innocent, some less so—which had begun within a few days of her arrival at the convent. The relief and novelty of being well away from her father and his bullying had given way to the reality of the deadly dull existence of day-to-day life amongst the valiantly virtuous.

"But I am sorry about the poor beetle. I like beetles; there are so many different kinds, some so pretty, all shiny bronze and green and blue and black. Not as much as I like bees, of course," she confided to the Queen of Heaven, who seemed disposed to hear her out.

"I never thought much about bees before I came to the abbey. Papa would never let me help old Crisp with the hives. 'Not fit employment for a lady of the Second House,'" she parroted in her father's bombastic tones. "You'd think being cousin to the king made me unfit for anything other than being cousin to the king."

Kaia's introduction to the interesting world of bees had been at the behest of Mother Superior, who, after casting about for suitable work for her spirited young charge, had hit upon the idea of apprenticing her to Sister Euphemia, the abbey's enthusiastic beekeeper.

"If we study the bee, we come to recognize those virtues the Good Lord encourages us to nurture in ourselves," Sister Euphemia had instructed Kaia. "The hive is a shining example of domestic order, good housekeeping, and loving nurture of the young. If we wish to appreciate obedience and good cheer, we have but to follow the swarm as the queen leads her loyal subjects in search of a new home."

Kaia forbore to point out to the well-meaning sister that she entertained no such wishes. What Kaia wished—and what her father forbade her, thereby sparking resentment and rebellion—was to learn to read. Wished with all her heart.

"Nonsense," Lord Kurinon had brayed. "What need have you of learning? A man does not want learning in a wife."

There it was, the crux of the matter if her father was to be believed: A man did not want learning in a wife. Certainly her father had not, gifting—if such it could be called—her mother with eleven children, five of whom died in infancy. Kaia was the youngest of the six girls who survived, and a sore trial to her father. Not only because she was yet another female to get off his hands, but because Lady Kurinon, having again failed to produce the desired son and seeing the determined look on her husband's face that boded another stint on the birthing stool, had opted for the embrace of her God rather than that of her husband.

"Shining example, my foot," huffed Kaia as she dutifully made the sign of the cross and wandered away from the Lady Chapel into the stillness of the high, dark nave. The bit of information that Sister Euphemia had conveniently omitted was that a queen bee was an adulteress through and through, who led the males on a merry chase through the skies, then abandoned them to disappointment and, ultimately, starvation. An adulteress *and* a murderess. Hah!

As the hours of the night deepened, Kaia took to wandering a vague circuit up and down the aisles, through the choir, behind the altar, then up the worn steps to the gallery and back down. She traced inscribed letters on memorial plaques and stone slabs with finger and toe, proud that at least she knew some of her letters, which her friend Morgana Dhion had taught her.

Kaia finally came to rest upon the padded bench provided for the comfort of elderly nuns who could no longer kneel at prayer on the stone floor. She arranged herself on her back and stared up at three adoring marble cherubs who perched upon the capital of a nearby column. Why, she wondered, did they fly about without their clothes on, whereas older angels were always garbed in ample robes that concealed their more intimate attributes? Did they even *have* intimate attributes? If so, what purpose could they possibly serve? Angels didn't . . . couldn't . . . wouldn't be allowed to . . . would they?

Kaia giggled. Imagine the Archangel Gabriel delivering the good news to Mary with his shaft dangling about!

That got her to thinking about the beautiful stained-glass window in the south transept that depicted a disturbingly virile angel Gabriel doing just that; modestly attired, of course, in flowing scarlet garb, his wings flames of cerulean blue and gold, but with an unmistakable bulge.

Unbidden there arose unpleasant memories of the many suitors, from the spotty of face to the wrinkled gray, who had come to her father's hall, not to kneel at her feet but to look her over like a prize mare. In vain had Kaia awaited the appearance of the one man in the world she would cheerfully sell her soul for: Lord Eben Dhion, armiger of the Ninth House.

Eben Dhion, Eben Dhion . . . Every girl in the Dominion fantasized, dreamed, and drooled over the Golden One, that beautiful man with his long, dark hair gleaming with strands of dark gold and palest amber, and that splendid body and impossible teasing ways.

Kaia had known Eben from the time she could barely reach his knee. For close to sixteen years Morgana's brother had been her brother too: vexing at times, as a brother was wont to be; gentle at others when soothing her little hurts and humiliations; impish as he charmed her out of sulks and snits. As the years passed, they had become competitors of sorts, each vying to outwit the other with ever more devious pranks and outrageous tales. Kaia would find her silk shifts flying from the battlements; Eben would awaken with his nightshirt sewed to his bed linens. He would find a bewildered frog in his soup; she would discover worms wriggling in her bath.

Eben was forever rescuing Kaia from her reckless impulses. He had plucked her from a lily pond on his estate when she took it into her head to see if she could sit on a lily pad like the little frogs did. It had not occurred to her at age five that one must learn to swim if one was to venture into water above one's knees. There had been that incident when she and Morgana, ages eight and six respectively, had set out to explore the long tunnel that connected the great house to the riverbank a quarter mile distant. They had clung to one another in terror for more than four hours—their candle having sputtered out about halfway along—before their absence was discovered and Eben came in search of them. He had rescued her from the tops of trees, the back of a runaway pony, and the bottom of a dry well.

When she was younger, Kaia would never admit that she rather enjoyed being rescued. She always stormed off in a snit after he had roundly chastised her for her recklessness and for dragging Morgana along with her. Nor was she aware that somewhere around her twelfth year her escapades were designed to attract his particular attention; being rescued by anyone else was not at all the same. The mouse incident had been one such occasion, and after that fateful day, Kaia Kurinon would never again think of Eben Dhion as a brother.

"Come up from there at once. If you fall, I'm going to kill you."

"If I fall," Kaia shouted up at Eben, *"you won't have to."* Sixty feet ought to take care of it nicely, she thought.

"Whatever are you doing down there, Kaia? What can you possibly be thinking?"

9

"Mouse," she shouted.

"Of course, a mouse. It would be," Eben muttered. "Don't move, not a muscle, Kaia." He started shouting orders for guards to bring a rope and a pulley; spread hay, mattresses, anything soft at the base of the wall.

The brown baby mouse in question, whose first venture into the big world beyond the nest under the stairs had dropped him a good seven or eight feet down onto a narrow ledge, burrowed deeper into the folds of Kaia's blue gown.

"You have only yourself to blame," Kaia informed it. "I trust you've learned a valuable lesson this morn."

It occurred to Kaia that she was about to learn one too. Eben would see to it. He'd not lay a hand on her, she knew, but her ears were going to be ringing when he was finished with her. "Always leaping before you look," she could hear him say.

Too true, she reflected. Particularly in the present circumstance. But what else could she have done? The piteous little squeaks had been heart-rending, and when she peered over the parapet and saw that quivering little form on the ledge, she had not thought twice about going after it.

She shaded her eyes as she peered up at Eben's furious visage. "I'm going to have myself lowered down," he told her. "I'll tie you against me and they'll haul us up. And then we're going to have a little talk, you and I."

Kaia didn't like the sound of that at all.

"But, Eben, what about the mouse?"

"Drop it."

"I most certainly will not."

"Put it in your pocket. God's teeth, Kaia, it's a goddamn mouse."

"What if it falls out?"

Eben visibly held on to his patience by the slimmest thread. "Then we'll scrape it up and give it to the cats."

Kaia could not believe her ears. "How can you even think of such a thing, Eben Dhion?"

"I can think of a lot worse things right now, Kaia," he said through clenched teeth. "Now put the damn mouse in your pocket or I'll kick it clear to the village when I get you back up here."

"You are not a nice person," Kaia informed him.

"You will excuse me if I am not offended, my lady," Eben snarled, "but there is somewhat of a crisis going on here and I haven't the time."

"Sorry, mousie," Kaia said as she tucked it in the pocket of her apron. "He's an ill-tempered old fart."

She watched as a pair of rough brown leggings appeared above her, then strong thighs closely confined in soft leather, and then . . . well, right at eye level that inconvenient bulge that men must carry about with them. Men seemed to spend an inordinate amount of time worrying about their bulges. They bragged about them, or if they were not of sufficiently grand proportions, padded their hose to make them appear larger. They scratched at them and were continually moving them to the left or right. Kaia often wondered how men could manage at all, and was glad she had not been born with a bulge of her own.

"Put your legs around my waist, Kaia," Eben ordered when he reached the ledge.

"What?"

"Just do it. If we start swinging out of control, the rope's going to break."

Kaia glared at him. "I most certainly will not."

"Kaia," he warned.

11

"It would be indecent. People will see."

"Believe me," he said dryly, "people have already seen enough to entertain folks around their hearths for years to come. If you look down you will see that half the village is gathered below with an excellent view up your gown."

Kaia looked down at the village folk who were grinning up at her. She shrieked.

"Now will you do as I say?"

Kaia threw her arms around his neck and hung on for dear life as he lifted first one of her legs to his waist and then the other. He looped the end of the rope around both of them several times and tied three strong knots.

"Are you ready down there, my lord?" someone shouted.

"Ready. Now."

Kaia buried her face in Eben's neck. "Did you groan? Did I hurt you? Eben, I'm sorry; it's just that I'm so frightened and—"

Eben gritted his teeth. "No, you didn't hurt me. Just don't wiggle like that."

"Oh. Yes, I see." Or rather, she felt. The bulge, which was pressed precisely at the juncture of her thighs, was definitely larger—and warmer—than it had been a moment ago.

"Can't you control yourself?" she snapped. "We're dangling sixty feet in the air in front of hundreds of people. Just for once, can't you set your, um, proclivities aside?"

Eben growled. "And how do you come to know of my proclivities?"

"I just do. They're common knowledge. Let's not speak of it anymore."

"Oh, let's do," Eben contradicted. "It seems to be a topic of some interest to you."

"I assure you, it is not."

"*You brought it up,*" Eben reminded her.

"*Only because you're throbbing.*"

"*You're far too young to know of such things, lady brat.*"

Kaia glared at him. "*I most certainly am not. You may not have noticed, but I am twelve years old. I know things.*"

Eben grinned. "*Things? I should like to know what things you think you know.*"

"*Just things,*" Kaia said, nose in the air, "*of which a real lady does not speak.*"

"*I see,*" Eben replied gravely, only half hiding his smile. "*I apologize then, my lady, if I have offended you. I shall endeavor to shield you from the evidence of my proclivities in future.*"

But she hadn't been offended, Kaia thought as she settled herself more comfortably on the hard bench. Truth be told, she had been aroused for the first time in her life. That day up on the battlements, a girlish infatuation had flowered into womanly desire.

Eben had been twenty-three and armiger of his House for nearly six years. At the impossibly early age of seventeen it had been necessary for him to ascend to the High Seat of his House when his father lost his wits from a virulent fever of the brain. Eben never lost his mischievous ways entirely, but the careless youth and the insouciant brother gave way to the graver man.

He had never been the brother of her flesh, but he saw himself as such in spirit. Kaia knew he would never think to offer for her now. Eben Dhion the man would never see her as a woman to be desired, wed, bedded. Ever she would be the sister, little Kaia.

A few tears and many deep sighs later, Kaia drifted into

a delicious dream of Lord Eben Dhion kneeling at her feet vowing eternal devotion. Clothed. Alas.

Clickety-click, clickety-click.

Kaia's eyes popped open as the unexpected sound trailed down the north aisle close by her bench and faded around the back of the altar. Her first thought was that it must be the church cat, performing its holy office by keeping the sanctuary free of vermin. But the value of a cat lay in the silent stalk; it wouldn't be clacking about, forewarning the poor mousies of their imminent sacrificial fate.

A dog, then, long nails striking stone. What in the name of all that was holy was a dog doing in the church? And how had it gotten in?

Kaia crept after the noise, praying that a slavering beast wasn't about to leap out at her from the darkness, or worse still, deposit fleas upon her person. It was very dark behind the altar. There was no sign of the dog, but a narrow crack of light showed beneath the door to the modest chamber where visiting priests and monks were housed when they sought shelter in the convent from the rigors and dangers of the road.

The thick wooden door muffled the conversation between two men within. A deep, commanding voice carried the greater part of the discourse, accompanied by a litany of "Saints preserve us!" and "Surely you don't mean?" and "Upon my word!"

Kaia's disappointment at not finding the elusive dog was banished by a raging curiosity as to what was transpiring in the priest's room. Hardly daring to breathe, she pressed her ear to the door.

It took but a few moments for Lady Kaia Kurinon's world to change forever.

Clickety-click, clickety-click.

Kaia squeezed her eyes shut and feigned sleep as best she could after rushing down the aisle and throwing herself upon the bench. Wherever the dog had gone, it was back. Perhaps it had been in the room behind the altar all the time Kaia's ear was glued to the door. When the door opened unexpectedly, she only just managed to avoid being caught in the act by scampering behind a silk arras and sprinting through the choir.

A cool, wet nose snuffling against her cheek, the lap of a rough tongue upon her nose, doggy breath—Kaia could not help herself; she peeked out through thick lashes into eyes as black as her own. A huge hound regarded her with an air of polite interest and canine aplomb.

"Nice doggie, good old doggie," Kaia soothed in case the beast was not the friendly sort. "Did Mother exile you too? You didn't relieve yourself in the garden, did you?"

If it had, the hound was not about to own up to it. As it seemed a nice enough dog she sat up and gave it a tentative pat. It nuzzled her hand, demanding more attention, then sat at blissful ease as Kaia toyed with its velvet ears.

"Come, I'll let you out. At least one of us should be free tonight." She led the way to the low door that opened onto the garden. The dog bounded out into the soft night air, then wheeled about and trotted back.

"Thank you, my dear."

"My pleasure, dog."

It was not until she was back on her bench examining

the night's astounding revelations that it occurred to Kaia that she had distinctly heard a dog speak to her. And smile. Yes, the dog had most definitely thrown her a mischievous grin as it melted into the shadows. Under any other circumstances, the realization would have been astonishing enough, but Kaia had even greater marvels to contemplate.

Somewhere, far beyond the Western Isles, in a world that existed impossibly far in the future, all girls were taught to read and write. They were encouraged to explore the world beyond the women's solar, the nursery, and the prison walls of a father's or husband's keep. In another time and place a girl could marry the man of her choice, and keep bees if she wanted to. Somewhere, sometime, a girl could realize the innermost desires of her heart if only she dared fly high enough and far enough to find them.

Lady Kaia Kurinon intended to be that girl.

Chapter Two

"Right off the bake-house roof, if you can believe it. The foolish girl got it into her head she could fly. Fly, I tell you. She landed smack on my squire, broke his arm when he tried to catch her. The poor lad was never the same with a sword again." Lord Kurinon's voice skated from sanctimonious outrage to self-pitying whine. "I do not know what the world is coming to, Jibril. In my day women knew their place."

16

Apparently, five cups of rare Gascony wine had not been sufficient to assuage Lord Kurinon's indignation when the order and peace of his world had been disturbed. He tossed the empty cup to an alert servant and snatched a full one from the boy's ready hand.

"She wanted to learn to read. Heaven preserve us," he declared, throwing wide his arms and splashing wine over the delicate carpet of ivory silk figured with scarlet and golden carp. King Jibril winced. He was particularly fond of that carpet. It had made the journey from Cathay over towering peaks, trackless deserts, and roiling seas, only now to be abused like sodden rushes in the meanest hall as his infuriated uncle strode back and forth across Jibril's solar.

"I have five other daughters—five, God help me—and did any one of them ever want to read? Of course they did not," Lord Kurinon assured the world. "They're good girls, well married, content with their lot in life. I have heard nary a word of complaint from them in all their days. Kaia's mother, God bless her soul, hadn't a thought in her pretty head, but she was a good breeder, I will say that for her. Kaia has been nothing but trouble from the start. Killed her poor mother in the birthing . . . wild . . . always up to mischief, concocting all manner of foolish tales. Pestering me day and night with questions, questions, questions."

Spent for the moment, Lord Kurinon flung himself into a chair, tipped his cup, found it empty, and demanded another.

King Jibril took the opportunity to regain control of the interview, which by rights should have been his from the moment his uncle stormed into the palace to report that

Lady Kaia Kurinon had run away from the convent of the Sisters of Valiant Virtue with, his uncle repeated over and over, *a man of the cloth*. Jibril had allowed his uncle a certain amount of latitude, as befitted a member of the royal family, but enough was enough.

"Calm yourself, Uncle," he said in a tone that hinted his uncle had better do as bidden or else. "There is nothing to be achieved if we lose our heads. Kaia is impulsive, yes, but I expect she has realized her error and is even now safely back in the convent."

Jibril had always known that his young cousin Kaia was cut from a different cloth than her older sisters; different from most women Jibril knew, for that matter. Excepting Syrah, his beloved wife and queen, who fourteen years earlier had kidnapped, imprisoned, and sold him back to his father like a bull in the marketplace. Now, there was a woman cut from a different cloth.

Syrah was not a woman to run away from her problems. If anything, she was all too ready to seize the sword to vanquish them. Kaia might be different, but Jibril rather thought not. His cousin might not be inclined to face up to her problems—who could blame her, given the sheer stupidity and intractability of her father?—but she would run toward something, not simply throw up her hands and abandon the field.

Jibril moved around to perch on the front of his desk and surveyed the small group gathered in his solar to address the emergency the disappearance of the Lady Kaia had occasioned. Prince Obike Zebengo, Jibril's adopted brother and chief of the Dominion's security, leaned his solid bulk against the mantel and regarded Lord Kurinon with ill-concealed distaste. Kalan Ankuli, Jibril's childhood friend and now commander of the kingdom's land forces, lounged nearby. Orini, Jibril's personal aide and captain of the royal guard, had remained by the door as was his deferential custom. Queen Syrah had been delayed, having to sort out some matter pertaining to the princess royal. Her brother, Lord Eben Dhion, had been summoned and was due to arrive at any minute.

"Let us review the situation together," Jibril began, using the exact phrase favored by his late father when working through a difficult problem. "Kaia was last seen in the church two days past, having been confined there by the Mother Superior for some mischief involving, if I understand it aright, a beetle."

"A beetle, I ashk you," Lord Kurinon growled to his wine.

"A Brother Absalom, on his way to face his bishop over some transgression of his own, was resident at the convent at the time of Kaia's disappearance."

"Transhgreshon."

"The following evening, both Kaia and Brother Absalom were nowhere to be found."

Lord Kurinon half rose from his chair. "Wanton!" he shouted.

Jibril held up a hand. "Now, Uncle, it does not necessarily follow that they left the convent together; merely that each disappeared on the same day. Brother Absalom may have continued on his way, while Kaia—"

"Abshalom will pay for this," Lord Kurinon vowed. "If he thought shelibashy a high prish to pay for his vocashon, wait until he finds his shaft shtuffed down his throat and his ballocksh—"

19

"I believe there was some talk of a strange dog about the place," Jibril interrupted hastily as a servant opened the door wide to admit a very pregnant Queen Syrah. She waddled across the room to a comfortably furnished chair that Jibril held for her, and plopped down with a sigh.

She smiled up at her husband. "Who is stuffing what down whose throat?" she inquired.

Jibril fixed Lord Kurinon with a kingly glare. "We have finished with that particular topic, have we not, Uncle?"

Lord Kurinon subsided into his chair with a barking belch.

"We were discussing a strange black hound seen around the convent grounds about the time Kaia disappeared, my dear, although I cannot think what that has to do with anything," the king continued. "Since we know little, save that both Kaia and Brother Absalom are missing, we must set aside for the moment trying to reason out why they disappeared, and concentrate instead on where they are now, either singly or together. We must initiate an exhaustive search. Obike, you will use your, er, unusual contacts to discover what gossip there may be in the taverns. Kalan, you will direct the search. Orini, you will accompany Lord Kurinon back to his hall to await Kaia's return, should she be headed that way."

Lord Kurinon surged out of his chair. "The devil you shay," he snarled, quite forgetting that although Jibril was his nephew, he was also his king. "I'm going after the ungrateful wretch, and when I find her I'll beat her until she cries mershy. Thish time I'll see that she learns her place once and for all."

An uncomfortable silence settled on the room.

Jibril studied his uncle for a long minute. "You have beaten Kaia?"

"Well, of coursh I've beaten her, Jibril. How elsh to deal with a woman who dishobeys her lord and mashter? Women understand a good beating—"

"Do . . . we . . . indeed?" Syrah had managed to gain her feet and was lumbering toward Lord Kurinon with the obvious intent of doing some serious bodily harm herself.

Jibril moved to head off a bloody massacre on his beautiful silk carpet. "Now, Syrah my dear, what my uncle meant—"

Syrah smiled a thin smile; her eyes fixed on her prey. "Oh, I know what he meant, Jibril, but I would know his reasoning better. Would you care to elaborate, my lord?"

Lord Kurinon was not so far into his cups that he did not recognize an enraged lioness when he saw one, not to mention an enraged queen.

"I beg pardon, Your Majeshty. I mishshpoke. It'sh hard on a father . . . Kaia being my youngest and all, you unnershtand."

Lord Kurinon subsided into his chair and was heard from no more.

"Lord Eben is without the gate!" "Lord Eben is within the gate!" "Lord Eben has crossed the threshold!"

Squeal followed upon squeal, shriek upon shriek as every lady of the court within sprinting distance rushed to the great hall, craning their heads this way and that, hoping for a glimpse of the phenomenon known throughout the land as the Golden One. Cheeks were pinched for a becoming blush, lips bitten for a kissable aspect, bodices lowered, hair smoothed, breath freshened with pastilles of mint and sprigs of parsley. The rustle of silk and velvet swished through the upper corridors as pining widows, disappointed wives, and sighing virgins gathered in the musicians' gallery, elbowing one another as they jockeyed for the best vantage point.

Down below in the great hall, where they had no business at that time of day, a phalanx of female servants set to fussing and bustling. They polished plates that already gleamed like the noonday sun. They straightened perfectly hung tapestries. They peered beneath tables in search of nonexistent vermin.

"Uncle, Uncle!" The royal children, trailed by anxious nursemaids, clattered down the great staircase, screeched and skittered across the expanse of marble floor, and attached themselves to various parts of their grinning uncle's person.

"You're late, Uncle Eben," cried six-year-old Oriana. "It's ever so exciting. Great-uncle Kurinon is in such a state because Kaia is missing from the convent. A dog ate her."

"Don't be silly, Oriana," Crown Prince Akritos, a worldly twelve-year-old, scoffed. "She's been ravished! By a priest, Uncle!"

Eben cocked his head to consider this extraordinary piece of news. "No, that can't be right, Akritos. Priests are not permitted to ravish. I expect what happened was that the priest ate Lady Kaia. They say the food is terrible in the monasteries. All the poor monks get to eat are pickled dromedary skin, stewed goat's nose, and slimy green slugs—

22

and that's the special food they get on the Sabbath. Kaia must have looked pretty tasty to him."

Cries of "eeeuw" and "icky" echoed across the vast hall as Eben shook off sticky little hands, disentangled his left leg from the adoring clutches of a three-year-old nephew, and strode down the long hall toward the king's solar.

"That must be my brother," Syrah sighed as Eben entered the crowded room.

"Word is that Lady Kaia has been ravished by a dog and eaten by a priest," Eben announced in great good humor as a page shut the solar door directly in the face of a particularly persistent lady of the court. "A sad fate, but it could have been worse. The priest could have ravished the dog and Kaia been obliged to eat them both."

"Someday, Eben," the queen scolded, "the children are going to believe your preposterous stories."

Eben placed a quick kiss on Syrah's upturned nose. "Would you prefer, Sister, that I tell them the truth, which is often far more outrageous than any tale I can concoct?"

Lord Kurinon had leaped to his feet at Eben's entrance. Here, after all, was the man he had set his sights on for his youngest daughter: Lord Eben Dhion, who held the High Seat of the Ninth House with its many manors and vast, fertile acreage; who had the ear of the queen and carried far more influence than he himself could ever hope to wield with his royal nephew.

"Lord Eben," he managed without burping, quite as though they had chanced upon one another at some entertainment. "What a pleasant surprise," he enunciated with utmost care. "I hope you are quite well."

Forgetting for a moment that Kaia was herself missing, his diction started to slip as he assured Lord Eben that "Kaia will be sho shorry to have mished you."

"You appear to be remarkably calm under the circumstances, my lord," Eben observed. "A canine-ravished daughter consumed by a ravenous priest does not appear to weigh heavily upon you."

"Not ravished, no indeed, not ravished, a virgin still," Lord Kurinon babbled, seeing all his hopes for a union of the Second and Ninth Houses going to hell.

Syrah threw Eben a repressive look. "Really, Eben, that is quite enough."

"Yes, Eben," the king echoed, choking back his amusement, "quite enough." Taking his uncle by the arm—Lord Kurinon was now close to tears, whether from too much drink or the sure knowledge that Lord Eben wouldn't touch a deflowered daughter with a ten-foot tilting lance—Jibril led him to the door and bade a servant show His Lordship to a chamber where he might lie down and collect himself.

As Lord Kurinon stumbled away clutching the arm of the page, Alya, the dowager queen, sailed in.

"What is all this fuss about little Kaia?" Queen Alya inquired as Jibril moved forward to conduct her to a cushioned chair beside his wife. "The children tell me she ravished a priest and has gone missing.

"I cannot fathom," she continued as she made herself comfortable, "how an eighteen-year-old girl would go about ravishing a full-grown man. I suppose it is possible for a woman to fall upon a man when he least expects it. He must be ready, of course—men seem always to be ready, do they not?—but she would hardly be equipped to do so, if I have it aright. These days women get up to the strangest things, so perhaps they have invented some clever way to ravish. In our day we seduced, of course, but I expect that's just old-fashioned. I really must keep up."

Having delivered this short meditation, the queen looked about inquiringly at the shocked assembly. Commander Ankuli's complexion had taken on the hue of an overripe plum, while Captain Orini's veered more toward the persimmon. Obike Zebengo was examining his fingernails with singular interest. Queen Syrah was busy smoothing her voluminous sky-blue gown over her swollen belly, while Jibril had simply closed his eyes and was shaking his head in disbelief. Even Eben, who had elevated the outrageous to a fine art, was speechless in the face of this extraordinary train of thought by the dowager queen of the Dominion.

A trill of nervous giggles emanating from beyond the half-open doors to the king's private garden punctuated the awkward silence. Ever vigilant for the monarch's safety, Obike pushed away from the mantel, strode across the solar, and disappeared into the shrubbery.

"Let go, Obike. Ouch! That hurt," an outraged female voice yelped. "Put me down, you big lummox."

"Now, is that any way for a lady to talk?" Obike was heard to growl.

"I can say whatever I . . . Eeek! I'm sorry, I'm sorry." Evidently, the female in question had capitulated, as she was soon being propelled into the solar by a firm hand on her back.

"Someday I'm going to get you for that, Obike

Zebengo," sixteen-year-old Lady Morgana Dhion vowed. "See if I don't."

Syrah made known her displeasure at having found her young sister eavesdropping outside the king's solar. "I should have suspected. Morgana, you will go to your chamber at once. I will be up to deal with you later."

Morgana glared at her sister. "I have just as much a right to be here as you do. More," she added with a defiant tilt of her chin.

Jibril folded his arms across his chest. "And just why is that, Morgana?"

Morgana was not one to be easily cowed, but when Jibril became brother-in-law, father figure, and king all in one stern package, he was a force to be reckoned with.

She managed to stand her ground. "Kaia is my dearest friend. She is practically my sister. We're soul mates."

"Soul mates?" The very notion was bound to bewilder the king. In the world of the male of the species, a man had comrades-in-arms, peers, friends—in his case, subjects—but what a soul mate might be he couldn't imagine. He hoped the Lady Morgana was not alluding to the peculiar liaisons between women or between men that occasionally revealed themselves to the public gaze. Heaven only knew what train of thought Queen Alya would be moved to voice on that subject.

"We tell each other everything. She is the only one in the whole world who understands me. And now she's gone," Morgana wailed, and burst into tears.

Syrah immediately regretted her severity. It was true: Morgana and Kaia were as close as sisters. Morgana must be terrified for her friend. Syrah tried to rise to go to comfort her sister, but her ungainly bulk had her plunking back into her chair with a decidedly unqueenlike grunt.

Eben had already gathered Morgana in his arms, her teary moans and hiccups of distress muffled against the soft russet velvet of his tunic. "We'll find her, Morgana, never fear. All will be well, you'll see," he crooned, although he wasn't so sure himself that something dire had not befallen little Kaia.

"No, it won't," Morgana wailed. "She's gone away and she won't ever be able to come back."

Eben set his sister away from him but kept his hands on her shoulders. "What do you mean, 'won't be able'? You know something about her disappearance, don't you?"

"No. Yes. I can't tell you."

By this time Syrah had managed to leverage herself from her chair with the aid of Commander Ankuli's strong arm. "Morgana, sweet, as you love your friend, you must tell us what you know. She may have unknowingly put herself in danger. Your silence could add to her peril. Think you she would hesitate to break such a promise to you if she feared for your safety?"

Morgana shook her head. "I gave her my word, Syrah."

"Morgana," Jibril's stern voice cut in, "Lady Kaia is a member of the royal family. As such, her safety is a matter of grave concern to our country. Your failure to assist us in this matter could be construed as treason."

Eben scowled at the king. "Now, wait just a minute. You've no right . . ." His voice trailed off as it occurred to him that where kindness might not achieve the desired result, the stern word of the monarch would.

The king motioned to Morgana. "I would have a word

with you in private, Morgana." He ushered the sniffling, apprehensive girl into the garden.

"As your king," he said more kindly when they had walked on a little, "it is my duty to command you to tell me where Kaia is, but I give you my solemn vow not to reveal secrets between the two of you that do not bear on this matter."

Morgana searched his eyes for a moment, pulled a tear-stained letter from the pocket of her gown, and trembled as he scanned it.

Jibril's eyebrows shot up. "Has she gone mad?"

"I don't know," Morgana moaned. "I don't know what to think."

"I'm damned if I do, either."

The king's mouth was a thin, angry line as he led Morgana back into the solar. She ran across the room to curl up on the carpet beside Syrah's chair, where she laid her head upon her sister's knee in search of comforting caresses.

Jibril cleared his throat. "Morgana has given me a letter she received from Kaia. It is in the hand of this Brother Absalom, but the signature, awkward as it is, is most certainly Kaia's. We must conclude that it is genuine and not the work of some blackguard. It does not appear that Kaia has been kidnapped; she left the convent voluntarily. I have promised Morgana that I will read only those portions of the letter that are relevant to Kaia's disappearance." He looked over at Morgana. "I will keep that promise."

"Dearest Morgana, my true sister:
With heavy heart I write to tell you that I am going away
with Brother Absalom, who is kind enough to pen this

letter as Papa will not allow me to learn to read and write. He is a good man and will keep me safe, so you must not be afraid for me. Merlin—yes! Merlin, the great sorcerer himself—told Brother Absalom that there is a time far in the future when the world is full of miracles and people can do anything they want to do. Even girls! People can fly there, too, and you know how often I have imagined flying through the sky like a bird. Imagine, Morgana, girls can choose their own husbands! Only you know who I would marry if only he would ask Papa, but he never will because he won't see that I'm all grown up now. I shall never marry since I cannot have him."

Here Jibril paused, scanning ahead past girlish confidences that Morgana, not to mention Kaia herself, would not wish to share with present company.

"But here, dear friend, is the sad thing: We will be traveling eight hundred years into the future. If we go we can never come back. There is a magic spell that will take us there, but it only works going forward, not backward. In order for the spell to work, we must travel to the Western Isles and there find a circle of standing stones where magic spells may be cast. Forgive me for leaving you, but Papa will never relent, and I cannot continue to live in ignorance and darkness. Since the love of my life shall never be mine, I cannot bear to live in a world where he will marry another.

"Remember me and pray for me, Morgana, for I shall never forget you."

"Waaahhhh," wailed Lady Morgana.

"Good heavens!"

"What man?"

"Poor child."

"What *man?*"

"Women. Leave it to a woman to believe such . . ." That from Commander Ankuli, whose opinion about the intelligence of the fair sex was cut short by a dark look from Queen Syrah.

"What man?" Eben Dhion shouted.

This uncharacteristic outburst from a man who dwelt behind a carefully crafted, affable aspect startled the company into silence.

A small smile played about the king's mouth. He could not resist having a bit of fun at his brother-in-law's expense. "Why, she speaks of Brother Absalom, of course."

"Not that man," Eben gritted out. "This swine who has broken little Kaia's heart."

"Really, Eben," said the queen, "I do not believe this man's identity is germane to the present problem."

"The hell it isn't."

The king caught his wife's eye and waggled his eyebrows. Her eyes widened and her lips formed a silent "oh" as she took his meaning.

Jibril returned to the matter at hand. "I agree with Syrah. Our immediate task is to find Kaia. This notion that some magic spell will send her into the future is lunacy. We will deal with that when we come to it. At the moment she is upon the roads without proper escort and therefore at peril. If they think to sail to the Western Isles, they will likely travel toward Galiana where a merchant ship might be found to take them on. We cannot, under any circumstances, allow her to set sail. Admiral Arcos informs me that pirates have attacked a number of merchant ships of late. One of the men he captured confessed that Ranulph Gyp is behind these raids."

"Ranulph Gyp!" Syrah and Eben exclaimed together. Nothing had been heard of their duplicitous, licentious cousin for more than a decade. His attempt to seize the hall of the Ninth House and force Syrah into marriage had resulted in his permanent exile from the shores of the Dominion.

"We believe he has taken up where that damnable pirate, Najja Kek, left off," the king continued. "For every one of the bastards I hang, it seems that two spring up. Your cousin is far too craven to be in the business alone. I feel certain he must have an accomplice. The admiral is on his way to the capital to give me his full report."

Eben had gone very still. His hatred for the man who had tried to rape his sister and steal his patrimony had not dimmed over the years. Syrah had asked for mercy for their cousin in order to heal the rift between the Ninth and the Twenty-seventh Houses, and the late king had sent Ranulph into exile when Eben was only fifteen. The bastard lived, and Eben was glad of it. Eben was a man now, and once this business of Kaia was taken care of, he intended to settle the score with Ranulph Gyp once and for all.

Eben forced his attention back to Jibril.

"The road from the convent to Galiana runs along the south coast," the king was saying. "That is where we must concentrate our efforts. Orini, you will accompany my un-

31

cle to his hall and prevent him from going in search of her himself. I can't imagine that Kaia will return home to face another beating. When she is discovered, we will bring her here to live at the palace. Where the devil are you going?" he demanded.

Eben was halfway to the door with murder in his eye. "I'm going to teach Lord Kurinon a lesson he won't soon forget. That poor child, beaten by that—"

The king had no need to order Eben to desist, for the page had already scuttled aside from the doorway and in his place loomed the bulk of uncompromising muscle that was Obike Zebengo.

"Let me pass," Eben snarled.

Obike just grinned.

"Get back here," the king ordered.

Eben whirled and strode toward Morgana. "You knew of this, Sister? You knew that bastard beat her and did not tell me?"

Now Commander Ankuli moved to block Eben's path toward Morgana and the queen. No one who knew him would ever believe Eben Dhion would raise so much as a finger to harm either of his sisters, but his fury had Morgana shaking and even Syrah looking faintly alarmed.

"Sit down, Lord Dhion," roared the king in a commanding tone not to be ignored.

Eben threw himself onto a bench and raked his fingers through his hair. "I don't know what's come over me."

The king abandoned his casual perch on the edge of his desk and paced back and forth. "So, to recap, Orini will take my uncle to his hall. Obike, you will first escort Morgana home in the event Kaia comes to her senses and seeks sanctuary with her; then canvass the underworld for news and gossip. Kalan, organize a search network throughout the island; station men at all ports, market towns, and major intersections. Eben, you will begin at the convent. Interview the Mother Superior. Find their trail and follow it. They cannot have gone far in just two days.

"I cannot fathom what this Absalom person thinks he is doing dragging a member of the royal family off to heaven-knows-where. Perhaps he does not know who she is, but even so, he must be God's own fool."

Jibril signaled the end of the meeting. Eben stalked from the room and, heedless of the mooning looks and fluttering hearts he left in his wake, quit the palace in a dark mood indeed.

"I don't want that big lummox taking me anywhere," Morgana declared as she swept from the room, her little chin in the air. Obike followed close behind, grumbling that he would be happy to give her a good hiding along the way if she misbehaved.

Commander Ankuli escorted the dowager queen, who was heard ruminating, "It sounds rather delightful, doesn't it, this world Kaia is off to? A woman taking the husband of her choice: what a novel concept. I shall have to think on it. I don't expect the men like it very much, but then, men must always be in control, mustn't they? I don't think I would want to go myself; sea journeys do not agree with me. Merlin, imagine! I thought him a myth. What I cannot understand is the spell working only forward. I believe Merlin is said to live backward in time, which is his forward, of course. But then, if our forward is his backward and . . ."

The queen's cheerful voice echoed away down the hall, and the general hubbub occasioned by the exodus was silenced as the solar door closed behind the people. Jibril stood behind his wife's chair and began to knead her shoulders. She arched her neck this way and that like a cat directing a caressing hand.

"Mmmm," she purred as the king's hands slipped down over her swollen breasts to encompass the huge curve of the royal tummy. "It was Eben that Kaia spoke of, wasn't it?"

"The girl is smitten."

"Eben and Kaia. It would be a splendid match."

"I must admit I never thought of it," Jibril murmured into the crook of his wife's neck.

Syrah laughed. "Neither did he, I'll warrant. I believe my brother is about to discover that little Kaia isn't so little anymore."

Chapter Three

Eben's mood had not improved the following morning. It had taken the utmost self-restraint to sit through the morning meal without vaulting over the table and seizing the whining Lord Kurinon's scrawny neck between his hands and throttling him. Somehow Eben had maintained a pleasant demeanor, and only those who knew him well recognized the predatory look in his dark blue eyes.

As Eben departed the sumptuous chambers set aside for his use when he wished to stay at the palace, the ample, powdered, and scented bosoms of Lady Yagur sailed into view. Normally, Eben would have employed his legendary charm to send her on her way; she might have failed to achieve her objective but would have believed he thought her absolutely captivating. Today, however, he declined the ongoing offer of the pleasures of her bed with a curt suggestion that she return to her hall and allow her husband to avail himself of her singular talents before the old man went to his grave.

Lady Yagur was succeeded by a spotty maidservant beckoning him into a cramped closet, a lurking laundress, and the strapping twin daughters of Lord and Lady Brute, who described in graphic detail the ecstasy Lord Eben would find in their dual embrace. As he descended into the great hall, Eben plastered an intimidating scowl upon his brow to prevent more of the same, and managed to gain the stables without further flattery, entreaty, or outright solicitation.

Disgust with Lord Kurinon and the aggressive wiles of females in general soon led to a blossoming anger at this Mother Superior of the Sisters of Valiant Virtue for locking Kaia in a dank, dark church all night. Eben could only imagine how terrified the poor thing must have been. And what of that sour old nun who couldn't take an innocent jest? Eating one measly beetle was not the end of the world. Insects were said to be most nutritious.

Image after image of Kaia Kurinon marched through Eben's mind as he rode on toward the convent of the Sisters of Valiant Virtue.

At the stone marker six leagues from the city, four-year-old Kaia was darting about his legs with two-year-old Morgana in toddling, shrieking pursuit.

At the ten-league marker, he was hauling her kicking and scratching off a page who had made the mistake of telling her she was just a dumb girl.

At fifteen leagues, she was storming off in a snit because he had trounced her at draughts three games in a row.

At twenty-nine leagues, she was giggling madly in the shrubbery, having drunk far more wine than any sensible twelve-year-old could handle.

At forty-seven leagues, she was whirling in a spirited country dance, her long, pale hair flying about her flushed face, her gown a trailing pink flame twisting about her slender form.

As Eben brought his white Arabian gelding to a halt before the outer gate of the convent, a vision of the near future took shape in his mind: Kaia cursing him roundly as he turned the iron key in the lock of the topmost chamber of the east tower of his hall, where she would eat naught but worms and water for a month as penance for running off in this harebrained manner and worrying everyone half to death.

And, had he been even remotely aware and able to articulate it, for growing up into a desirable young woman before his very eyes.

The interview with the Mother Superior did not go as Eben had expected. She was not a heartless old biddy but a gentle, capable soul, who took upon herself full blame for Kaia's flight. The sister who accompanied her was not the bitter old beetle-eater but Sister Euphemia, a chipper keeper of bees, who was prepared to leap to Lady Kaia's defense at the merest hint of calumny against her young charge.

"I do not believe we need fear for Lady Kaia's virtue if she keeps to the company of Brother Absalom," Mother assured Eben. "He is a timid, elderly soul, quite unprepossessing, and not at all interested in worldly matters.

"Except," she continued, "insofar as they pertain to inquiries into the discipline of natural philosophy. That is, I believe, where he ran into difficulty with his abbot, who feared Brother Absalom's experiments with various herbs and potions might be luring him into the murkier waters of investigating the casting of spells and such. I am not privy to the particulars of the matter, but I understand it was nothing heretical, just crossing the boundary of legitimate scientific inquiry. So it is not to be wondered at that some passing charlatan, posing as a wizard, might persuade him that he could travel into the future."

Eben related what particulars of Kaia's letter to Morgana that Jibril had seen fit to share, and revealed that Lord Kurinon had taken a whip to the girl more than once. Mother Superior blanched and the loyal beekeeper burst into tears upon learning of Lord Kurinon's mistreatment of their Kaia.

Mother crossed herself. "God forgive me, I cannot say I liked the man. Had I only known."

"You mustn't blame yourself, good lady. Only my sister knew of it, and Kaia made her promise not to tell."

"To think a man would beat a child for wanting to learn to read and write," Sister Euphemia burst out. "Does he not know that in this day and age many girls of her station are taught?" She shook her small fist in the air. "I would give him a good tongue-lashing, I would. He would rue the day he—"

Mother held up a hand. "God will deal with Lord Kurinon in His own way and in His own time. It is not for us to judge or condemn. We must, instead, set our minds to assisting Lord Eben in finding Kaia and bringing her under His Majesty's protection."

Mother Superior related to Eben all she knew of Kaia's stay at the convent. With fond smiles she recalled Kaia's ingenious but harmless pranks, her keen intelligence, her way with bees. She dredged up everything she could remember about Kaia's last evening at the convent and the appearance of the strange dog in the convent precinct.

"Sister Xanthe reports that one of the spare habits is missing from the laundry," Mother concluded. "As are some provisions we send to the sisters in the orchard for their noonday meal."

Sister Euphemia bristled. "Kaia is no thief. How dare anyone—"

"That is quite enough, Sister Euphemia. No one is accusing Kaia of any such thing. I discovered a gold disc in the alms box, which I'm sure is Kaia's reimbursement for whatever she took for her journey."

"You must find her, Lord Eben," the beekeeper pleaded.

Mother Superior laid a delicate hand on Eben's arm. "Yes, find her, my lord. Before her father does."

"I will, good lady. And hell will freeze over before Lord Kurinon so much as lifts a finger against little Kaia again."

That night, Eben Dhion dreamed of bees. An undulating sea of bees, sweeping across meadows of wild iris and rambling rose and soaring above wind-whipped waves. And of the lithesome queen, she of huge dark eyes, who flew high and wide in her new world, and came to rest upon his breast, and there sank her stinger deep into his heart.

Chapter Four

"They must be tiny horses." Kaia frowned into the fire as she contemplated the possibility of a four-wheeled metal box that carried people along the roads with the horses inside rather than out.

Brother Absalom closed his eyes, trying to picture the conveyance. "Or a very large box."

"Birds I could understand. One could fit a great many small birds into a metal box to make it fly through the air. But Merlin said the horses that pull the box are inside, so where would the people ride?"

Brother Absalom could offer no answer to that question, nor to the many hundreds Kaia had plagued him with in the past two days. He had become rather weary of repeating "I couldn't say" and "We shall have to wait and see, shan't we?"

The elderly monk was beginning to wonder if it had been prudent to allow Kaia to accompany him. She had won out in the end by the simple expedient of badgering him half to death. First, he'd agreed to relate the full history of his association with the great sorcerer, Merlin, beginning when the magician had materialized out of thin air in his workroom at the abbey of Milo the Mild, and ending with each and every revelation vouchsafed him in the church of the Sisters of Valiant Virtue. The next thing he knew, he was sneaking away into the peach-colored dawn with Kaia mounted behind him upon his ill-tempered nag.

Of course, Brother Absalom would never allow Kaia to accompany him into the future. He intended to send her back to the Sisters of Valiant Virtue before he took passage on a ship to the Western Isles and the mysterious circle of standing stones Merlin had instructed him to find. In the meantime, why not let the girl enjoy a breath of freedom? Like as not, she would soon be wed and turn her attention to the happiness of her husband, the nurture of her children, and the management of her hearth, as was proper according to the laws of God and the Church. He only hoped that her husband would grant her the boon denied by her father and not think the less of a wife with learning. Absalom decided he would teach her to read and write as they journeyed westward. Perhaps then she would find it in her heart to forgive him for leaving her behind.

The good brother did not deceive himself that his decision to take her with him was altogether altruistic. For all her nagging and impetuosity, Kaia possessed an inner light and optimistic energy he had forgotten existed during his ascetic and lonely years in the abbey. He had known from an early age that he had no true vocation. Had the Good Lord seen fit to set him upon a different path, he would very much have liked to marry and to father sturdy sons and pretty, lively daughters. Daughters like this spirited girl.

Absalom believed that where one joy had been denied him, another had been granted: the life of the mind. He had enjoyed the freedom to pore over the hundreds of ancient texts in the abbey's library and pursue his studies in natural philosophy. He had been fortunate in the long tenure of his abbot, who had indulged Absalom's passion to conduct his modest experiments in the musty storage room in the cellar beneath the refectory.

That forbearance had come to a lurching halt two weeks earlier when the bishop had ordered Brother Absalom to come to the capital to defend himself against the charge of practices that might be construed as heresy. The course of that journey—and his life—had veered off into the fantastic the night a black hound had scratched at the door of his room behind the altar of the convent of the Sisters of Valiant Virtue, and had revealed to him a world where a man might pursue his studies without fear of ridicule, or the stake.

As he ventured into the darkness beyond the fire to see to his personal needs, Brother Absalom reflected that he knew almost nothing of Kaia. By her speech and bearing, he surmised she must be of noble birth, one of the flock of chattering girls who boarded for a time at the convent to see if they might have a religious vocation. Brother Absalom suspected that Kaia's father would be all too happy to have his daughter off his hands, but from what he had learned of Kaia's pranks, he doubted that God had a religious life in mind for her.

41

He shuffled back to the fire, wrapped his short, thin frame in woolen cloak and blanket, and lay down upon his side. He could see Kaia's huge eyes, molten black in the red glow of the dying embers. No doubt that keen little mind was hard at work.

"Brother Absalom, why were you on your way to see the bishop? What offense had you committed?"

The question caught him off guard. "I, er, may have tried one experiment too many."

Kaia leaned forward, her eyes glinting with eager interest. "Experiments? How very exciting. Can you cast spells? Could you turn Papa into a pig?"

Brother Absalom pursed his lips and frowned at her through an explosion of burning sparks. "I do not cast spells, child. That is magic, and one must be wary around magic. It must only be used for the good. There is white magic, you see, which is good, and black magic, which is bad. I'm afraid using magic to turn a man into a pig falls into the latter category. The line between the two is not so clear as one might wish, which is why I do not dabble in it at all. That does not mean that I would not find the study of it of great interest, of course."

"I don't think it would be black magic," Kaia reasoned. "He could be a pig until he learns his lesson and promises to be nicer, and then you could turn him back into a man. That would be a good deed, wouldn't it?"

"There is no point in discussing it. I cannot turn a man into a pig, nor would I if I could, not even for the sake of his immortal soul. Such things are best left in the hands of the Almighty. I am perfectly content with my herbs and potions and pots and such."

Truth be told, Brother Absalom's more exotic experiments had made him one of the less popular members of the Worshipful Brotherhood of Milo the Mild on more than one occasion. There had been that unfortunate episode with noxious gas, when every soul in the abbey precinct was sent retching and reeling through the gates when he tried to rid the dormitory of fleas by spraying a mist of bile of fish about the place. The fleas returned to take up residence after only three days, but the monks were forced to sleep outside for near a month.

Then there was the incident that became known far and wide as the Fiasco of the Fleece. The abbey's extensive flocks had been producing wool of rather poor quality for several seasons. Brother Absalom hazarded a suggestion that some supplement to their diet might remedy the situation. To that end, he puttered about in his little laboratory in great secrecy for some weeks until he finally emerged with a leather pouch filled with a harmless-looking orange powder, which he instructed the herdsmen to pour into the water troughs from which the sheep drank.

Everyone sat back to await the results.

The wool that season was the finest the abbey had ever seen. It was thick. It was tight. It was silky.

It was orange.

"You haven't answered my question," Kaia said. "Why did your bishop summon you?"

Brother Absalom would rather slice his tongue from his mouth with his own hand than relate the particulars of that ghastly incident, especially to the delicate ears of a young woman.

He fluttered a hand. "It was nothing; just a minor mix-up in a recipe."

Kaia was relentless. "It must have been a serious mix-up if your bishop is considering charges of heresy against you."

Serious? Brother Absalom thought. Catastrophic was more like it. Who would have imagined that mistaking "gnats" for "ants" would result in his having to barricade himself in his cell with the brothers baying for his blood and the abbot threatening excommunication? What should have been a simple restorative tonic, properly brewed from ants steeped in daffodil juice, had, with the substitution of gnats, translated itself into a draught that had the entire abbey in a raging sexual frenzy for two days. If Merlin hadn't wandered by to rectify the situation, Brother Absalom was certain the mob would have broken through the abbey's tall iron gate and hunted down every virgin, wife, widow, and hag in the nearby village.

"I do *not* wish to discuss it." Before Kaia could inquire further, he niftily changed the subject. "Of what house are you, my dear? I have been secluded for so many years that I can scarce recall who is who outside my abbey's walls."

Kaia shrugged and tossed a bit of wood into the flames. "It's of no consequence."

"If we are to travel together, we should know something of each other."

Kaia tried to steer the conversation away from herself. "What about you, Brother?"

"I may be the son of a noble house, but I really cannot say for certain. I was abandoned at the abbey as a baby. My swaddling clothes were of silk, and tucked into them was an offering of gold coins. I expect I was born outside the bounds of holy matrimony, but of my parentage nothing is known. You have not answered my question, my dear," he reminded her.

"The Second House," Kaia mumbled.

Absalom, whose hearing was not all it had been twenty years ago, wondered if he had heard aright. Had she said the *Second* House?

He shot up to a sitting position. "You are of the Second House?"

Kaia avoided his eyes. "As I said, it matters not."

Oh, it mattered. Even in the cloistered world of the abbey of Milo the Mild everyone knew about the family of the Second House. The lord of the Second House would be the brother of the late King Ahriman Chios, which meant that Kaia's father was not merely Lord Kurinon but Prince Kurinon, uncle of the present king. That could mean only one thing: *Kaia was first cousin to King Jibril himself.*

Brother Absalom clapped a hand to his heart and prayed that it would start beating again, the sooner the better.

Fearing he might be falling into some kind of fit, Kaia hastened to reassure him. "Really, Brother Absalom, it doesn't matter who I am. Papa will be glad to be rid of me. I suppose he might send one or two men after me just for show, but they'll soon turn back and that will be the end of it."

Brother Absalom's voice erupted in a spurt of strangled squeaks. "The letter I wrote. Who is this friend of yours, this Morgana?"

This time Kaia's words might have strained the hearing of a starving owl on the hunt. "Queen Syrah's sister."

"What?" Brother Absalom mouthed, his eyes wide with horror as the gates of hell opened before him.

"My friend Morgana is younger sister to the queen," Kaia repeated, a little louder this time.

"Aaaggghhh!" Brother Absalom gurgled as his eyes rolled back in his head and he fainted dead away.

He awakened from his swoon in the chill hours near dawn, crawled into the bushes to heave up the contents of his stomach, and gladly plummeted back into the temporary sanctuary of sleep. God only knew there would be time enough in the morning to contemplate the punishment that awaited a man who had kidnapped a member of the royal family. Lady Kaia was naive in the extreme to believe it would be but one or two indifferent men on their trail.

It would be the whole damn army.

The black hound rested on its haunches well back in the shadows at the edge of the clearing. It rose, stretched, and metamorphosed into the tall, elegant figure of a man in a midnight-blue cloak studded with citrine suns and sapphire stars. A small diamond winked from his left earlobe, and rings of curious design graced the long fingers of both hands.

The great magician Merlin regarded the sleeping travelers with a complacent smile. He had been delighted to arrive on this pleasant small island of generous people adrift in the great Southern Ocean. Half a century spent wandering the northern lands ravaged by mindless wars and plagues of every kind known to man and God had put him in an irritable frame of mind. He was never sure how he knew when the time had come to move on—or back, as it may be—but the silent signal had finally come. With his usual flair for the dramatic, he had gladly left those tedious years behind in a burst of green flame, and found himself in the presence of one Brother Absalom of St. Milo's abbey. The good brother, understandably befuddled at finding the tall stranger in his makeshift laboratory one misty morning, had proved a delightful study: quite the typical absentminded professor Merlin recalled from his time in the twenty-first century.

Merlin's instincts told him that his great destiny did not lie in this time and place. That was yet to come. It was not given to him to live a full life each time he "arrived," as it were, but each manifestation seemed to have some purpose, and it was incumbent upon him to find the purpose out as quickly as possible and play his part before the next call came.

Occasionally he had use of his full powers, but more often he served only as a catalyst, mentor, or counselor. He could neither make nor alter history; only ensure that those whom he met upon his long journey moved through their own lives in accordance with what was written for them, just as he himself must.

Of course, if he could brew up just a little innocent mischief and mayhem for his own amusement in the course of events, well, that made each visit all the more interesting and enjoyable.

He had immediately discovered at least one reason for this particular incarnation and had set the wheels in motion, sending Brother Absalom on a quest for a future that promised freedom to explore every aspect of natural philosophy to his heart's content without fear of ridicule or censure, not to mention the insanity of the Inquisition. The charming girl, too, had leaped at the opportunity to live in a world where education for women was looked upon not as a novelty or privilege but as a necessity for the good of all.

Merlin had decided to shepherd his charges to the Circle of Standing Stones in canine form. Dogs were always underfoot and rarely taken much notice of. More important, they were less likely than other small meaty beasts to find themselves fricasseed and served up on a platter with overboiled cabbage. Besides, he fancied he made a rather elegant hound.

Merlin suspected that his own journey would continue beyond the Circle of Standing Stones, to what and where he could not know. Moreover, if his instincts did not fail him, there would soon be others upon the road in full cry for his unique talents.

With that delightful prospect in mind, man again became beast, and the black hound dozed off with a contented sigh.

"Has everyone gone out of their minds?" King Jibril bellowed. He stormed down the great staircase and slammed into his solar. "We're trying to have a baby here."

The court physician pattered along in his monarch's wake. "Two, actually, sire. I think we can expect Her Majesty to deliver the second babe any moment."

"I know that," the king snapped. Syrah had made her

feelings quite clear on this unexpected development by grabbing the ear of her royal consort and giving it a good twist.

If she hadn't already been in a black mood at finding herself still on the birthing stool, the news that Morgana had taken it into her head to go in pursuit of Kaia had transformed his wife into a raging harridan. It had been all that Jibril, the doctor, and Syrah's stalwart personal maid, Mayenne, could do to keep his wife abed when news came that Morgana had outfoxed Obike Zebengo by slipping a sleeping potion into his ale, and disappeared in the company of Eben's fourteen-year-old squire, the harelipped Jocco.

Only the fact that there was another child wriggling about in her belly had prevented Syrah from vaulting onto her palfrey and joining the chase. And had Jibril not just left the dowager queen in the royal birthing chamber with his wife, he would not have been surprised to learn that his mother, too, had taken to the road.

"Find Morgana," Jibril snapped at an incensed Obike Zebengo. "Find them all and bring them to me. In chains, if necessary."

A page skidded through the solar door, tripped over the edge of the silk carpet, and fell flat on his face before his sovereign. "Sire, the queen, the queen."

"Find them or she'll kill me," Jibril snarled at Obike as he strode from the room.

"Hell, she'll probably kill me anyhow," he was heard to growl as he took the stairs two at a time to welcome another little princess into his home and heart.

* * *

An eagle sailing the thermal currents high above the emerald isle of the Dominion that fine summer day might very well have wondered at the odd parade of determined souls—seekers, dreamers, pursuers, and pursued—that straggled along fifty leagues of the south coast road.

And circling round and round them all, a black hound grinning from ear to floppy ear.

Chapter Five

"My nam is Kaia. I can reab anb rit. I am a goob reaber."

Kaia frowned as she chewed thoughtfully on the twig of fragrant sarsaparilla she had peeled and sharpened to use for her writing stick. Something didn't look right. Words sometimes had letters in them that one couldn't hear if spoken aloud. Kaia thought it a silly rule, but Brother Absalom was adamant that she had to put them in anyway. Aha! There should be an 'e' at the end of the words 'name' and 'rite'—that was the problem. She squeezed them in and sat back on her heels to admire her handiwork.

Propped beside her against the sun-warmed brick wall of the old inn, Brother Absalom snoozed, snored, and drooled, while the great black hound that seemed to have adopted them sprawled in canine abandon, dreaming doggy dreams and occasionally chortling or guffawing.

After two days in its company, Kaia wasn't all that surprised at what could come out of this dog's mouth. A dog that could smile and talk would be a dog that could chortle and guffaw. Not that it had all that much to say, but it had shepherded them through the terrible storm in the dark of night to the shelter afforded by the overarching eaves of the inn when Brother Absalom had lost his wits entirely as a cascade of lightning strikes crashed about them. A sure sign, the good brother had wailed throughout the ordeal, that the Lord did not look down with pleasure upon the present enterprise and the gates of hell were even now yawning wide to receive them.

Close by, spread along the crossbars of a sagging split-rail fence, their damp garments steamed in the rising warmth. The contents of their cloth satchels lay drying in bright patches of blue, white, and brown on a sward of sweet pasture beyond the fence, and the crumbs of their morning meal—dried sprats, hard yellow cheese, and aromatic new-baked bread—were being borne away by an enterprising army of small brown ants.

Kaia scooted down to lie with her head nestled on the warm flank of the twitching hound, and stared into the clear blue vault of the sky above. She was well pleased with her adventure so far. It was a pleasure tempered somewhat by the voice of conscience that was ever perched upon her shoulder whispering of duty, ingratitude, selfishness, rashness, and regret. If it whispered now, after only two days on the road, how it would roar when she stepped into the Circle of Standing Stones and prepared to leave the only world she had ever known.

The niggling thought pushed its way to the forefront of her mind again that a journey of eight hundred years into the future and beyond the edge of the world might be an excessive undertaking just to get out from under Papa's thumb. But she was already making wonderful progress with her letters under Brother Absalom's gentle tutelage. Perhaps the true path to learning lay in the sheer desire to do so and the application of the will. Such desire must not be constrained by ignorant men such as her father, who could see no more worth in a woman than her marriage portion and her body as the keeper of their treasured seed.

Kaia took up her twig again and smoothed a small patch of dirt for her next effort. "Lorb Eden Bion is a dlinb doody."

No, that didn't look right either. The problem didn't lie in the thought itself—Eben Dhion *was* a blind booby— but all her Bs and Ds had gotten backward somehow, and there were still letters missing here and there. She set to the task of identifying the errors and fixing them before Brother Absalom awoke. He was touchingly proud of her quick and steady progress, and she in her turn was equally eager to please the dear old thing.

How could Papa be so backward in this enlightened day and age? Had some madness seized him that rainy morning when he discovered her in the chapel at her secret daily lesson with Father Olli? The normally placid old priest had been on the verge of tearing his hair out over Kaia's spirited objection to the letter 'c': Why should Cs sound like Ks in some words, Ss in others? The upshots of that unpleasant confrontation with her father had been the ig- nominious departure of poor Father Olli and her own ex- ile to the convent of the Sisters of Valiant Virtue.

What evil would come to the woman who could read the holy word, the noble poetry of the ancients, the thrilling romances of Camelot, a recipe for snail and lamprey pasty in a hot green sauce? Even more curious, what measure of evil could a woman unleash upon the world with such learning? From what the mysterious stranger had told Brother Absalom that night in the convent church, girls in the far future could study whatever subject interested them, and put their knowledge to good use in any number of "professions." What professing had to do with it Kaia wasn't quite sure. In her world, one professed one's vows to enter the religious life. Perhaps each trade had a sisterhood? Might a girl choose to study bees and then make a profession to enter, say, the Good Sisters of the Holy Hive?

"Hey, stop that, you stupid dog," Kaia exclaimed. The black hound had surged to its feet and all but obliterated most of Kaia's carefully revised words. "Now look what you've done."

"Quiet, child," the dog growled, its nose in full twitch. It trotted away across the courtyard, now bustling with the usual business of the morning: travelers, peddlers, pilgrims, beggars, loungers, and lurkers. Cart wheels creaked, horses whickered, donkeys brayed; a pet mynah bird squawked obscenities. Children dashed about with no clear purpose; an early-rising harlot sashayed through the growing throng, her purpose all too clear.

Kaia's annoyance quickly turned to apprehension as she watched the prowling hound. This was not a dog that indulged in aimless conversation or undue alarm. Something was definitely amiss. Foreboding turned to outright panic when the dog came loping back and with a curt "Soldiers" pounced full on Brother Absalom's chest.

"Move, move," the dog said, pushing them both into concealing shadow around the corner of the inn.

"Wha . . . why . . . huh?" Brother Absalom muttered as he awoke reluctantly from a pleasant dream in which books and parchments grew upon trees like ripe fruit ready for the plucking. "Oh my, oh my," he groaned as the full measure of the approaching horror dawned.

"We are doomed," he cried. There followed a litany of "Hail Marys," interspersed with odd bits of the Twenty-third Psalm. "The Lord is my shepherd . . . full of grace . . . yea, though I walk through . . . the womb . . . the valley of the shadow—"

"Hush!" Kaia whispered. "They haven't seen us."

Three pairs of eyes, two human, one canine, peered around the corner as ten soldiers in the black and scarlet livery of the king's own guard trotted importantly into the courtyard. Stable boys rushed forward to take hold of the reins, hawkers milled about them, beggars importuned, and the harlot perked up at the unexpected possibility of good trade so early in the day. The innkeeper's fat wife appeared at the door wiping her hands on her apron. A buzz of expectant interest stirred in the crowd.

"Stand back," ordered the leader of the troop. "I come on important business for His Majesty the King."

Kaia had to clap her hands to her mouth to keep from screaming as she recognized none other than Kalan Ankuli, commander of the king's land forces. She didn't have to wonder what that important business might be.

Ankuli swung down from his mount and strode over to station himself authoritatively upon the worn stone doorsill that led to the inn's public drinking room. Idle boys balanced precariously upon fences and posts, maids leaned from upper-story windows, and a group of close to a hundred nuns and monks who were on a pilgrimage to one of the holiest shrines in the kingdom, St. Polyp's Pillar, pressed forward.

Commander Ankuli drew a tightly rolled scroll from his belt and looked out over the excited crowd, whose number had nearly doubled as news spread like wildfire that there were great doings at the inn. Although a public hanging was probably too much to hope for, perhaps some miscreant was to be taken into custody, or even better, pilloried. An old woman selling produce was suddenly doing a brisk business in overripe fruits and vegetables suitable for throwing.

The crowd fell silent as the commander unrolled the scroll and cleared his throat.

"Hear ye, hear ye! By order of His Most Serene Majesty, Jibril Mekon Jirod Chios, be it known that a reward of ten gold discs is offered for information leading to the safe return of Lady Kaia Ellora Kurinon, age eighteen—"

Here Ankuli's voice was drowned out as the crowd erupted with exclamations of surprise and horror and cackles of anticipatory greed.

". . . for Thou art with me . . ." mouthed Brother Absalom.

Ankuli was forced to raise his voice to be heard. "Lady Kaia Ellora Kurinon," he repeated, "age eighteen, beloved child of Prince Konstantin Kurinon, honored sixth daughter of the Second House, esteemed and valued cousin in the first degree to His Majesty . . ."

By now Brother Absalom was well beyond the outermost limits of reason or any sense of self-preservation whatsoever. The Twenty-third Psalm had inexplicably segued into the 108th: "Moab is my washpot; over Edom will I cast out my shoe . . ."

Commander Ankuli droned on. ". . . last seen two nights past within the confines of the convent of the Sisters of Valiant Virtue at Capiri . . ."

Kaia could not have moved from the spot had a herd of dehydrated dromedaries been bearing down upon her on a rampage toward a distant oasis.

". . . in the company of one Brother Absalom of the abbey of the Blessed Milo the Mild . . . abduction . . . high treason . . ."

With a strangled squawk the brother in question crumpled to the ground.

"God save the king!" Ankuli concluded.

"God save the king!" echoed the crowd.

"God save us all," Kaia whispered as her muscles turned to mush and she slid down the wall.

God help her when he got his hands on the little minx.

Lord Eben reined in his horse as he returned to the crossroads after a fruitless detour ten miles northward to a long-neglected, weed-choked shrine. A walleyed old man had assured him it was indeed the destination of the thousands of religious folk on the road this day. As it turned out, Eben had found only three monks of some obscure order, sprawled nearly insensible beside the road. They had been similarly misdirected, and had come to the conclusion, after a night of strong drink and convoluted theological discourse, that it was the intent of undertaking the pilgrimage that God deemed important, not actually arriving at the destination. They need travel no further. Besides, they had only eighteen bruxa left among them for enough wine to fortify them for the remainder of the journey.

Eben dismounted and led the sleek stallion to a spring-fed stone trough that had served travelers upon the coast road since time immemorial. He was not a man to be easily discomposed or angered, but he was discovering that the least inconvenience, delay, or distraction on this damnable mad pursuit across the island was a sore test of his usual unflappable demeanor. Little Kaia might think she could lead him on a merry chase and not pay the price, but Eben had plans for her, he most certainly did, and the price would be high.

Some miles back he had discarded the notion of locking her away in the east tower and feeding her naught but worms and water, because that would mean she would be on one side of a stout, iron-studded door and he on the other. Why should he deprive himself of the pleasure of seeing a slimy worm wriggling its way past those cherry-ripe lips, over the sweet wet warmth of that sassy little tongue, sliding sinuously down the long white column of her throat? He shouldn't. He wouldn't.

In fact, after all the trouble she'd put him through, he deserved to see it close up, which would mean he'd have to tie her up so that she wouldn't leap at him in a fit of pique as she had done so many times as a child. Likely she would take exception to eating worms, so he'd probably have to feed them to her from his own hand, twining his fingers through that glorious golden hair to tilt her head back as he dangled the writhing creature before her horrified eyes. She'd resist, of course, and he would have to trap her against his body to keep her still, her breath coming in short, sharp gasps, breasts heaving, twisting against him . . .

Try as he might to banish such inappropriate images—this was, after all, little Kaia he was lusting after—he could not will away his arousal.

It was going to be a truly uncomfortable ride to the Inn of the Bishop's Bastard.

Chapter Six

Kaia crouched behind a huge boulder high on the slope above the inn and watched the black hound disappear into a weathered woodshed behind the stable. While the crowd was still well occupied with talking excitedly about Commander Ankuli's electrifying announcement, Kaia had towed an ashen-faced Brother Absalom behind her up the hill to their present place of concealment. From this vantage point she could see not only the inn yard, stables, and outbuildings, but a good stretch of road in either direction.

Enterprising individuals were already circulating through the crowd, casting a suspicious eye on every female between the ages of nine and ninety. Others were scattering east and west in a hunt that, as the news spread, would soon have half the kingdom upon the roads, and prove, without a doubt, a boon to every strumpet, pickpocket, swindler, and highwayman from Capiri to Galiana.

After a few moments a man attired in the robes of a moderately prosperous merchant emerged from the wood-shed, so tall he had to bend nearly double in order to pass beneath the low lintel. He wended his nonchalant way through the bustling stable yard to the front door of the inn, where he waved off several persistent peddlers and disappeared into the cool shadows within. Where the dog had got to, Kaia could not imagine, but her attention was now drawn to a distant rider approaching from the east, whose evident mastery of his mount and strong, erect carriage vaguely reminded her of someone, although she couldn't put her finger on who it could be.

"We are doomed, done for, child." Brother Absalom quivered beside her. "We cannot escape. We must give over and throw ourselves upon the mercy of the king."

"It is not the king I'm worried about," Kaia said. "It's my father. He's going to kill me."

"Surely not, my dear," exclaimed Brother Absalom. "Banish you, perhaps, to a life of prayer and contemplation, which is not so terrible as you might suppose, especially if you happen to find yourself in a convent with an adequate library. You will have books enough to last you a lifetime. That is what you desire, is it not? What more could you wish for?"

A husband of her own choosing, Kaia thought. Love, passion, children. Eben Dhion.

"I, on the other hand," he gabbled on, "am headed for the gibbet if I am unlucky, the block if the Lord is merciful. Better the swift cut than the long drop, assuming, of course, that the blade has been properly sharpened. My one great fear is that someone will not have measured the rope correctly: too short and the break is not quick and clean, too long and one is left dangling with one's toes dragging upon the ground. Then they must cut you down and begin all over again, which cannot be pleasant, but which, now that I reflect upon it, would allow me more time for prayer before I kneel at last before the Throne of Judgment—"

"Please, I beg you, be silent and let me think," Kaia interjected before Brother Absalom could launch into a rambling recitation of his expectations of the afterlife.

The crowd below had begun to disperse when the tall stranger stepped from the inn, followed by Commander Ankuli and his men. They stood for some time in earnest conversation. Occasionally the merchant would wave his arm back toward the coast road. After several minutes, the soldiers moved off toward the stable yard to find their mounts. The merchant bade them farewell and sauntered across the road, where he gathered up Kaia's and Absalom's garments and stuffed them into the satchels. Stopping for a moment to buy a bag of gingered nuts from a young girl, he began the long climb to the crest of the hill. He reached the boulder and leaned against it, trying to catch his breath.

"I'm not getting any younger," said he.

Kaia eyed the tall stranger closely. It did not take too great a leap of the imagination to realize that she was face to face with the greatest wizard ever to walk the earth. The appearance of a loquacious hound in the convent church at the same time Brother Absalom was in deep conversation with a mysterious stranger behind the altar, and the goings-on in the woodshed—enter a hound, exit a man—must be the final confirmation. She had, however, not been formally introduced to him, which Kaia felt was somewhat remiss of Brother Absalom.

"Good day, sir," Kaia began with a graceful little curtsy. "I am—"

"I, um, hesitate to contradict you, my good sir," Brother Absalom interrupted her, "but to be strictly accurate, you are. Getting younger, that is. I can't say that I understand how it came about, but He who can move mountains holds His own counsel. Now that I think on it, it cannot be that different. You have no more idea of your past than others have of their future. Traveling in either direction leads us all to the same destination. In your case, you see, you should say rather, 'I am not getting any older.'"

Kaia grinned at the thought of Brother Absalom and dear old Queen Alya, a lady much given to rambling thought herself, comfortably seated before the hearth on a dreary evening, ruminating and rambling singly or together, most likely at cross purposes.

"Perhaps," Kaia said kindly, "we could explore this conundrum at a less precarious moment. If you would just allow me to introduce myself—"

Merlin fixed Brother Absalom with a steely stare. "I, at least, sir, have the comfort of knowing that in the not too distant future I shall be able to skip up this hill like a young billy goat, while you will have to be carried up it upon a litter."

Brother Absalom's chin shot up a notch. "As you say, sir. My comfort is that, while I grow wiser upon my litter, you will be romping about with all the reasoning power of that goat."

At this point Kaia gave up all hope of effecting a proper introduction and hastened to intervene before a simple discussion escalated into a ripping row. "Well, I don't know about you two, but I'm not about to sit here quibbling while my cousin's soldiers are likely to seize me at any moment and cart me back to the convent. We must think what to do."

"Change into the sister's habit, child. Be quick about it," Merlin said.

"I really fail to see—" Absalom began.

Merlin aimed a pugnacious chin in the monk's direction. "Where do you hide a tree?"

"A tree?" Absalom inquired, forgetting for a moment their dire predicament. He loved riddles. "Let me see," he mused. "A tree, a tree. Where does one hide a tree? I suppose it would depend on the size of the tree. Could you be more specific?"

Kaia groaned as she fished about in her satchel for the gray tunic and white veil she had procured from the convent's laundry. She smoothed out the creases as best she could and headed off to a nearby thicket to change. She had caught the man's meaning at once.

"Size doesn't matter," said Merlin with a decided glint in his eye.

"Of course size matters!" the monk countered. "Surely if you have a big one that is thick about the base, it would be much more difficult to conceal from the observant eye beneath one's garment, for instance, than a seedling which one could easily tuck away. So you see, size would always determine where you would put it."

"Oh, not really," murmured Merlin, and with a lascivious grin ambled back down the hill in the direction of the woodshed.

"But what about the riddle?" Brother Absalom called after him.

"It's a forest," explained Kaia, who had by now reappeared swathed in the habit of the Sisters of Valiant Virtue. "You hide a tree in a forest."

"What in the world has that to do with our situation?" demanded Brother Absalom, somewhat put out that he had not been able to come up with such an obvious answer himself.

Kaia swept her arm toward the throng of monks and nuns who were milling about in the inn yard.

"Oh, yes, I see. How clever. But . . ." Absalom hesitated. Here, thought he, was a most fortuitous moment to dissuade Kaia from her present course and get her to return to the convent, as he had planned all along. Not to mention extricate himself from grave peril and perhaps save his immortal soul.

He got no further than venturing a timid "My dear—" before Kaia shrieked and sank to her knees.

"What, what?" Brother Absalom cried, his head practically swiveling full round atop his neck as he searched out the cause of her alarm. Certainly the sight of the black hound loping up the hill toward them would not occasion such horror as now overspread her countenance. The scene below remained much as it had been, as far as he could see, although the mounted troop of soldiers had now been joined by an imposing young man, upon a splendid horse caparisoned in a bright saddle blanket of blue, green, and gold. That he came of a noble house could be easily surmised. That his appearance boded ill, if Lady Kaia's reaction was anything to go by, was a certainty.

Chapter Seven

Think.

If ever a moment called for clarity of thought, careful analysis, strategic cunning, the triumph of the will over ungovernable emotion, this was that moment.

Unfortunately, Lady Kaia Kurinon had not a single thought, coherent or not, in her head. She could not have discerned the difference between a squire and a squash. Nor could she have outwitted a five-year-old in a game of Twelve Men's Morris.

Of raw emotion there was no insufficiency.

Ebenebeneben . . .

Blindboobyblindbooby . . .

"I'm sorry—did you say something?" Absalom whispered beside her. He placed a comforting arm about her shoulders. "I fail to see cause for your present distress, my lady. Merlin has come up with a most ingenious plan. Do you recall how the Lord our God led the children of Israel from bondage and closed the waters of the sea over

64

Pharaoh and his armies as they pursued them? Surely He will do no less for us if we ask nicely."

He paused as the implications of such a development dawned. "I believe I misspoke." He frowned. "The present circumstance does not merit such an emphatic response from our Lord as did the exodus of His chosen people. The king's men are, after all, only following orders, and I should hate to see the waters come upon them. But then Pharaoh's legions were also under orders, so—"

"Please, you're giving me a headache," Kaia groaned. She had, to some degree, recovered her wits, although her eyes were still closed tight against the sight of Eben Dhion come in search of her.

Or had he? Perhaps he was simply upon the road on some business of his own. The man probably didn't even know she had been sent away to the convent, much less that she had left it. Unless Morgana had betrayed her; she was, after all, Eben's sister, and might very well have suffered an attack of bad conscience and showed him . . .

The letter. Oh, God, the letter! What had she dictated to Brother Absalom; had she revealed Eben's name?

Seizing the front of Brother Absalom's tunic in both fists, she commenced shaking the terrified monk, demanding he recall what he had written down for her—every damn word.

"Really, my dear," he stuttered, "I hardly think even this perilous moment calls for such language. The Lord does not look with favor—"

Kaia wanted to howl in frustration. "Eben Dhion," she said through clenched teeth. "Did I mention Eben Dhion?"

"If you will release me, child, I may be able to think a bit more clearly. There, that's better. Well, let me see. You mentioned a man." Here he gave her a benevolent little smile. "You seemed quite fond of him, if I recall. There was a name . . . let me see now. Creon? No. Dobon? Hmmmm. Really I cannot recall, but I feel certain it had Ds and Bs in it. I suppose it could have been this Eben Dhion.

"God help me, God help me," Kaia wailed.

Brother Absalom cleared his throat. "While you're requesting our Lord's assistance, perhaps you should apologize for your language. It may better dispose Him toward our cause."

"Oh, all right. We need all the help we can get. I'm sorry for my bad language, God," she said, quite like a dutiful child apologizing to her papa for some misdemeanor or other.

"There, now that we've tidied up the loose ends, let us see what is going on below," Absalom said briskly, suddenly feeling quite chipper now that God had been mollified.

Kaia squeezed her eyes shut. "I can't look. You tell me."

Absalom peered over the boulder.

"Well, the king's men have gone on their way. The wrong way, I might add. I believe Merlin saw to that. Oh, now your young man has dismounted and . . . Well, bless me, what's this? Where did all these women come from? They're swarming about him like bees around a platter of sweetmeats. Now they're tugging him into the inn. Good heavens! A fight has broken out; two women are rolling about in the dirt . . ."

"Of course," Kaia muttered. "They would."

The black hound had settled onto its haunches, listening with ears cocked to this exchange, smiling all the while. Now it rose, stretched, and nudged Kaia to her feet. "Enough. We must be on our way."

Down the hill they went, quite openly now that Ankuli and his men had disappeared back along the coast road toward Capiri and Lord Eben Dhion was well occupied in the tavern with fending off half the fertile females—and a few who were well beyond that blessed state—from the local village. They melted into the crowd, well concealed in the stream of pilgrims in their black, gray, brown, and white habits as they set off westward along the road. To the left, the turquoise waters of the Southern Ocean swept in majestically to break against the base of towering russet cliffs.

Kaia was in command of herself once again. She could not recall a time when she had lost her head like that. She felt exhilarated and saddened by turns as she trudged toward an uncertain future.

Had Eben Dhion come after her?

And if so, and far more important, why?

Damn all women to hell.

Eben had extricated himself from hand-to-hand skirmishes with falchion and dagger more easily than he had finally escaped the clutches of the gaggle of willing wenches back at the inn. One, who would not be denied, had somehow managed to slip her hand beneath his tunic and into his breechcloth, taking his member hostage and refusing to let go until he took her above stairs and demonstrated its renowned prowess. Eben's wildly erotic dreams of the past few nights had featured a bewitching nymph who provided pleasure beyond any he had ever before experienced, and although the wench who now had a firm hold upon him might have tempted him at one time, he could envision no other than the black-eyed beauty with the fall of golden hair. Fifty bruxa had eventually gained the release of his unwilling shaft.

No torture devised by devil or man would wring the admission from Eben Dhion that the woman who had writhed beneath him in his dreams was little Kaia Kurinon. He did not want to know it himself.

Eben urged his horse forward. In the far distance around a sweeping curve of the cliffs he could see the flowing stream of pilgrims. Kaia would be among them. What better means of concealment than to hide in plain sight? She had purloined a nun's habit from the convent, since she could not very well go about in the fashionable attire of a daughter of the Second House without exciting curiosity and attracting attention.

It was not long before Eben was trailing along behind the pilgrims, holding his mount to a sedate walk as he searched for Kaia in the large crowd. The tonsured heads of monks shone in the bright sunlight, bobbing along among the white-veiled heads of the nuns. He saw any number of gray habits, which might or might not be the habits of the Sisters of Valiant Virtue; other orders wore gray too. He focused his attention on the nuns, but could not very well guide his horse through the crowd as if he were cutting out a wild filly from the herd.

He kept his eye on those whose veils were pulled unusually close, as though to conceal their faces, ignoring those whose gait proclaimed them to be of advanced years and the obviously far too tall, too short, or too rotund. He was clearly at a disadvantage at the back of the column, so he guided his horse up a gentle incline and moved forward at a pace commensurate with the walkers.

Kaia was here. He could feel it.

How he missed her on the first pass he would never know, but as he trotted back, he espied a lithe little figure in gray angling through the crowd and drifting along on the edge closest to the cliff. There was a furtive quality to her movements. He was certain it was Kaia and that she had spotted him.

Eben gloated. She was well trapped between the crowd and the cliff. It would be easy enough to simply pluck her up into his lap. The game was up, and by the saints, when he had her in hand, she would feel the full measure of his—

He was distracted for only a split second when a large black hound darted nearly beneath the hooves of his mount, but it was time enough for his quarry to make her move. When Eben looked up, the little gray nun was sprinting toward the edge of the cliff.

And then she was gone.

Chapter Eight

When his teeth had rotted from his mouth, his hair gone gray, and some gnarly old priest with garlic on his breath was praying at his bedside for the salvation of his immortal soul, Lord Eben Dhion, venerable scion of the Ninth

House, brother-in-law to Jibril the Great, the Golden One of revered memory of an entire generation of the women of the Dominion, knew he would still go weak at the knees at the mere thought of this moment. He teetered at the edge of the precipice desperately searching the jagged rocks below for the mortal remains of his little Kaia.

Far, far below, spent waves eddied through rock pools and were drawn back out to sea. No sad little form lay crumpled and crushed there. No gray habit floated upon the retreating waves. Kaia Kurinon had vanished into thin air.

Eben could not believe his eyes, would not believe. He searched for some way to climb down, and that was when he saw a small figure scrambling down a dangerously steep and narrow path cut into the cliff.

Throwing off his sword belt, Eben slipped over the edge and went after her. He lost sight of her as he slid and slithered, sometimes upon his posterior, and by the time he reached the bottom she was nowhere to be seen. The tide was coming in, but there would be caves and hidey-holes enough along the base of the cliff where a slim, agile young woman could hide. With much muttering and cursing, Eben set out to hunt her down.

It wasn't as though she had intended to hurl herself into oblivion. She'd been heading for a tangle of stunted trees that had somehow managed to anchor in the thin rocky soil atop the cliff. Some had toppled over to form a dull gray/brown barricade behind which she had thought to hide. And then, quite suddenly, she was catapulting over the cliff edge and dropping a good five feet onto a crude path where she lay sprawled in shock for a few seconds before gathering what wits she had left and making for the beach below.

Kaia glanced up once to see the magnificent figure of a man poised against a blinding sky with his long hair whipping about his face. From this distance she could not distinguish his features, but she would know him anywhere. He leaped down onto the path and was lost to sight around a sharp bend.

Eben had come for her. Rat-a-tat-tat.

He cared. Ratatatta-ratattata-tat.

He would woo her, wed her, bed her.

He would . . .

Wait. What made her think he would come for her of his own volition? He could have wooed, wedded, and bedded her, had he so desired, in the first place, and then she wouldn't be running about the countryside in a nun's habit like a madwoman. But he hadn't, and that bore some thinking about.

Creeping through a wilderness of fallen debris, Kaia discovered a crawl space just her size between a mammoth boulder and the base of the cliff. She had just tucked herself into its deep shadow when Eben finally gained the beach. He looked left, then right, and to Kaia's relief set off in the opposite direction.

Oh, he was looking for her, that was true enough, but he looked angry enough to spit fire. Most likely, Jibril had dispatched him to find her, and when he did, he would throw her over his saddle like a sack of grain and dump her back at the convent and ride away forever.

"You're here," Eben shouted into the wind. "I know you're here, Kaia. Now be a good little girl and come out."

Kaia went cold, hot, pale, flushed. *Little girl?*

"I'm going to count to ten, Kaia. One . . . two . . ."

Oh, so Lord Eben thought she would play that game, did he?

"Three . . . four . . . five . . ."

Well, he could count up to a gazillion, or however many numbers there were. Kaia Kurinon wasn't going back to the convent, or to her father, or to mooning over a lackwit reprobate who could not get it through his thick, albeit lovely, skull that she was *not a little girl* anymore.

"Now I'm getting really angry," Kaia heard Eben say a few minutes later as he started poking through the boulders not fifty paces from where she hid. She couldn't stay where she was; she'd have to make a run for it. Since there was nothing to lose, she stuffed her skirts into the cord about her waist, crawled out, darted from boulder to boulder, and finally broke into an all-out run down the hard-packed sand-and-pebble beach.

The ensuing spectacle would be the talk of the kingdom for years to come. There was Lord Eben Dhion, seventeenth armiger of the Ninth House, Special Counsel to His Majesty the King, and brother to the queen, in flat-out pursuit of a nun in the habit of the Sisters of Valiant Virtue—later identified as the Lady Kaia Kurinon, born of the late Princess Kurinon, sixth daughter of the Second House, niece to the late King Ahriman of revered memory and the dowager queen.

And if that were not extraordinary enough, the fact that the lady's skirts were hitched well up on her thighs, revealing for all the world to see an occasional glimpse of a very fine little backside, would become the stuff of bawdy tales, songs, and jests of troubadours down the years.

Pursuer and pursued could only be eternally grateful that the real entertainment would be hidden from the cheering mob up on the cliff by the fortuitous presence of a projecting headland around which they disappeared from view.

Chapter Nine

Eben could scarce believe his eyes, nor could he drag them from the sight of the two firm, succulent globes of little Kaia's pert behind bouncing along ahead of him. Had he not been in hot pursuit because his quarry was a reckless, infuriating, cunning minx, he most certainly would be for far different, less noble, reasons.

The exact moment when the pursuit became something other than what it had begun as is uncertain, but it may have been when Kaia, realizing that she could not outrun him, swung about like a cornered gazelle to face the tiger head on and make a valiant last stand. To her surprise, the desperate maneuver brought Eben to a stumbling halt. Just as Diana, moon goddess of the ancients, had punished the youth who had dared spy on her as she bathed by turning him to pale, cold marble, Eben Dhion might have been a statue with a look of utter amazement on his face and his muscles, all his muscles, hard as stone.

All that could be heard above the whoosh of the incoming tide were the harsh cries of gulls and the sound of labored breathing as Kaia and Eben faced off across a ribbon of soft black sand and took one another's measure.

"I am not going back."

"Yes, you are."

Kaia dodged to the right, the left, the right again.

He lunged; she danced back out of reach.

"You can't make me."

"Oh, you think not?"

They might have been two giddy children dancing around one another after a shrieking chase around the upper bailey, but the heated looks that flashed between them were anything but childlike. Prey was no longer really seeking to escape, and predator was now stalking to satisfy the ancient hunger of the male for its mate.

"You're an idiot, Eben Dhion," Kaia shouted.

"An idiot?"

"You don't understand. You will never understand. I want to learn to read and write. I can do that in the future. I can fly . . . I can keep bees . . . I can live by my own rules. You're a man, you can't understand. You can do anything you want. It's not fair."

By now Eben was in no frame of mind to try to reason with her. The brief flash of a smooth, firm belly and, below, the object of a man's desire, and long, slim legs that a generous God had designed to wrap around a man as he pushed into warmth as sweet as honey was, frankly, driving him insane.

Unaware that she was nearly naked from the waist to the tops of her boots, Kaia could not know that the look

74

in Eben's eyes was a lust so strong he thought he would die if he could not take the treasure before him. But she could not ignore the pounding of her own heart, the rush of blood through her veins, and the flashes of heat in her most secret place. If he so much as touched her with a fingertip, she couldn't be held accountable for her actions.

Run, escape, urged her mind. *Stay, surrender,* countered her body.

There was no time to debate the matter, even if she'd had the presence of mind to do so, because Eben chose that moment to spring forward, wrap his arms around her, and bear her down onto the soft sand.

For a breathless moment they simply stared at one another, tip of nose to tip of nose, and then slowly, very slowly, his mouth settled on hers. And took possession.

She knew the first thrilling taste of him as his tongue teased her lips open and found hers. He tasted of spiced wine—sweet, intoxicating—and smelled of leather and horse and the salt sea; then of rosemary as his damp hair brushed her cheek.

When he shifted, Kaia panicked and grabbed at his tunic lest he leave her alone with this heat spiraling through her body, her breasts tingling, and the aching place between her legs that seemed so empty. She groaned with relief as he settled between her thighs, hard and heavy.

He reached down to loosen the cord at her waist, and slipped his hand up beneath the habit to caress her breasts. "So soft, so soft," he murmured as he explored down over her hard belly and smooth, smooth thighs. He cupped that place that so craved his touch, only his. The moment when his fingers slipped into her and he touched and teased her most secret place, all thought fled and Kaia no longer knew who she was or where, or whose touch could ignite such sweet fire there.

And then she was flying, truly flying in a way she never could have imagined. Soaring up and up until . . . until . . .

"Let it happen, let go," a voice urged.

"I'm afraid," cried another voice, her voice.

"I'm here. I'll catch you."

Kaia flew.

"Yes, that's it, yes."

And strong arms caught her as she drifted down.

Eben slipped an arm beneath her and pulled her hard against him as his own need threatened to overwhelm him. He moved against her, slowly at first, then more urgently. He could wait no longer, reached down to free himself.

"I need you," Eben groaned against her neck. "To be inside you . . . Kaia . . . Kaia . . ."

He froze. Something was wrong here, someone—

"Oh, God! . . . *Kaia?*"

In all his life never had Eben's ardor deserted him so abruptly. Never had thought, if such it could be called, rushed from his nether regions to his brain so quickly. Never had the tolling bell of conscience jangled so fiercely as at the moment when Eben Dhion raised his head and realized the woman who lay sprawled beneath him in erotic thrall was his sister.

Well, no, not his sister, not really, but close enough; doubtless enough to damn him to hell for all eternity, or at the very least draw down upon his head the wrath of the priests, of every noble house, and the contempt of every man, woman, and child in the kingdom.

Rearing back as though a cobra swayed before him ready to strike, Eben flung himself aside and scrambled to his knees. Kaia had not yet fully recovered her senses and gazed up at the trailing feathers of clouds with slumberous, unfocused eyes, as though returning slowly from a sea journey to some exotic clime and unwilling to accept that the ship was coming to anchor.

"Oh, God, I am so sorry, Kaia. Forgive me." He snatched at her skirts, tugging them loose from the cord at her waist and draping them over the sweet gate he had only moments before sought to breach.

He sprang to his feet, stormed this way and that. "Mad—I must be mad. That's it, I've lost my mind. *Kaia*. What ever could I have been thinking?"

Such frenzied reflection and remorse would not be reassuring to any woman, virgin or not, who had just been so pleasured. Kaia climbed to her feet with slow deliberation, adjusted her habit, and shook the sand from her tousled locks. She fixed Eben with a look that would make any man with a modicum of sense hold his tongue and back away to a prudent distance.

She crossed her arms across her chest and cocked her head. "You appear to be distressed, my lord."

Eben was too distraught to apprehend his danger. "Of course I'm distressed. A man of principle does not . . . his own sister . . . mortal sin . . ." he babbled to the heavens.

Kaia glared at him. "I am not your sister."

"You might as well be," said Eben, waving his arms

about. "I've known you since . . . well, since the day you were born. You spent more time in my hall with Morgana than you did in your father's. I have always looked upon you—"

"Have you?" demanded Kaia.

"Have I what?"

"Looked at me. Really looked at me."

Eben's eyebrows went up. "Of course I've looked at you."

"As a woman?" she challenged, stalking a circle around him.

Eben sensed a trap. "Well, er, you're but eighteen, not exactly a woman. Almost."

"A child, then?" Kaia inquired, far too politely.

He needed to gain some control here, Eben thought. "Well, yes, if you must know," he said, coming to a standstill and settling his hands on his hips. He wasn't about to back down in the face of her growing fury.

"Was I a child a few minutes ago?" she shouted. "Did a child incite your passion, harden your body, drive you beyond coherent thought?"

Eben, of course, had no answer. She certainly had been no child, but the most exciting woman who had ever lain beneath him. No, definitely not a child in that moment. But he'd cut off his right arm before he'd admit it.

He had no choice but to steer the conversation toward safer ground where he could be sure of himself. He must go on the offensive.

"Only a child would be so rash as to set out on this harebrained scheme of yours. You have half Jibril's army out in search of you. The future!" He gestured contemptuously.

"Only a lackwit would believe such nonsense. Some charlatan has drawn you in for some dark reason of his own, and you have not one iota of common sense if you believe him."

"You know nothing about it," Kaia snapped. "Merlin himself has been there, and he would have no reason to lie. He knows a spell to send us there. I can learn to read and write, I can—"

"You can do that here," Eben countered, abandoning any attempt at reasoning with her about some mythical sorcerer.

"My father would have me live in ignorance all my life," Kaia yelled into the rising wind. "Yes, just like a child. That is how men wield their power over us. Keep us in ignorance, keep us children, send us from the rule of our father's house to that of our husband's."

She threw up her hands in disgust. "And we go like sheep because we don't know any better. Well, I know better now. It doesn't have to be like that, it doesn't—"

"Not all men are like your father, Kaia," Eben interjected hastily before she became hysterical. "Jibril will bring you to the palace, where you can study with the best masters in the kingdom."

The first wavelets of the incoming tide eddied ever closer, but Kaia and Eben would likely not have noticed a thirty-foot tidal wave thundering toward shore.

"And what then?" Kaia yelled. "What good will my learning do when I am married off to some sour old man and find myself in childbed year after year? When I must have the scriptures read to me and interpreted for me by a priest—a man, naturally—and I am beaten when my hus-

79

band finds me with pen and parchment in hand, as my father did?"

Kaia's fury exploded into a flood of tears. When Eben made a move toward her to offer comfort, she backed away and threw up her hands to ward him off. "No, don't touch me," she sobbed.

"Kaia," Eben said gently, "Trust Jibril. Trust us all to see that you do not live this life you fear. You will never return to your father's hall. We will find you a husband who—"

Something in the way Kaia's head jerked up and her eyes went hard stopped Eben in mid-sentence With great deliberation she wiped her eyes on her sleeve and straightened up, every bit the imperious noblewoman she had been born to be.

Eben breathed a sigh of relief. The storm appeared to have passed. He held out his hand to her with a winning smile.

"Come, little one. All will be well, you'll see."

So unexpected was the scream of frustration and rage that rent the air that Eben stumbled and landed flat on his back. A little wave washed over him. Sputtering and spitting sand, he clambered to his feet. Before he could properly collect himself, Kaia was off, pelting back down the beach.

"Oh, hell," Eben snarled and went after her.

Far ahead, Kaia could see what looked at first like a flock of birds flapping toward her. With her waist-length hair streaming behind like her a golden pennant, she ran toward it, and soon saw that the brown and gray, white and black that she had supposed were wings were in fact the habits of a gaggle of perhaps twenty nuns, who had launched a rescue party for their imperiled sister.

The beach was narrowing now as the tide began to pour in, and Kaia had no time to veer around them as they raced toward her. At the very last moment, they parted like the Red Sea to allow her through, then closed ranks again when they saw Eben pounding toward them.

He never stood a chance.

Lord Eben Dhion, armiger of the Ninth House, went down beneath an onrushing horde of vengeance-bent brides of Christ.

Chapter Ten

"I suggest you wipe that grin from your face or I shall be compelled to do it for you."

Eben glared at Obike Zebengo through his one good eye. He raised his cup and winced at the sting of the rough wine on his split lip.

"What the devil are you doing here anyway?" he demanded.

Zebengo had arrived at the Inn of the Bishop's Bastard just as Eben, supported by two sturdy farmers, was being assisted down from the back of a cart carrying a number of curious, snuffling piglets to market. A small boy trailed behind leading Eben's stallion, and a straggling parade of gawkers hastened to catch up. The pilgrims had continued on their way, having satisfied themselves that there would be no encore to the thrilling events on the beach. The little nun had scrambled up the cliff face, plowed through her applauding audience, and disappeared into thick woods, trailed by a shrieking monk and a frolicking black hound.

Obike leaned back in the inn's most commodious chair. "A few miles back I heard there was excellent sport to be seen here—extraordinary, actually. I just couldn't resist. Imagine my surprise—"

"Enough," Eben growled.

"Imagine my surprise," Zebengo continued airily, "to find none other than Lord Dhion himself being borne from the field of combat, where, apparently, he had gone down to defeat in hand-to-hand combat with twenty virgins hell-bent on saving one of their sisters from a fate worse than death. You don't see something like that every day. I simply had to come."

"You're enjoying yourself, aren't you?" Eben growled.

"Immensely. Since I don't see Lady Kaia tied across your saddle, I must assume she made her escape."

"I would have had her if it hadn't been for those crazed nuns," Eben complained. He shuddered at the memory.

"This whole thing is utter madness," he declared. "We cannot allow Kaia to board that ship. If Gyp should get his hands on her . . . When I get hold of her I'm going to send her home under armed guard, and then I'm going after that bastard."

Obike shifted in his chair and cleared his throat. "Better double that guard. We've got another little fool who's run away. Two, actually."

Eben's head snapped up. "Who?"

"Morgana."

"Morgana? My sister Morgana?" Eben's voice was too quiet, too controlled. "And?"

"Your squire, Jocco."

It was too much. Eben leaped to his feet and slammed his fist into the wall. "My sister is running around the countryside with my squire?" he roared. "Unchaperoned? Where the hell were you, Zebengo, when this happened? You were supposed to take her back to the hall for safekeeping."

Obike Zebengo was a mountain of a man. He had been a prince in his own land once, then a slave, and then a prince again when the late King Ahriman purchased his freedom and made him his adopted son. He quailed before no man, and no man would willingly tempt him to anger. He rarely showed emotion, but in the face of Eben's righteous anger his discomfiture was evident.

"She put a sleeping potion in my ale. I didn't awaken until the following morning. By then they were gone."

Eben stormed around the room tearing at his hair and letting loose a stream of remarkably colorful invectives. "What in the name of God was she thinking?"

"She left a note. She's gone in search of Kaia, to bring her back. She's feeling guilty, I gather. As for Jocco—"

Eben threw himself into his chair and splashed wine into his cup. "When I get my hands on him, I'll—"

"Hold on. Before you have the lad drawn and quartered, you should know that he believes in this 'future' business and thinks the healers of that day could mend his disfigurement. He discovered Morgana's plan and determined to go with her to protect her. And Morgana has only to smile her little pixie smile at him and he'd follow her to the ends of the earth."

"Little Kaia, my sister, my squire," Eben muttered into his cup. "Wizards, delusional monks, magic spells, beetles, bees. Everyone's gone mad. I've gone mad."

Obike nodded. "I'd say that about sums it up."

Crouched before a fire that seemed much too small, encircled by a night that was much too black and far too long, Lady Morgana Dhion reflected that the blame for this whole terrible situation lay squarely on her own shoulders. She should never have promised Kaia not to tell about the beatings; had they known, Jibril and Syrah would have put a stop to them at once. She should have gone to the convent with Kaia. She had no business hiding Kaia's letter for two whole days. She was guilty, guilty, guilty.

Of course, the fact that she and Jocco were hopelessly lost was entirely his fault.

The road that ran parallel to the coast some miles inland would take them to Galiana just as well, he'd said, and there would be less chance they would be apprehended.

Of course he knew where they were going, he'd said. She was wont to worry overmuch. They could just retrace their steps. . . .

Oh, *now* he knew where they were. . . . .

Wait, he knew a shortcut. . . .

No, there was no reason to ask directions. . . .

Well, perhaps he was a bit disoriented, but it couldn't be far to the main road now. . . .

How could he think, with her nagging him at every turn?

84

He couldn't help it, Morgana decided as she watched him emerge from the shadows with an armful of dry twigs. He was, after all, a man, and all in all, a rather sweet one.

They had plowed steadily westward through thick woods and tangled undergrowth until it became impossible to see in the deepening dusk. They finally set up a little camp to wait out the night. If they didn't get their bearings soon, Morgana thought sadly, they would never reach Galiana in time to catch Kaia before she sailed away forever. And Jocco would live out his life with his ugly harelip, sad, lonely, and feared save for the friendship and compassion of the family of the Ninth House.

"I have thought of a new riddle," Jocco announced proudly in the strange, lisping speech he had devised to compensate for his inability to pronounce certain letters.

Morgana smiled. He had never learned to read and write, but he had a remarkable memory. He could name every troubadour who had performed in the hall of the Ninth House, and was ever reciting poetry, singing nonsensical ditties, and concocting jests. Few had the patience to listen closely so as to make sense of what he was saying, but he positively glowed when he had an audience, even an audience of one.

He built up the fire and settled down beside her.

> *"What is heavier than the lead?*
> *And what is better than the bread?"*

Morgana made a great show of trying to reason out the riddle; she'd heard it before but didn't want to hurt his feelings by coming up with the answer too quickly. "Aha!" she cried at last.

> *"Sin is heavier than the lead,*
> *The blessing's better than the bread."*

"Very good," Jocco acknowledged. "But that was an easy one. Try this."

> *"What is sharper than a thorn?*
> *What is louder than a horn?"*

"Let me think," said Morgana. "Thorn. Horn. A woman's tongue? No. It works for the first line, not the second: horns are not necessarily sharp. A voice would be loud, but not a tongue. Hmmm. Oh, I give up. Tell me."

> *"Hunger is sharper than a thorn,*
> *And shame is louder than a horn."*

Morgana clapped her hands and laughed. "That is so clever, Jocco. I don't know how you do it. Perhaps you will be a troubadour in your new world."

Jocco looked wistful. "How can I be a troubadour with my mouth twisted so and my teeth sticking out? People will only laugh at me more."

Morgana's heart went out to him. "The healers will fix your mouth, you'll see. And then you will tell your jests and stories and sing your songs, and people will flock from all around just to hear you."

"You think so? Oh, if only—" He stopped suddenly and peered uneasily into the darkness beyond the fire. "Did you hear something?"

"Yes," whispered Morgana. She scrambled to her feet

and clapped both hands to her mouth. The slavering beasts and fire-breathing monsters of a hundred childhood nightmares might be lurking just beyond the firelight.

Jocco thrust her behind him, drew a long, wicked knife from his belt, and tensed to face whatever menace lurked in the shadows. He felt no fear: Lord Eben had trained him well. He would fight to the death to protect Lady Morgana.

"Sheathe your weapon, son," a deep voice said.

Morgana felt only a fleeting sense of relief that she was not to be torn apart by a pack of hungry wolves or crushed in the jaws of an enraged mother bear in defense of her cubs before it dawned on her that they faced a far more dangerous animal: man. Who could know what diabolical fate awaited her at the hands of thieves and murderers and ravishers of helpless virgins?

"Show yourself," Jocco demanded.

At first they could see only a pool of shadow against the greater darkness, the faintest shape of a very tall man; then, inexplicably, a sprinkling of silver stars and crescent moons sparkled upon the form.

The apparition did not so much as step from the darkness into the firelight as flow from it.

"Good evening," it said. "I hope I didn't alarm you."

Jocco did not relax his defensive stance. "Who are you?"

"What are you?" Morgana chimed in.

"I am Merlin."

The knife slipped from Jocco's hand. "*The* Merlin?"

Merlin shrugged. "I know of no other."

Morgana could barely contain her excitement. "Kaia's Merlin?"

Laughter shone in his ancient eyes. "Lady Kaia's Merlin,

if you like, and Brother Absalom's. Young Jocco's Merlin. Yours too, Lady Morgana."

"You know who we are?"

"Of course." He chuckled. "And where."

"Well, thank goodness for that," Morgana declared. "Jocco has gotten us well and truly lost—"

"That is not so, my lady." Jocco bristled. "I know exactly where we are."

"Really?" she inquired in a honeyed voice. "Where exactly are we?"

Jocco stood tall. "Here. We are here. We can be nowhere else."

"That is the stupidest—"

"Well said, young Jocco," Merlin interjected before the argument heated up further. "You have the makings of a philosopher. I think, however, you wish to be somewhere else. If you will come with me, I will lead you there and you will find those whom you seek."

Jocco smiled a smug little smile as they put out the fire and followed the wizard into the night. "I told you so."

Morgana rolled her eyes. "Men."

Chapter Eleven

There were secrets one did not share even with one's closest friend, or speak in the sacred precinct of the confessional no matter how much one needed absolution. Better to hold one's counsel or repent in silence.

Morgana would hear the story eventually—it would be on the lips of every living soul in the kingdom by tomorrow's sunrise—but Kaia could not bring herself to speak of what had transpired the previous day on the beach. In the abridged version she told Morgana, Eben had caught up with her several miles from the Inn of the Bishop's Bastard. A chase had ensued, and Kaia had managed to break loose after a brief tussle.

The recitation was suitably theatrical for Morgana's sake, enhanced with a goodly amount of fanciful detail and heart-pounding drama. Even had she wished to confide the intimacy she had shared with Eben, Kaia would have been at a loss for words to describe the indescribable.

At sixteen Morgana was still ignorant of her own carnal nature, but then again, two days ago, in her wildest fantasy of what might transpire between a man and a woman in the marriage bed, Kaia could not have imagined her own.

It had been Eben Dhion who had shown her. And recoiled in horror when he realized it was Kaia—*little* Kaia—who lay beneath him. In the night Kaia knew not whether to weep or rage, damn him to hell or imagine him on top of her again.

And the worst of it was the realization that if he would not satisfy his own need for her as he did for other women, what hope then that he would ever love her?

"Ahem, if I may have your attention, ladies and gentlemen." Merlin frowned down at the four of them. "We must hasten to Galiana. There each of you must look into your heart and decide if you wish to continue on. Right now Brother Absalom seems to be the only one who has fully committed himself. I believe Lady Kaia may be having some second thoughts. Squire Jocco seems to believe he will find a better future, a kinder world, but is not yet sure. The Lady Morgana had no intention of traveling into the future when she set out after her friend, but she may be sufficiently intrigued to wish to join us."

"You know if it is a better, kinder future," Jocco said. "You have been there. You have only to tell us. Then we can decide one way or the other."

Merlin paced slowly back and forth before them, his head bent in deep thought. "No man can choose his time, not even I. He is born into it and must make what he can of what he finds there."

"But the spell gives us the power to choose," Kaia objected.

"You choose only to leave one place for another. I could impart to you a certain amount of knowledge, but it would avail you little. A newborn arrives in his world with a certain kind of knowledge too; it is called instinct. But he does not yet know who he is; he must live his life to find out. You do not know if you will arrive as the same person who departed. You too must live your life there to find out."

A thoughtful silence settled upon the group. Merlin's words cast an entirely new light on the enterprise.

Brother Absalom was the first to speak. "A very interesting philosophy, but you are quite wrong, sir, and I fear your words verge on heresy. Scripture states quite clearly that a man can do naught but tread the path that God intends for him."

Merlin did not look at all concerned that he might be speaking heresy. "I expect it does say that; I do not consult scripture overmuch. However, if anyone should know about arriving in a new world and living the life destined for him there, it is I, and I can assure you that any knowledge I carry with me avails me little. I could expound for days on the theory of free will, and not one of you would have the faintest idea what I was talking about."

Absalom perked up. "Free will? I don't believe I know the term."

"You wouldn't. No one has conceived the idea yet. But soon, soon." Merlin smiled. "Come, my friend, I shall explain."

They wandered off through waving grasses. Exclamations of surprise and consternation drifted back as Absalom tried to wrestle with the astounding new concept of free will.

Kaia, Morgana, and Jocco stared at one another.

"I really don't understand a word he said," Morgana admitted, "but I think this is a very bad idea and you will all live to regret it. Kaia, dear friend, I beg you to reconsider."

"Well, I know I shan't change my mind," Jocco declared. "I have no family that I know of. Save for Lord Eben and you two, I have no friends to speak of. There is no remedy here for my deformity. What have I to lose?"

And I, thought Kaia, but knew in her heart that she had far more to lose than she cared to admit.

"We've lost them."

Obike and Eben focused on the ribbon of dusty road below. They could see for a league in either direction from the windswept brow of the hill. Now that the pilgrims had left the coast road and turned northward toward St.

Polyp's Pillar, there was far less traffic passing by. Kaia would surely have abandoned the habit and assumed a new disguise; it would serve it no purpose to search for her among the pilgrims.

In any event, Eben Dhion was not sure he wanted to come within flailing distance of a nun ever again. Although he could now see out of both eyes after the application of a foul-smelling poultice by an even fouler-smelling old woman at the inn, Eben still sported a spectacular purplish-black bruise around his eye socket. He'd suffered far worse in his life, but he did not take being humiliated well and had concocted a number of vivid scenarios in which Kaia Kurinon would receive her due.

"I think we should abandon the search," agreed Obike. "We can reach Galiana tomorrow night if we ride hard. They cannot possibly have gotten ahead of us. All we need do is wait for them to come to us.

"Besides," he added, "I have need of a good meal and a willing wench in my bed." He glanced over at Eben, who was still in a foul temper from the events of the previous day. "It wouldn't do you any harm, either."

Chapter Twelve

So this was what it felt like to be a woman in the world of the Saracen. Kaia found it strangely liberating. Swathed in an ankle-length black veil that Saracen women were required to wear when appearing in a public place, she was comfortably shielded from the appraising gaze of men. She had pinned the veil in place with a small silver brooch. Only her eyes were visible, and Merlin had emphasized that they must all keep their eyes downcast to emulate the modest demeanor Arab men insisted on in their women. As the cart rumbled along, she reflected that there was a difference between looking at the world and looking *out* at the world.

The others had reacted with varying degrees of enthusiasm when Merlin decreed that they should complete the journey disguised as Muslim women. Morgana thought it wildly romantic. Jocco wasn't at all happy to be cast in the role of a woman, but found a certain relief in being able to hide his deformity behind the veil. It was Brother Absalom who put up the most resistance, fretting over the heresy of assuming the garb of the infidel. Cast as chief wife, he spent the larger part of the journey perched up on the seat beside Merlin in heated theological debate.

The wizard looked impressive in the garb of a man of high caste: a loose white tunic and a black turban wound about his head, with the extra length dangling between his shoulder blades. He sported a bushy black moustache and beard.

Kaia, Morgana, and Jocco had been assigned the roles of second, third, and fourth wives, and bounced along with much grumbling in the back of the cart.

Merlin finally acceded to demands for a rest so that his companions could see to their personal needs. They would easily reach Galiana by evening; there was no real hurry. He was finding the whole charade immensely enjoyable; so much better than his previous incarnation in the rat-infested, plague-ridden cities of the north some decades in the future. He wanted to take full advantage of this pleasant interlude. Heaven only knew where he was headed next.

He was just rounding up his charges when twelve riders appeared around a bend in the road: Eben, Obike Zebengo, Commander Ankuli, and the men of the king's guard.

Four wives froze.

"Keep your heads. Do exactly as I say," Merlin ordered.

Brother Absalom reacted to the present circumstance as he always did when he was on the verge of losing his wits. This time he launched into a fervent recitation of the plagues visited upon Pharaoh when Moses commanded him to let his people go.

"'And if thou refuse to let them go,'" proclaimed Brother Absalom "'behold I will smite all thy borders with frogs. And the river shall bring forth frogs in abundance, which shall go up and come into thine house and into thy bedchamber, and upon thy bed, and into the house of the servants and upon thy people and into the ovens—'"

"For the love of heaven," Kaia begged, "hold your tongue. You cannot be a Muslim woman proclaiming Holy Scripture."

The search party drew up in a cloud of dust.

"Peace be with you," Eben said as was proper when greeting a man of Islam.

"And with you, praise Allah," the tall man replied.

"I see you are taking a rest from the rigors of the road," Eben continued. "It is very hot, and our horses require water." He unfastened a leather flask from his saddle pack.

"We have some excellent wine with us. We can mix it with cold water from the spring. It will make a most refreshing drink. I hope you and your ladies will join us."

Merlin placed his palms together and dipped his head in a respectful bow. "I am honored, good sir, but the Prophet forbids us spirits."

"Of course, of course. I apologize if I offended you," Eben replied.

"Not at all, good sir, not at all," Merlin assured him. "I will be pleased to join you if only to enjoy pleasant conversation."

The men were now brushing off the dust of the road and heading in the direction of the sweetly bubbling spring with their own flasks. Eben joined them.

"Draw your veils more closely," Merlin commanded as he shepherded his "wives" to a grassy knoll nearby. "Sit. Fix your eyes upon the ground."

"' . . . will I bring the locusts into thy coast: And they shall cover the face of the earth: and they shall eat—'"

"Brother Absalom, you will cease your insane babbling this minute," Merlin snapped. "Squire Jocco, a woman glides; she does not gallop. Lady Morgana, stop trembling. Lady Kaia, I must insist you keep your eyes modestly upon the ground. There," he said as they sank into a huddled mass of black cloth. "I think that will do. Not a word now." He headed back to where the riders were unfastening their heavy sword belts and making themselves comfortable in the cool of the shade.

"Your daughters?" a soldier inquired, wondering what the women looked like beneath their strange garb.

"My wives," Merlin replied.

95

"Good Lord," the soldier exclaimed. "You have four wives?"

"As you see," Merlin acknowledged. "Allah wills it so."

Kaia strained to hear the men's conversation. Had she not known better, she would have believed that Merlin was exactly what he presented himself to be. She only hoped his "wives" appeared equally credible.

Eben had remained at the spring for some minutes, rinsing dust from his hands, face, and hair. As he started back, he decided to take a closer look at the women; not so close that he would offend their husband but enough to satisfy his curiosity as to their ages and, if such could be deduced from the eyes only, their beauty or lack thereof.

He bowed deeply to the women. "Peace be with you."

Not one responded with the customary "And with you." That surprised Eben, who had met with many diplomats and traders and their families at Jibril's court. The women might not always voice the appropriate reply, but they did at least nod.

These women huddled so close to one another that they appeared to have four heads perched atop one enormous body. Eben could sense their profound discomfort—more like fear, actually—at finding a strange man not five paces from them.

"A man values modesty in his woman," said the merchant, who had suddenly appeared beside Eben. "Praise Allah, I am so blessed in my house."

"It is a virtue our women would do well to emulate," Eben observed. "We have allowed them far too many liberties. As a result they come to believe they are the equal of men. They think to make their own decisions without the proper guidance of their fathers and husbands, and attempt to join in the rational discourse of men, when they have but the minds of children and require our guidance at every step."

A gasp and flash of angry dark eyes drew Eben's attention to one of the women in the back of the group. She appeared to have taken grave exception to this casual observation. He eyed her thoughtfully.

"In fact, a foolish girl—nay, two foolish girls—are the reason we ride," Eben explained. "They have taken it into their heads to run away, and I am commanded by the king to retrieve them so that they can be punished accordingly and instructed in proper womanly ways."

"How very distressing," Merlin murmured, gently guiding Eben back toward the men sprawled beneath the trees. He very much feared Lady Kaia's reaction to the man's rather pointed remarks. It would not surprise him if blood were to be spilled.

Merlin was just assisting his charges into the back of the cart when Eben, who was making some minor adjustment to his stirrups, remarked, "It is merely a matter of curiosity to me, and I hope you will not be offended if I inquire as to your destination, sir."

Merlin took up the reins. "Not at all, sir. We travel to Galiana, there to take passage to Lyda, where I have further business. From thence we return to our home."

" ' . . . and it became a boil breaking forth with blains upon man and beast . . . ' "

"Your women do not seem to be enjoying the journey," Eben observed. The three in the back of the cart were clinging to one another, and the chief wife who rode beside the merchant had drawn her veil full over her face so that not even her eyes could be seen. She seemed to be praying, although Eben could not catch the muffled words.

"My wife is a woman of great religious fervor," the man explained, squeezing Brother Absalom's shoulder. "She praises Allah day and night."

Eben smiled. "Yet another virtue. Most commendable."

The merchant nodded. "As you say, sir."

"Since Galiana too is our destination, perhaps you can assist me in finding those I seek."

A muffled groan came from one of the women huddled in the back.

"But of course," the man said. "In what way, sir?"

"These are no common girls," Eben explained. "One is a young cousin of the king himself; she travels in the company of an elderly monk. My sister, too, is missing, as is my squire, although they took to the road a few days later."

"Most distressing," the gentleman replied somberly, "to have one's women abroad in the world unprotected and likely to get up to all sorts of mischief. I shall certainly keep an eye out for them."

"We will take lodging at the Seven Curses Inn tonight," Eben informed him. "You may find me there if you should have any intelligence of them."

Two leagues down the road Eben signaled Obike to pull up. "I have been thinking. Our friend back there has four wives."

"Four too many, if you ask me," observed Obike.

"Does it not occur to you that two when added to two amounts to four?"

Obike frowned, then threw back his head and laughed. "Yes, I believe it does."

Chapter Thirteen

Kaia would not be swayed. Morgana marshaled what arguments she could, but she was not given to deep reasoning and in the end was reduced to pleading and tears.

"How can you leave behind those who love you? Does our friendship mean so little? Who will look after you? What will become of you? How will you make your way?" Morgana sobbed.

Kaia had asked herself the selfsame questions again and again in the past days, and had found no answers. When she considered the formidable obstacles she would face, alone, in an unknown place and time, her decision and stubborn determination appeared heartless, irrational, inexplicable, and rash even to herself. It would break her heart to part with her friend. Although Morgana was two years her junior, they had shared their joys and sorrows, questions and secrets, hopes and dreams as they grew up together.

"I will miss you more than you can possibly imagine, Morgana," she said, choking back her tears, "but there are things you do not know; things that have happened to me you cannot understand."

"Tell me," Morgana cried. "I will try to understand. What has happened that you cannot confide in me? Do you no longer trust me? I have always kept your secrets. I never told how your father hurt you; it was he who confessed it to Jibril. I would never, ever tell anyone about how you love my brother and are so sad he does not love you. As God is my witness."

Kaia turned to the window and gazed out over the harbor of Galiana. Sailing vessels of every description, large and small, sleek and well weathered, foreign and domestic, bobbed on gentle, moon-clad waves. A few denizens of the port were still out and about, intent on their errands and secret business of the night, while drunken seamen searched out the few harlots who had not yet found their beds after a hard night plying their ancient trade.

"I do not love Eben," Kaia said flatly.

"Of course you do," Morgana insisted. "You have always loved him."

"I did once, it is true. I know now that it was the fantasy of a foolish young girl."

Morgana pulled the rough blanket from the bed they shared. She stepped to the window, draped half of the blanket around Kaia's shoulders and half around her own, so that they stood cocooned in a stray shaft of moonlight.

"What has happened to change your mind, Kaia? Surely one does not just pluck love from one's heart and discard it like a faded flower?"

"I don't know, Morgana. I feel as though I don't know anything anymore: what I believe, what I want, why I do the things I do. Nothing is as it first appears, especially love."

"You've changed." Morgana sniffed. "Since your papa sent you away, you are not the same person."

"No," said Kaia softly, "I am not."

Brother Absalom tested the water with one bony toe. It was not as cold as he had feared, so he ventured out until it washed about his knees. He had never bathed in the nude before. In fact, they did not often bathe at the monastery, and on the rare occasion the brothers were herded out to the hideously cold Lake Zando, they removed neither their breechcloths nor their hose, so as not to incite the lust of any female who might pass by. Not to mention one another.

It was most stimulating, he thought, though he could not imagine splashing about in water that would close over one's head as Jocco was doing some way out. If God had intended a man to swim like a fish, He would have provided him with fins and gills, was Brother Absalom's considered opinion. God had created man in His own image, and no one had ever suggested the Creator was possessed of fins and gills.

In the early days of their acquaintance, Merlin had gone so far as to suggest that man had descended from a fish! Brother Absalom very much feared Merlin skirted dangerously close to heresy and might even have tried his hand at black magic. Hell must surely await him, a fact that saddened the kindly old monk. He brightened at the sudden thought that Merlin might escape such a fate. One died and went to heaven, hell, or more likely purgatory after one *died*. Merlin lived toward his birth, not his death. That would mean . . . well, Absalom had no notion of what it

101

might mean. He would posit the question to Merlin on the morrow. He quite looked forward to bracing theological discourse to break the tedium of the sea journey.

"Ho, Brother Absalom, will you not come in?" Jocco shouted before he dived below the surface again.

Absalom waited anxiously until Jocco reappeared. He had grown rather fond of the lad, and he wished with all his heart that he could ease the pain he had suffered in his short life. Brother Absalom had encouraged Jocco to tell his story over a meal of mutton, bread, and black-bean potage they had taken at the inn where Merlin had deposited his "wives" before he went into the town on his own mysterious errands. Despite a dispassionate recitation of his experiences, Absalom knew that beneath Jocco's words lay a grief that could not be told.

How Jocco had been born into a family of some wealth; sent to a wet nurse in the village for his first two years, an outdated custom still practiced amongst some people of his class. How his parents, disgusted and shamed by his twisted mouth, would not reclaim him; in fact, repudiated him altogether.

Jocco would not speak of his early years, but Brother Absalom could imagine the cruelties he must have endured, shuffled from place to place, taunted and reviled, until he finally found himself on the streets of Suriana, where Eben Dhion had discovered him pawing through garbage behind a bake house, and taken him in. In the hall of the Ninth House, Jocco had found the first real kindness of his life and a certain amount of respect, despite his harelip. He had worked hard to become a page and eventually squire to the lord armiger himself.

"It is time you came out now, lad," Brother Absalom called. "You will catch a chill."

Why, he sounded exactly like a father calling to his son, Absalom realized with surprise.

Chapter Fourteen

Eben would reflect later that in thinking himself so very clever he had only managed to deceive himself as well as be deceived. It did not sit well with him; his pride and complacency had almost led to disaster.

At ease in the certainty that Kaia and the others were going about disguised as Muslim women and therefore easily marked, he set off the next morning to discover what ships were undergoing repair and refitting, hiring crew, and taking on stores in preparation for departure. He went alone; Zebengo was still abed with a foxy little wench, and likely to awaken with a sore head and even sourer disposition. Eben had, of course, been besieged with offers of diverse pleasures the previous night—one in particular taxed the imagination as to how it could be accomplished—and finally escaped to his room, where he was forced to bar the door lest the clothes be torn from his body and his person violated. He had no taste for a quick tumble, no matter the incentive. There was only one wench he wanted to get his hands on, not for bed sport, he assured himself, but for taking across his knee and applying the sound paddling the wretched child so richly deserved.

That particular train of thought sent Eben skidding down the slippery slope of inevitable male preoccupation, which in turn let loose a flaming arrow of lust straight to his loins. He was obliged to retire into a shadowed doorway to regain command of himself and adjust the drape of his tunic. He forced the vision of Kaia Kurinon's delectable derriere from his mind and continued down the hill toward the harbor.

Four vessels large enough to undertake a lengthy sea voyage lay alongside the long breakwaters that jutted out like two embracing arms around the inner harbor. The tide was full out, and a wide expanse of mud, slimed with seaweed and stinking refuse from the town, had marooned dories, coasters, and all manner of fishing boats. On the quayside, Eben could see the carts and rough wooden shacks of a thriving market and hear the shrill cries of hawkers, while a short distance along the pebbled strand a father and son played at Halfpenny-Prick and a large black hound leaped and cavorted around them.

It was a pleasant scene, and Eben strolled along in the warm sunshine in no particular hurry, since no ship could sail until the next day's high tide. He had plenty of time to locate his prey and set his trap.

A handsome two-masted vessel drawn up at the far end of the nearer of the two jetties caught his eye. As he drew near he could see a number of carts drawn alongside, filled with sacks of grain, kegs of ale and vats of oil, and all the provisions necessary for a journey of some weeks. Chickens clucked and pecked at one another in crowded cages; a milk cow gazed out at the world through soft, dumb eyes;

sheep bleated; pigs oinked. Since most sailing vessels usually provided only dried and salted meat and fish for a journey, Eben concluded the passengers aboard this vessel must be persons of some means. A wealthy Muslim trader might very well choose such a congenial passage.

"Aye, sir," the captain replied when Eben inquired as to his destination, "we sail on tomorrow's tide for Gijon with two ports of call at Evros and Calpe."

"How many passengers does she carry?" Eben asked.

"Twelve. Any more than that and they're biting each other's heads off two days out. We cater more for goods, and I'm glad to take on traders who prefer to travel with their merchandise rather than trust intermediaries. They're willing to pay more for their passage, they are. As a matter of fact, only yesterday a distinguished Muslim gentleman paid passage for himself and his wives, four of 'em if you can credit it. Got two merchants bound for Evros, but they only got two wives each. Ain't natural, if you ask me. I don't mind saying it's always a problem having these ladies in their veils and such aboard. Their men is mighty suspicious if one of my lads just as looks at one of 'em. We had bad business two—no, three—trips back. One of my lads took to one of them women. Can't imagine why, since he couldn't see nothin' but her eyes. Don't much care what a woman's eyes look like; I'm more interested in what's down below, if you get my meanin'." He waggled his eyebrows and smirked. "Anyhow, her brother went after little Ninu with the wickedest lookin' knife I ever seen. Near gelded the poor lad. Had to set him ashore at Tripos, get him stitched up."

If this intelligence had not been enough to convince Eben that his supposition had been correct—that Kaia and the others would continue on in their disguise, swathed from head to foot as they had been yesterday—the sight of the Muslim gentleman himself coming toward him did.

"All praise be to Allah, good sir, again we are well met," said that gentleman, according Eben the respectful greeting of his people. "I am just completing plans for our journey. A fine vessel, is she not?"

"Very fine," Eben replied. It occurred to him to wonder for the first time just who this man was and how he had come to play a role in this mad escapade. He was far too tall to be Brother Absalom, as described by the Mother Superior. Kaia must have great faith in him to keep their secret. But who was he?

"We sail tomorrow on the afternoon tide," the man said. "I am glad to be on the homeward leg of this journey. My wives complain constantly, and contend among themselves for my attentions in the night." He grinned and spread his hands in a helpless gesture. "But I am, as you see, just one man, and not so young as I once was. Yet I manage, Allah be praised.

"I must be about my business, sir. Much to do, much to do. By the by, I have kept an eye out for those you seek, as you asked, but alas . . . Perhaps you have already nabbed your fugitives?" he inquired hopefully.

This man, whoever he was, played his part well, Eben thought. A clever man. But not so clever as he might think. His game was up, and when Eben had Kaia and the others in hand, he would make it his business to discover exactly who was aiding them, and why.

Eben offered his hand in parting. "No, but I am confident it will not be long."

"You seem quite sure of yourself, sir."

Eben smiled politely. "Not without reason, I assure you. Farewell and Godspeed. Somehow I think we shall meet again."

"Oh, we shall certainly meet again," Merlin murmured to himself as he went on his way. "But I fear you are in for quite a surprise, Lord Eben."

"Where do you hide a tree?" Brother Absalom asked.

"That's easy. In a forest, of course," replied Jocco.

"Oh, you've heard that one."

Jocco stuffed a huge meat pie into his mouth. "Everyone's heard that one." He swallowed the last of the pasty and announced, "Now it's my turn."

"I warn you, lad, I'm quite good at riddles," Absalom boasted, praying he would not humiliate himself if the riddle proved too difficult.

Jocco wiped his mouth on his sleeve and recited:

> *"My house is not quiet, I am not loud;*
> *But for us God fashioned our fate together.*
> *I am the swifter, at times the stronger,*
> *My house more enduring, longer to last.*
> *At times I rest; my dwelling still runs;*
> *Within it I lodge as long as I live.*
> *Should we two be severed, my death is sure."*

Jennie Klassel

Brother Absalom gazed down at his boots, up at the sky, hemmed and hawed. "I know!" he declared. "A fish in a river!"

"Very good. But that was an easy one," said Jocco. "Try this."

> *"Oft I must strive with wind and wave,*
> *Battle them both when under the sea*
> *I feel out the bottom, a foreign land.*
> *In lying still I am strong in the strife;*
> *If I fail in that, they are stronger than I,*
> *And wrenching me loose, soon put me to rout.*
> *They wish to capture what I must keep.*
> *I can master them both if my grip holds out,*
> *If the rocks bring succor and lend support,*
> *Strength in the struggle. Ask me my name!"*

"Let me think, let me think," said Absalom. "Sea . . . something in the water. Strong in the strife . . . perhaps a storm? Aha!" he crowed. "It is an anchor!"

Jocco realized he was up against a canny opponent indeed. He searched his mind for the hardest riddle he knew. Yes, this would surely stump the smirking monk.

> *"What is greater than God?*
> *More evil than the devil?*
> *The poor have it,*
> *The rich don't want it,*
> *And if you eat it, you will die."*

Brother Absalom's mind went blank. This was dreadful. Was he to go down to ignominious defeat at the hands of a fourteen-year-old who could neither read nor write? The humiliation, the—

"God's ballocks!" Jocco exclaimed.

"That answer makes no sense at all," Absalom snapped. He sent Jocco a very dark look indeed. "And may I say that although there has been a great deal of theological debate on the issue among the greatest minds of the Church for many years, we have as yet no real proof that God possesses such parts, and it may very well verge on heresy to attribute them to Him. I should take care if I were you."

"Not God, you dolt, Lord Eben!" Jocco was on his feet now, pulling his cap low on his brow and taking off at a brisk trot down the strand.

Absalom was at a loss. "Lord Eben's ballocks?"

Then, catching sight of Eben striding down the quay not fifty paces away, he let out a strangled shriek, leaped from the wall on which they had been sitting, and fluttered away after the squire.

"This is so tedious," Kaia complained, pacing first one way and then the other in their little room.

Morgana neatly folded the last of the black veils and set them in a battered chest in the corner. "Merlin has forbidden us to go out, and I quite agree with him. Eben and Obike are probably scouring the streets for us right now."

Kaia threw herself on the bed and stared up at the blackened beams of the ceiling. "It's not fair. Brother Absalom and Jocco have gone into the city, and we're dressed in the same clothes as they. We have only to bind up our hair and wear the straw hats."

"That's true, but they walk like men," Morgana pointed out, "whereas we have the wider hips and, er, more ample posteriors. Not to mention breasts. Men stride, we sway."

"These tunics are big enough to disguise our breasts," Kaia grumbled. "Besides," she added, jumping up and swaggering about the room, "it's easy enough to imitate a man. You just strut about like a cock of the walk, pretending you're lord of all you survey, and crook your finger at every woman you pass to come and satisfy your every need."

Morgana giggled as Kaia struck an imperious pose, nose in the air, legs wide, clenched hands braced upon hips. "Come to me, woman," she commanded in a deep voice. "Tend to me. Wash me. Fill my belly. Stroke my—"

"Kaia!" Morgana gasped in horror, then collapsed on the floor in a fit of laughter. "You are outrageous. If your papa heard you say such a thing, he would . . . well, he would send you off to the convent and you'd have to run away all over again."

"Well, he's not here," Kaia replied with spirit. "He's far away and probably in his cups already though it's not even noon. And spitting mad," she added with satisfaction.

The sound of feet pounding up the stairs and along the bare boards of the passage made Kaia and Morgana suddenly clutch one another in horror. They were discovered. In a moment two very angry men would throw wide the door and all hell would break loose. Eyes wide with fright and apprehension, they sat frozen and awaited their fate.

"Not in there, in here," a voice wheezed, as though the man had run a great distance and was near collapse. The door flew wide, and Jocco and Brother Absalom fell into the room all in a tangle.

"Close the door, bar the door," the monk cried.

Kaia scrambled to her feet, threw the bolt, and stared down at the panicked duo. She ran to the window and searched this way and that for any sign of pursuit.

"I don't see anyone," she reported.

"There. On the quay," Jocco managed. "Lord Eben."

Morgana could not stop trembling. "He saw you? Did he recognize you?"

"I don't think so," Jocco gasped. "But he was there."

"God's bones, Jocco," Kaia grumbled, "if he didn't see you, why are you running about like madmen?"

Jocco and Absalom stared at one another.

"I don't rightly know," the little monk admitted. "It seemed like a good idea at the time."

Kaia threw up her hands. "It was a terrible idea. He'd be far more likely to take notice of two maniacs crashing about the town. If he did see you, he'd have followed you here and that would be the end of us. But as there's no one in the lane save an old beggar woman, it appears we're safe enough for the moment.

"In fact," she continued thoughtfully, "since these peasant clothes have proved such a good disguise, and since Eben is bound to be looking for Merlin's 'wives,' I think I'll just take a stroll myself."

Jocco threw himself against the door, arms extended. "You will not leave this room, Lady Kaia," said he.

Kaia glowered at him. "And just who is it who will stop me, *Squire*?"

"I will stop you, my lady," Jocco replied stoutly. "It is my sacred duty to protect you."

"And I," added Morgana as she stepped in front of Jocco.

"And I," Brother Absalom declared, positioning himself beside Morgana with arms folded across his chest and an uncharacteristic scowl upon his face.

Kaia glared at the three and threw up her hands in disgust. "This is absurd. I ran away from the convent so I could go where I would, make my own choices, and be free. I might just as well be locked in my father's keep or a hermit's cell, for all the good it's done me."

"It's for your own good, my dear," the monk said kindly.

"Spoken like a true man," Kaia retorted, and retired to a corner, where she spent the remainder of the day sulking and wondering why in the world the simple desire to read and write and choose her own husband and keep bees and learn to fly had become so damnably complicated.

Chapter Fifteen

They would have nowhere to run, nowhere to hide.

Eben Dhion surveyed his trap with the satisfaction of a man who knows he cannot fail. Short of plunging into the sea, Kaia would have no avenue of escape, but because Eben would not put even that act of lunacy beyond her at this point, two of Jibril's guard, dressed in the rough garb of fishermen, were patrolling the waters around the *Sea Maiden*.

Other guards scouted the bustling market and kept watch along the shoreline. Zebengo stood like the fabled Colossus at the head of the breakwater. Once the "merchant" and his "wives" stepped foot on the jetty, they would be well and truly snared.

Eben himself had taken up position halfway out on the jetty, where he lounged against a piling that provided a good spot to observe the pulsing parade of life in either direction. Kalan Ankuli perched upon a stack of crates nearby. The only difficulty Eben could see lay in the large number of people thronging the jetty on business of their own.

Seamen, traders, and travelers chattered, gossiped, and contended in a dozen languages. Peddlers cried their wares, gulls their discontent. Rigging groaned, hulls grated against ancient wood, sails flapped in an indifferent breeze.

Eben reached down to fondle the silky ear of the black hound that had materialized out of the crowd and settled on its haunches at his knee. He recalled seeing it on the beach the previous day. It looked remarkably sleek and well fed for a stray, yet there appeared to be no master nearby. Eben found the dog a pleasant companion to while away the time with.

Suddenly, far down the jetty to his left Eben saw Zebengo, who stood a good head and shoulders above the crowd, waving and pointing. Eben leaped to his feet as four dignified men in Arab dress made stately progress through the crowd. Four figures swathed in black trailed a few steps behind, their veils drawn close about their faces. Eben signaled to Ankuli, and they took up position.

"Halt, in the name of the king," Eben commanded.

The leader of the group stopped short in surprise. "Allow us to pass, sir. You can have no business with us."

Eben saw immediately that the man before him was not the same one he had met on the road the previous day— he was far too short—but he could not dismiss as mere coincidence that four veiled women accompanied him, evidently on their way to board the *Sea Maiden.*

"Where is the leader of your party?" Eben demanded.

"Praise be to Allah, sir, I am the leader of this party."

"Where is the other?"

"Other? There is no other. I am he."

"You are he?"

"I tell you, I am he."

"These are your wives?"

"I cannot see, sir, how that can be any business of yours," the man replied carefully.

"You will see soon enough that it is my business."

The man's dark eyes narrowed, his thick black mustache quivered, his hand slid to the hilt of a jeweled dagger at his waist. "You are mistaken, sir," said he with dangerous courtesy. "I am an ambassador to the court of your king. These women are the wives of my brother, here, and myself. We are bound for Calpe on the *Sea Maiden.* Let us pass."

"You may pass, of course," Eben said, "but the women, whether they be your wives or the wives of the other, are mine."

"I repeat, there is no other, so these cannot be his wives."

"Aha! But if there were an other, these would be his wives, is it not so?"

The Arab gentleman was now convinced that the stranger was mad. "Very well. If you will have it so, sir, then I am the other and these are my wives."

"They are not. They are mine," Eben replied.

"You think these women are *your* wives?"

"Of course they are not my wives, you fool. You have just said that they are the wives of the other."

"There is no other!" the Arab gentleman shouted in exasperation.

A small crowd had gathered. Despite the scrupulously civil tone of the conversation up to that moment, something interesting was going on here. With any luck, a good fight might be brewing.

"Let me see if I have it aright," the Arab continued through clenched teeth. "You want my women."

"They are my women."

How long this inane exchange would have continued is anyone's guess. Fortunately, they were interrupted by Commander Ankuli shouting, "God's bones, Dhion. Look!" He pointed toward the shore.

Eben looked. "Hell and damnation!" he roared. "Hell . . . and . . . dam . . . nation!"

Ankuli was already elbowing past the Arabs and plunging into the crowd. So shocked and incensed was Eben that for a moment he could not take his eyes from the unfolding scene before him.

Obike Zebengo was thundering along the quay in apparent pursuit of . . . Eben could not actually see from where he stood whom Zebengo was chasing, but he knew. Oh yes, he knew.

By the time Eben gained the shore, Ankuli was far ahead. Zebengo had almost reached the land end of the other jetty and was now engaged in what appeared to be a shoving match with the black hound, which had reared up on its hind legs and planted its front paws firmly against Zebengo's massive chest.

And further out on the jetty, three figures were sprinting toward a ketch whose oarsmen were readying to row it out into deeper water before the foresail was raised.

"Damn, damn, damn." Eben had no hope of catching up to them if he continued along the quay and down the long jetty. Zebengo might do it if he could shake off the dog. Even Ankuli had an outside chance if he really put on speed.

Eben looked around wildly, hoping to commandeer a small boat, but the water near shore was too shallow for a launch. The malodorous mudflat stretched a hundred yards beneath the jetty, but at the far end the three-masted ketch almost had sufficient draft to sail.

Eben assessed the distance, observed the relative speed of pursuers and pursued, weighed his options.

He chose the mud.

Kaia thought her lungs were going to explode right out of her body. The *Apostle* looked to be impossibly far away. Jocco was well ahead of her, but she knew that Brother Absalom must be far behind. Morgana had given it up before she even reached the jetty, and had collapsed in a storm of tears and self-recrimination.

It was like one of those strange dreams people had in which they ran and ran and ran without any idea where they were going, or why, or who was chasing them. They just knew they had to keep running or something terrible was going to happen.

Brother Absalom. She couldn't leave him behind. She skidded to a stop, whirled, and raced back along the jetty to where the poor monk was wheezing and groaning as he stumbled along.

"Run," he gasped, "or the ship will sail without you. Don't worry about me."

"It's not going to do me any good if you're not with me," Kaia snapped. She grabbed his arm and towed him along behind her. "And it's not going to do you any good either. You'll be hanged for high treason if they catch you."

If Kaia had intended to remind Brother Absalom that such a fate awaited if he did not pick up the pace, it did the trick. He put on a spurt of speed that sent him galloping wildly down the jetty, wailing all the way.

"Hurry, hurry," Jocco was shouting as they reached the *Apostle.* He held out his hand to haul Brother Absalom aboard. Kaia jumped just as the last line was cast off, and the boat began to move slowly away from the dock. Then, from out of nowhere, the black dog was racing toward the departing vessel and launching itself in a flying leap onto the deck. Kaia, monk, squire, and hound collapsed in a gasping heap, much to the astonishment of all aboard. It was by far the most interesting embarkation anyone had witnessed in recent memory.

"Full sail," the captain shouted. Sailors hauled on the sheets and the huge white mainsail billowed out in the freshening breeze. Kaia climbed to her feet and gazed back at the receding coastline. She could see the small figure of her dearest Morgana in the comforting embrace of Obike Zebengo as she wept into his tunic. But search as she might, Kaia could see no sign of the beautiful man she would love, in any time or place, for the rest of her life.

"Aieeeee!" Brother Absalom shrieked behind her.

Kaia spun around. There before her stood a figure out of a hideous nightmare. Slathered in mud, drenched in slime, dripping fetid brown water from the tip of its nose, and reeking of deepest hell, It glowered down at her through stormy blue eyes.

"If you have a moment, Lady Kaia, I should like to have a word with you," It said.

Chapter Sixteen

Tears. A woman's last resort, her final ploy when she cannot argue the point, knows she is at fault, seeks leniency.

Eben could not, would not allow himself to be swayed. Kaia was clearly in need of a firm hand. Certainly not the harsh discipline her father favored—beating a child was reprehensible—but thoughtful instruction that would address the problems of her unruly impulses and unrealistic expectations. Lord Kurinon was clearly incapable of understanding the female mind. He, Eben Dhion, would therefore undertake her transformation in the stead of the brother she had never had.

Braced against the gentle roll of the ship, arms folded sternly across his chest, grim of countenance, he looked down at the bent head of the contrite little figure on the hard, narrow bed. Her long hair, the color of new corn silk, had come loose in the course of her frantic run. It lay in a disheveled tangle upon the back and shoulders of her brown homespun tunic and fell in unruly waves about her face.

Eben resisted the urge to put a comforting arm around her shaking shoulders. She was weeping into her hands, and the sound of her remorseful tears tore at his heart.

He swiped at another rivulet of muddy water as it tracked its way down the length of his imperious nose. He had never felt so foul in his person in his life, but it was absolutely necessary to impress upon Kaia who was in charge here, and washing away the scum of the Galiana harbor would have to wait.

"I am most displeased," he began in his most lordly manner. "Your recklessness has put a good many people to a great deal of trouble. This fantastic notion that you can move through time has occasioned pain and anxiety in those who care for you that you have lost your mind. The impropriety of running about the countryside with some monk who may be madder even than you, and my own squire, who obviously hasn't a lick of sense, is unparalleled in my experience. That you can believe the ravings of

119

some charlatan who tells you he is a mythical wizard attests to the fact that you cannot be left alone for a moment without supervision.

"What, pray tell, have you to say for yourself, Lady Kaia?"

Having spoken his piece, Eben assumed a righteous pose to await her response.

Noisy sniffling and a low moan attested to Kaia's contrition, but Eben was determined to have the words from her.

"I—I—am—so . . ." she began but could not go on.

"Yes?" Eben prompted.

"I have never—seen anything—so very . . ."

"I'm listening."

"Funny!" she shouted. And threw herself back upon the bed. Her head twisted from side to side, her legs scissored through the air, and her fists beat against the coverlet. She could hardly breathe for laughing or see for the tears streaming from her eyes. "Ha ha ha ha ha! Oh, oh, oh! The look on your face . . . funniest thing I ever saw," she gasped.

"You find this amusing, Lady Kaia?"

". . . smell like a privy," she howled.

"A childish jest, perhaps."

"No, but you must admit—"

Eben had obviously lost control of the situation—if he had ever held it. Chagrin, exasperation, and finally fury swept through him, followed by a grim calm.

"Very well," said he. "Since you show yourself to be a child, I shall consider you one and act accordingly. You are to remain in this cabin for the duration of this voyage and the return trip. You will speak to no one, enjoy no diversions. You will have ample time to contemplate your transgressions and your future, which—and I shall see to it personally—will be spent in the contemplative life of a convent."

With that, he slammed out the door, threw the bolt, and stormed up to the deck, where Brother Absalom and Squire Jocco awaited his pleasure.

Eben appropriated the cramped cabin that Jocco and Absalom were to share, leaving them the choice of sharing the dank, dark forecastle with the unsavory crew or sleeping on deck. They chose the latter without hesitation.

Eben managed to wash off the filth in several buckets of seawater, fresh being unavailable for bathing purposes, and dressed in spare clothes donated by the captain of the vessel. With the exception of his boots, sword belt, and money pouch, he heaved the old clothes over the side with considerable regret as they had been rather fine.

Since there was no sense to be had from the monk at this point—he was far too frightened to give a proper accounting of himself—Eben went in search of Jocco. He found him in earnest conversation with an ill-favored young sailor of his own age with whom, apparently, he had a great deal in common. Eben motioned him to follow, sat him down on a vat of palm oil that was secured to the deck with stout rope, and fixed him with a steely eye.

"Explain," he said tersely.

Jocco poured forth the whole sorry story in an anxious,

rambling, disjointed monologue that was more apology than informative narrative.

"I couldn't let her go off on her own without anyone to protect her, my lord," Jocco tried to explain, "but she was determined, Lady Kaia being her closest friend and all. You mustn't blame Lady Morgana. She thinks it is her fault that Lady Kaia ran away. She wanted to convince her to go home."

"You could simply have informed someone of her plans."

"That's just it, my lord," Jocco cried. "I accompanied Lord Obike to the hall with Lady Morgana, and then he left, and you'd already gone, and Commander Ankuli, and I didn't have time to return to Suriana to inform His Majesty, and—"

"Yes, yes, I understand," Eben interrupted, "but you cannot tell me that you did not have your own reasons for setting out. I understand you believe all this nonsense about magic spells and the future."

Jocco fidgeted with the clasp of his belt. "As to that, my lord, I can't say. I don't believe it exactly, but I don't *not* believe it either, if you take my meaning."

Eben shook his head. It always required patience to wait until his squire got to the point, both because of his jumbled speech and because Jocco tended to be wary of speaking his mind. Had he been born to a kinder life, Eben suspected he would have been able to show the world that he did possess a quick mind. As it was, he was regarded with little respect, and thought himself the lesser.

"You either do believe it or you don't," Eben told him.

Jocco frowned. "I think, my lord, that it is more that I want to believe it. I want to be like other boys. I want maids to smile at me. I want to make songs and stories and riddles and speak them and not be laughed at."

Eben softened. He could have no answer to such a speech. Blessed as he was with fortune of birth, wit, charm, and a countenance and body most women desired, how could he chastise Jocco for wanting the same, or at least to be other than what he was? His deformity was an accident of birth, not, as the least charitable priests might decree, God's punishment for the sins of the boy's mother, or the wages of the original sin in the Garden, or the inexplicable will of God.

Eben could see that Jocco had steeled himself for the worst, and he smiled at the look of utter surprise on his squire's face when he clapped a hand on his shoulder and said, "You did well, lad. I thank you for seeing to Morgana's safety, but I fear you have been deluded by this charlatan's wild tales.

"Where is this man now?" Eben demanded. "He is not on this ship or I would know of it. He has taken your coin and absconded."

"Oh no, my lord," Jocco exclaimed. "He asked no payment for his spell. He says . . ."

He paused, wondering just how much he should tell his lord about Merlin. From close observation of the wizard, he had concluded that the black hound and Merlin were the same, although he had not himself witnessed the transformation.

"I am sure we will see him again."

Jocco decided to leave it at that.

Chapter Seventeen

In the end, Eben relented somewhat. Brother Absalom could visit Kaia in her cabin for one hour each day to continue her lessons. Jocco was permitted to deliver her food and sit with her for exactly five minutes. She was allowed no board games or other diversions.

Once each day she was conducted to the deck to empty her chamber pot and take the air. Eben undertook this duty personally. Sailors were a notoriously rough lot, and without the company of women for days on end would likely as not mount even a toothless hag to assuage their need. Kaia was far too tempting a morsel to be entrusted to the care of any but himself.

Arrayed in their righteous anger, they spoke barely a word to one another.

He would arrive at her door each morning and make a perfunctory bow. "My lady."

She would sail past him with her chin in the air. "My lord."

"Allow me," he would say politely as he took the chamber pot from her hands and emptied it overboard.

"I thank you," she would say with equal civility.

"Your chamber, my lady," he would announce when they went below deck.

"How kind," she would murmur as he held the door for her.

"Good day, my lady."

"Good day, my lord."

And then Eben would return to his own cabin and slam his fist into the wall and Kaia would throw herself onto her hard little bed and weep into her pillow.

Day followed upon day in much the same way. Night brought fevered dreams: she of him from which she would awaken furious with herself that she should crave the touch of a man who did not want her; he of her, a woman he could not allow himself to want.

On the second day out, Eben summoned Absalom to account for himself. It required all Eben's patience to draw forth a coherent story from the little monk, who kept veering off into fantastical tales of talking dogs, flying goats, and fishy mists. There was no doubt the man really believed that Merlin—yes, that Merlin—was exactly who he represented himself to be. A man of fascinating parts, great learning, and profound introspection, enthused Brother Absalom, if a little too arrogant in his manner and dismissive of Absalom's own humble opinions. In matters of theology, however, Brother Absalom feared—

"How came it that you allowed Lady Kaia to leave the convent with you?" Eben managed to interject before Brother Absalom launched into a word-for-word recitation of each and every conversation he had enjoyed with the great magician.

Brother Absalom pinkened slightly. "Well, as to that, my lord, try as I might to dissuade her, she would not be left behind. I even tried to sneak away while she slept. You cannot imagine how relentless she can be once she gets it into her head to do something."

"Oh, I can imagine well enough," Eben muttered.

"In my own defense, my lord, I must tell you that I planned to send her back to the convent when we had reached Galiana. She is young, and the young do not always take into account the true consequences of their actions. Lady Kaia has been unhappy. Her father appears to be a man of limited understanding and has not treated her kindly. She is in love with some young man who does not return her feelings. Her horizons stretch further, and her imagination is far more fertile than most young women of her class, yet she is not even permitted to read and write."

Brother Absalom paused for breath. "I think, my lord, Lady Kaia feels she has no choice but to leave, but I do not believe in her heart she really wishes to do so. She would regret it for the rest of her life. I would have found some way to prevent her continuing on with me."

Eben had never believed for a moment that this unassuming old monk was guilty of kidnapping and high treason. Now that he had heard the full story from both Jocco and Brother Absalom, he believed rather that they should be commended. They had assumed the responsibility of keeping watch over two headstrong young women, who might very well have brought catastrophe down on themselves with their lack of forethought and reckless actions.

"You truly believe in the spell this Merlin speaks of?"

"Yes, my lord, I do."

"I think you will be sorely disappointed, but I will not try to stop you. I will inform the king you are blameless; you need not return to Suriana with us. I have given Jocco leave to accompany you. I expect you will both find your way back to the Dominion sadder but wiser.

"Lady Kaia, however, will return to face what discipline His Majesty decrees. She and I will disembark when the ship calls at Evros for fresh supplies. If there is no passage back to the Dominion to be found there, we will await the *Apostle* on her return voyage from the Western Isles in three weeks' time."

Brother Absalom cast a worried look at Lord Eben. "I pray the king will be lenient with Lady Kaia. She is such a lovely young woman. Her only fault is, as the saying goes, she is wont to leap before she looks. In time she will mellow."

"It can't be soon enough," Eben muttered, and went in search of the captain to inform him that he would need to find two new passengers at Evros.

"Have you solved the riddle yet?" Jocco inquired.

"Oh, I'd forgotten all about it," Brother Absalom hedged. He had in fact spent hours trying to puzzle it out without success. He did not like to admit the young squire had him stumped. "How did it go? Something about snakes, I believe. Or was it clouds?"

Jocco smirked. "You couldn't solve it, could you?"

"Of course I could solve it." Brother Absalom bristled. "It's just that so much has happened, it's gone right out of my head."

They had made themselves a comfortable little place to sleep well out of the wind amongst the crates and cages on deck rather than share quarters with fourteen sailors who were unacquainted with the concept of either good manners or personal hygiene. For Brother Absalom it had the added benefit of having the rail handy; he had not taken to sea travel very well, or rather, his stomach hadn't. He was looking forward to the morrow when they would dock at Evros, and for two days at least he could sleep in a real bed, and with any luck sit down to a meal that would stay down.

Jocco, on the other hand, had taken to life at sea like a fish to water. The crew had no cause to taunt him for his disfigurement, as not one of them was any more handsome than he. Some had missing teeth, some no teeth at all. One had lost an ear, another an eye. They suffered all manner of maladies caused by poor diet and hygiene, and hideous scars caused by poor judgment in brawls in a hundred taverns and brothels. But Jocco's greatest joy lay in hearing their wild tales—some fantastical, a few with at least a grain of truth to them. He loved their rude jests and songs and bawdy talk.

Of the five of them—if one included the hound—only Jocco awoke to the pleasure of each day and the anticipation of the next. Eben brooded. Kaia sulked. Merlin did not take to the pitch and roll of the sea any better than Brother Absalom. In the evening when darkness fell and he could transform himself into human shape without causing consternation or downright panic among the crew, he and the little monk would take turns sipping from a bottle of syrup of ginger, which was said to calm the stomach and tighten the bowels.

"Oh, for some Dramamine," Merlin groaned as the ship climbed a high swell, rode atop it for a moment, then slid down the other side.

"Dramamine?" Brother Absalom inquired as he returned from the rail. His face had taken on the hue of week-old pea potage.

"A miraculous potion for seasickness in the form of a little pellet," Merlin informed him. "Late twentieth century."

Brother Absalom scowled at the magician. "It is a most annoying habit of yours to extol the efficacy of medicines of eight hundred years in the future that we require at the moment and cannot avail ourselves of."

Merlin waved off the monk's criticism. "Think of it as incentive. Now that you know it will exist, perhaps you will be the one to invent it."

"That makes absolutely no sense," replied Absalom. "This Dramamine must already exist if you have partaken of it. Therefore, I would have no need to invent it since it has already been invented."

Merlin felt a headache coming on. "You don't know it exists or that it must be invented."

Brother Absalom threw up his hands in frustration. "Of course I do! You have just told me so."

"Where is Albert Einstein when I need him?" Merlin inquired of the stars.

The little monk's ears perked up. "Albert Einstein? A man of science?"

Oh, no, thought Merlin, he was *not* going to try to explain the General Theory of Relativity to Brother Absalom.

"An old friend," was all he said.

"Oh. Anyhow," Absalom grumbled, "it takes all the fun out of it if one's invention already exists before one has invented it."

Merlin rose and stretched out his long frame. "You really must read *Alice in Wonderland* sometime," he remarked. "Lewis Carroll might have had you in mind when he wrote it."

The rising wind whipped his midnight-blue cloak about his legs. "Storm coming," he remarked.

Brother Absalom jumped up in alarm. It was true; one by one, millions by millions, stars were disappearing behind a scudding blanket of dark clouds. The wind had shifted around to the northeast; never a good sign for a ship attempting to negotiate the dangerous waters of the Gibralos Strait.

"Let us go below to confer with Lord Eben," Merlin said. "It appears we may be looking at a change of plans."

Chapter Eighteen

"Get below and stay below," Eben shouted.

"I won't. I want to help."

"The only way you can help is by staying the hell out of the way," Eben snarled. He pushed Kaia ahead of him and grabbed hold of the frame of the companionway to keep them both from crashing to the deck.

"Jocco," Eben yelled. "Take her down to her cabin. Tie her up if you have to. Where's that monk got to?"

"Here, my lord," came a muffled voice from within a crate previously occupied by two suckling pigs. The cook had done rather well with them, everyone had agreed, but as they had now passed on to whatever reward a pig could expect in the afterlife, Brother Absalom had selected the secured crate as an appropriate place to prepare to meet his own Maker.

"Sweet Jesus," Eben muttered. "Jocco, get him out of there. I'll take Kaia." Rather than risk a struggle with her, Eben simply threw her over his shoulder like a sack of grain and groped his way down the stairs to the tiny cabin from which she had somehow managed to escape when the storm broke over the *Apostle*.

"Put me down, you idiot," she yelped.

"Kaia, this is no time for childish tantrums," Eben growled as he deposited her on the bed. "You will obey me."

Jocco appeared at the door towing a terrified Brother Absalom behind him.

"I can't just sit here and do nothing while the ship goes down," Kaia cried.

"We're going down? The ship is going down?" screeched Brother Absalom, falling to his knees.

"The ship is *not* going down, you fool," Eben yelled, "but we're way off course. We missed Evros, and we're well out into open water. We need every hand up there to man the rigging and the helm."

He pointed to Kaia, who had already leaped up from the bed. "Except you. And you," he added as Brother Absalom made to scramble to his feet. Eben suddenly had a brilliant idea. "Brother Absalom, I charge you to keep Lady Kaia safe. Kaia, I charge you to keep Brother Absalom safe.

"That ought to keep them well occupied while we get this thing under control," Eben remarked to Jocco as they climbed back to the pitching deck.

* * *

Strangely enough, Kaia wasn't frightened, though she thought she had every reason to be. Eben wouldn't let anything happen to her. She knew that as surely as she knew the sun would rise each day.

He'd been so magnificent up there on the deck. Kaia admitted she wouldn't have been much help, but, Lord, she'd have been willing to strap herself to the mast just to watch him. He'd been amazing when the poor captain went over the side. With his hair whipping about his face, he'd taken command, shouting out orders with an authority that even seasoned sailors rushed to obey.

Sometime in the midst of the tumult he'd ripped off his wet tunic. His linen shirt and hose clung to every hard-muscled plane of his beautiful body. Kaia could not tear her eyes from the heavy bulge that had fired her passion when he pressed against her on the beach.

She started to giggle. Here she was, facing the greatest danger of her life, perhaps at death's door, and all she could think of was Eben's body.

"You're not going to fall into a fit of hysteria, are you, Lady Kaia?" Brother Absalom inquired anxiously.

"Probably not the kind you mean." Kaia grinned.

"Oh. I didn't know there was more than one kind."

"Neither did I until recently," she said.

"Perhaps it would help to calm our nerves if you explained what kind of hysteria you are referring to."

Kaia rolled her eyes. "Some other time, perhaps. Let's talk of something else to take our minds off the storm. How about riddles? Jocco has a wonderful riddle. It goes: What is greater than God, worse than—"

"No, no," the monk cried. "No riddles today. I find I am tiring of riddles."

"But it's really quite easy," Kaia assured him.

"No riddles!"

Suddenly Kaia went flying as the ship was hit broadside by an enormous wave. She came down on top of the monk, knocking the breath out of him.

"Am I dead?" he inquired.

"No, you're not dead," Kaia assured him as she helped him up to a sitting position. "But I don't think it's going very well up there. Maybe we should—"

"Absolutely not, Lady Kaia," Absalom wheezed. "Lord Eben said I was to keep you here, and keep you here I shall."

"No, he didn't," she argued. "He said you were to keep me safe. That's not at all the same thing."

The door flew open. Eben dragged Jocco into the room.

"Look after him," Eben barked and slammed the door behind him.

Brother Absalom knelt beside the insensible boy. He began to cry. "Son, son, can you hear me? Are you dead?"

Kaia listened for a heartbeat. "Calm yourself. He's not dead. He must have hit his head. I'm sure he'll be fine. We'll leave him on the floor; he'd just roll off if we put him on the bed. Here, give me a pillow."

They did what they could to make the squire comfortable and prevent him from rolling about on the floor. Then they sat in silence and listened to the roar of the wind in the rigging and the shouts of the men as they fought to save the ship.

It seemed like hours but was in fact only a few minutes later when Eben slammed into the cabin and collapsed back against the door.

"The mainsail's split. Part of the rigging is coming down. It's too dangerous to stay up there. I've sent the men down to their quarters."

"We're to die?" Absalom whispered.

"But who's at the helm?" Kaia cried.

"Tall fellow. I don't remember seeing him before. He just gave me the strangest look when I ordered him below. I can't credit it, but he seems to know what he's about. I could swear he's actually enjoying himself."

Brother Absalom made the sign of the cross. "Thank you, God."

"You know this man?" Eben said.

A quick smile flashed between Kaia and the monk.

Eben narrowed his eyes. "Who is he? Answer me."

Kaia and Brother Absalom looked at each other, then at Eben.

Eben folded his arms across his chest. "No. Absolutely not. I refuse to believe—"

A deafening crack of lightning had every hair on every head standing straight out, and the clap of thunder that followed left every ear ringing. The ship bounced across the waves like a ball booted by a giant foot.

"We are doomed!" shrieked Brother Absalom as the four occupants of the cabin went flying and the small lantern that was their only light crashed to the floor.

Eben found himself flat on his back on the bed. A moment later something landed on him with a solid thwack.

134

"Aggghhh," Brother Absalom gurgled from somewhere near the door.

Eben tried to push the heavy weight off his chest. "Jocco? Where are you?"

"Here, my lord," came a groan from the floor beside the bed.

"Kaia?"

"Here," the something on top of him mumbled against his chest.

The wind still roared through the torn sails, but the ship had steadied somewhat.

"Is it over?" Brother Absalom groaned.

"I don't know," Eben said. "Everyone stay where they are. Stay calm. Brother Absalom, since you are given to prayer, perhaps now would be a good time to consult the Lord as to His intentions toward us."

"Yes, yes," the monk babbled, "pray, yes."

"I'm frightened, Eben." Kaia hid her face in the crook of his neck. "I don't want to die."

His arms came around her, strong and comforting. "We're not going to die, little one."

"I'm not little," she protested.

Eben smiled. "All right, you're not little."

"I'm a woman."

"Close enough," he murmured against her hair.

Brother Absalom had been searching his memory for something appropriate to their unhappy situation.

"I think Psalm sixty-nine might do," he declared out of the darkness. "'Save me, O God; for the waters are come unto my soul. I sink in deep mire, where there is no standing: I am come into deep waters, where the floods overflow me . . . ' "

Brother Absalom was well launched and rather enjoying himself by now. " 'I am weary of my crying: my throat is dried: mine eyes fail while I wait for my God. They that hate me without a cause are more than the hairs of mine head . . . '

"Hmmm. Perhaps *Jonah* would be better," he suggested to no one in particular. "Why didn't I think of it in the first place?

" 'The waters compassed me about, even to the soul: the depth closed me round about, the weeds were wrapped about my head. I went down to the bottom of the mountains: the earth with her bars was about me forever: yet hast thou brought up my life from corruption . . . '

"It seems to be getting a bit off the point here," Brother Absalom observed.

"Kaia," Eben said in a low tone, "about that day on the beach—"

"Mmmmm?" She touched the tip of her tongue to the warm skin of his neck. It tasted salty.

"Um, well, I should never have . . . allowed it . . . to happen."

The devilish little tongue had discovered his ear. "Why?" she whispered.

Eben caught his breath. "Well, for one thing, you are . . . and I am . . ."

The tongue traced the line of his jaw and described a feather-light line around his lips. "Yes, we are." He felt a little puff of air against his mouth. "Open."

"Now look, Kaia, this simply won't do—" he began, but

the tongue swept into his mouth and suddenly he found he really had absolutely nothing to say.

"Hush." Her hand cupped his cheek, and they sank into a slow silky kiss, the most sensual Eben had ever experienced.

Eben groaned.

"Are you in pain, my lord?" Jocco inquired.

"No, I am not in pain," Eben snapped.

"It certainly sounded like it to me," Brother Absalom chipped in. "I do wish the lantern hadn't gone out. I don't like being in the dark like this."

Pitch dark was just fine with Eben Dhion at the moment, essential in fact. "I'm fine," Eben managed as Kaia's hand slid down his body and slipped into his breeches. "Nothing to worry about," he mumbled as she cupped him.

"If there's anything I can do to ease your discomfort, you have only to speak, my lord."

"I assure you, Jocco," Eben ground out, "I have no need of your help at the moment."

"'. . . And the Lord spake unto the fish, and it vomited out Jonah upon the dry land.'"

Eben bucked as Kaia's fingers wrapped around him. He summoned up every shred of willpower he possessed not to move as she gently stroked and massaged him. Up and down and up and—

Bang, bang, bang!

"Everyone all right in there?" The door flew open. A bandy-legged sailor peered in at them. He grinned, catching sight of the activity on the bed. "I'd say so."

Before Jocco and Absalom could so much as turn their heads, Kaia had rolled to the side and Eben had flipped over onto his stomach.

"Storm's moving out," the sailor informed them. "Don't know how we got through, nobody at the wheel."

"Someone took the helm," Eben said. "I saw him."

"I was the first up," said the man. "Weren't nobody there except that dog. Thought for sure he'd gone overboard, but there he was, waggin' his tail like nothin' happened."

Brother Absalom clambered to his feet. "The Lord moves in mysterious ways, indeed He does. I for one need to get out of this cabin," he announced as he tottered out the door. Jocco stumbled along behind.

Kaia got to her feet and stood looking down at Eben, who still didn't dare move. She clasped her hands behind her back and cocked her head. "Will you be joining us above deck, my lord?" she inquired politely with all the social aplomb she might have exhibited at Jibril's court.

"Kaia," Eben growled.

"Or would you like to have a few moments alone to put yourself to rights?"

Eben glowered up at her. "Now listen here, Kaia, this sort of thing has got to stop."

Kaia frowned. "What sort of thing, my lord? I'm afraid I don't take your meaning."

"Kaia," he warned.

Kaia looked around in puzzlement, glanced back over her shoulder. "You are addressing me, sir?"

"Yes," he said through clenched teeth. "I am addressing you, my lady."

"Oh, yes, of course. I beg you will excuse me, my lord. I am usually addressed as *little* Kaia, and you quite confused me there for a moment."

Eben started to rise, thought better of it, and plopped back onto his stomach. "Just wait until I get my hands on you, brat."

Kaia executed a graceful curtsy. "I shall most certainly be looking forward to it, my lord," she said, and sailed from the room.

Eben Dhion groaned and buried his head in his arms.

Chapter Nineteen

With only its foresail remaining and a good portion of the rigging seriously damaged, the *Apostle* was now for all intents and purposes adrift. The oars, which were used to maneuver the vessel in and out of calm, shallow water in a sheltered harbor, were of little use against the rolling surge of open sea. There was no way to calculate just how far the ship had been blown off course, and the charts in the captain's quarters were of little use since they had no point of reference from which to begin.

Eben assumed command, as was right and proper given his station, but he had no real seafaring experience. He selected a sailor who seemed more intelligent and responsible than the rest—not to mention a good deal more sober—to captain the ship. Four men had been lost in the storm, including the original captain and the cook, so Brother Absalom was pressed into service in the tiny cooking shed on the foredeck. To his own amazement, the monk discovered he had a certain talent for cooking and managed to turn out reasonably palatable fare with what few stores remained.

Kaia was again confined to her cabin, not for disciplinary reasons but because her presence was inciting increasingly lascivious attention from some of the bolder members of the crew. Eben had been obliged to thrash the living daylights out of one man who had whistled to gain Kaia's attention and then had begun rubbing himself suggestively. Kaia herself had no wish to witness a repeat performance and so had raised no objection when Eben escorted her below deck, bowed, and with a curt "my lady" locked the door behind him.

As the days grew long, tempers grew short. Fights erupted over a game of dice, a missing hat, the last pasty on the platter. When Brother Absalom tried to organize a prayer service, a great brute with a wart on the end of his nose picked him up and dangled him head first over the side. Jocco got tangled in the rigging and would have hung himself had a man with a ready knife not raced to cut him down. The sun rose, the sun set, and not a speck of land was to be seen.

On the fifth night after the storm, unable to sleep, Eben offered to take the watch. "Right good of you, my lord," the sailor said. "This hound here'll keep you good company. Times I'd swear he understands every word you say."

Left alone, man and dog regarded one another; Eben with suspicion, the hound with polite interest.

"It occurs to me," Eben said, feeling like a fool to be conversing with a dog, "that everywhere I go, there you are. At the Inn of the Bishop's Bastard, on the road, on the beach at Galiana, on the jetty. You took on Obike Zebengo—there aren't many, man or dog, who have the courage to do that—and now you show up here on the *Apostle*. If I weren't a rational man, I'd say it's not much of a coincidence."

The hound settled onto its haunches and began scratching behind its right ear. "Damn fleas."

Eben opened his mouth, shut it, and regarded the hound through narrowed eyes. "I don't believe it."

The hound grinned.

"I still don't believe it."

If a hound could be said to shrug, then the hound shrugged.

"Show yourself, then," Eben demanded.

The dog stretched voluptuously and trotted off. Eben seated himself on a crate and waited to see what would happen. A moment later, a tall man in a midnight-blue cloak studded with silver stars emerged from the companionway. He bowed. "Allow me to introduce myself, Lord Eben. I am Merlin."

Eben passed the flask to the wizard. It was their third, and neither was, in the strictest sense of the word, sober. "I have to say I am deeply disappointed in you, sir," Eben said. "Surely a magician of your legendary reputation can bring us to safety. Wave a wand, or whatever it is you do."

"Would it were that simple," Merlin sighed. He tipped the leather flask to his lips and let the honeyed wine slide down his throat. "Ahhh. A fine Bordeaux. The truth is that as I grow younger my memory is not what it used to be. I can't remember names and faces. I am forever mislaying my wand. I forget the words of spells I know as well as I know the back of my own hand. In 1504 I was almost burned at the stake: wrong spell."

He passed the flask back to Eben. "Besides, I too must abide by what is written."

"Written? By whom?"

Merlin shrugged. "God, I suppose."

They sat for a while in companionable silence. They looked up at the stars; the stars looked down.

Eben finally spoke. "Can you really send the monk and my squire into the future?"

"Yes," replied Merlin. "That is one spell I expect I shall never forget, no matter how young I grow. It's very handy. You'd be surprised how often I've had occasion to use it. There is an entire body of literature on the subject, although they never really get it right. Science fiction, it is called. A contradiction in terms, if you ask me, but they will scribble away."

"The spell?" Eben prompted. Merlin was as likely to wander off on tangents as Brother Absalom.

"I couldn't send them off on my own, of course. The spell must be cast in a place of true power. There is no spot on the face of the earth as powerful as the standing stones of the Western Isles."

"I know one thing. Kaia will not be going," Eben stated flatly.

"If it is written, Lady Kaia will go," said Merlin.

"I won't allow it."

"You cannot stop her, son. It must be her choice."

"She's a child. She doesn't know what she wants."

"You may wish to think of her so," Merlin said mildly,

"if it suits your purposes. But not long ago she had no idea she had any choices at all. Now an entire universe has opened up before her. She will follow her heart, and I assure you it will be the heart of a woman, not a child."

Eben climbed to his feet and paced unsteadily back and forth across the deck. "She's impossible," he declared, running his fingers through his hair. "I never know what she's going to do next. She feeds beetles to old women, runs around the countryside dressed like a nun, hurls herself off cliffs. One minute she's prim and proper, and the next she's . . . well, she's not, if you know what I mean."

Merlin laughed softly. "An intriguing quality in a woman, wouldn't you say?"

"What I'd say is, she needs to be locked up for her own protection."

"And yours, I'll warrant," Merlin opined with a grin.

"And mine," Eben admitted wearily, and took himself off to bed to pass what remained of the night in blessedly dreamless oblivion.

Chapter Twenty

"Land ho!"

"Praise the Lord," shouted Brother Absalom. "Let us give thanks to our God who has delivered us from—"

"Not now, Brother," Eben growled, surveying what appeared to be an island, although it was difficult to tell at this distance. It might very well be a headland or peninsula of some greater land mass. "I think perhaps we should refrain from rejoicing until we learn what manner of people we may encounter here."

Brother Absalom was not to be deterred. He rather prided himself for storing up a bit of scripture to have on hand for every occasion. "'And the waters returned from off the earth continually, and after the end of the hundred and fifty days the waters were abated. And the ark rested in the seventh month on the seventeenth day of the month upon the mountains of Ararat. And—'"

"But we've only been at sea for eight days," Jocco piped up with that annoying habit found often in the young of stating a fact without a thought for the sensibilities of others.

"Cannibals, could be," offered the newly appointed captain, one Two-toes by name.

"Virgins?" suggested a crewman hopefully.

"Them Amazon women I heard tell of," enthused another. "Got only one breast, but hell, I only got one mouth, so what's it matter?"

"I think we're getting ahead of ourselves," Eben said dryly. "First we have to get ourselves there. We might get some work from the foresail, but I think we're going to have to use the oars."

"Calm enough, though it's hard to tell how far out we are," Two-toes observed.

"The men will row in shifts," Eben decided. "One watch on, one off. I doubt we'll make landfall before dark. That works in our favor. We'll have a chance to do some exploring before we're spotted or show ourselves.

"Right, gentlemen, let's get to it."

The crew scattered to their appointed tasks. Eben leaned on the rail and contemplated the island. He wouldn't have been able to put it into words, but he had the strangest feeling that the island had somehow summoned him; that it had all been ordained—Kaia's flight, this ship, the storm. He had come to this island to finish something in his life that had been left undone.

Merlin would have said it had been written.

No one with two ears attached to his head could doubt that Lady Kaia Kurinon was beyond furious.

"I am beyond furious," she yelled at the top of her voice.

Brother Absalom cringed. "Yes, yes, I can see that, my lady. Perhaps if you would just try to see the matter from Lord Eben's point of view—"

Her voice skated up another full octave. "I can't begin to find the words to describe how furious I am."

Brother Absalom stuck his fingers in his ears and thought she was doing rather well at it actually. He had never seen anything like it. Of course, he'd lived amongst men his entire life, so it was possible this behavior was to be expected in the gentler sex when they found themselves under stress.

Lady Kaia Kurinon stood upon her bed banging her little boot against the ceiling and announcing to the world in the most graphic terms her intention to geld the armiger of the Ninth House as soon as she could get her hands on his . . .

Brother Absalom's mouth dropped in shock. How came the highborn daughter of the Second House to know so many euphemisms for that portion of the male anatomy the Lord had provided for men to go forth, be fruitful, and multiply? Apparently, Lady Kaia had spent far too much time hanging about the kitchens and stables of her father's hall, where such words were bandied about.

It had been some time since Lord Eben had descended from the deck to inform Kaia that he intended to explore what he could of the island under the cover of darkness. Ten men were to go with him; three would remain behind to guard the ship. Kaia would remain in her cabin. Brother Absalom would keep her company. She would be allowed a game board so they could play tables or draughts; he might even be able to find a chess set on board. The door would be locked, of course, for her own protection.

"I see," Kaia had replied when he had spoken his piece. "I take it I am not even to be allowed to set foot ashore?"

"I have decided it would be better if you did not," said Eben.

"You have decided," she repeated.

"I have."

Kaia tucked her hands behind her and gifted him with a brilliant smile. "Let me understand the situation, my lord. You, the armiger of the Ninth House, are informing me, the daughter of a royal prince of the *Second* House and a princess in my own right if I choose to assume that title, that I am to be confined in this chamber indefinitely or until such time as I am returned to my cousin's court and thence to my father's hall. Do I have it aright?"

Brother Absalom thought it prudent to make a strategic retreat at this point, and sidled toward the door.

"Stay, Brother," Kaia ordered. "I want you to bear witness to Lord Eben's reply."

Eben raised a brow. "I think you have summed it up quite well, my lady."

Kaia did not appreciate his haughty manner one bit. "On whose authority do you make this decision?"

"On my own, my lady, since there is no one else of my station to do so."

Brother Absalom backed away. He did not like the look in Kaia's eye.

"I believe I have just explained that *I* am of your station; in fact, I am considerably far *above* your station. It cannot have escaped your notice."

Eben was fast losing patience. "As you say," he conceded with a slight bow, "but you do not possess the one qualification necessary to be entrusted with important decisions."

"I don't?"

"You do not."

Kaia waited.

"You are not a man. You are a woman, my lady. And if your recent behavior is any reflection of your talents in that direction, I think all would agree it is better that you obey me in these matters."

"Er, perhaps we should continue this discussion at a later time," Brother Absalom interjected before the situation got completely out of hand. "I'm sure Lady Kaia and I will be perfectly comfortable here. It's really quite cozy. We can play at riddles," he added brightly.

Jocco appeared at the door to inform Eben that the men were ready to depart.

147

Eben adjusted his sword belt. "We'll be back before dawn. The *Apostle* is well concealed in this inlet, and I have every confidence in the men I have assigned to see to your safety. Until then, my lady."

Kaia kept up her tirade until it became obvious that there was no one above to hear her, whereupon she plopped down on the bed and sank into a brooding silence from which Brother Absalom was unable to rouse her with a round of particularly clever riddles, or even a cheerful little homily on patience and the keeping of one's temper.

All her dreams of taking control of her own life were disintegrating before her eyes. No one would ever know how difficult it had been for her to take that first step into the unknown. Leave everyone she had ever loved behind and put her faith in a distant future. Believe that she could fly. Fly free.

And Eben, the friend of her childhood, her hero, the lover of her dreams, had revealed himself to be no different from other men. Lock up the women. For their own safety, of course!

Yes, he had called her a woman. It had not escaped her notice. But the word held no honor so long as he continued to treat her like a child. He might just as well have called her a fool.

What, then, determined when a woman truly became a woman? Surely not the loss of her maidenhead or the bearing of children, for most women were as much children in their husbands' halls as they had been in their fathers'. Therefore, if men would keep women children even unto their deaths, that could only mean that it was the woman herself who must make the determination. She must first believe it of herself and then prove it to her man.

Kaia Ellora Kurinon knew herself to be a woman.

Soon Eben Dhion would know it too.

Chapter Twenty-one

It was, perhaps, Brother Absalom's finest hour.

Lady Kaia too had risen nobly to the occasion, and although the outcome was not entirely as they might have wished, Brother Absalom later reflected that they had acquitted themselves rather well. The odds had not been all that good at the outset: a dozen fully armed soldiers against a sixty-two-year-old monk and an eighteen-year-old girl.

It was difficult to know the exact hour when the barbarians boarded the ship, but Brother Absalom believed it must have been shortly before dawn

Kaia was shaking him. "Brother Absalom," she whispered, "you must wake up. Something's wrong. Someone is creeping about on the deck."

"I'm sure it's nothing to worry about, just one of the guards," he assured her drowsily and tried to turn over and go back to sleep.

"No, really, you must wake up. Listen."

It was true. A board creaked. Something thudded on the deck. Someone swore a foul oath. A member of the crew would be moving about with more assurance. The activity above had a furtive air to it.

"We're trapped in here. What will we do?"

"The first thing is not to panic," Brother Absalom whispered. "No, I take that back. The first thing we must do is pray."

"Oh, for heaven's sake. We don't have time—"

"There is always time to pray, child," he said gently. "If ever we needed God's help, it is now."

Kaia was too shaken to object. Brother Absalom took her hand and softly recited the Twenty-third Psalm. Whether it was his touch or the beauty of the ancient words, she felt the stronger for it.

When he had finished, the little monk rubbed his hands briskly and whispered, "Now let us see how we can defend ourselves."

"We have our eating knives."

"True. But we are only two, and they may not avail us against a stronger force. We have no idea how many there are. Guile may be the better weapon."

"I don't understand."

"Here is my idea. If you recall, our beloved queen once outwitted an entire army by pretending to be a slop girl. She made her person so repulsive that no one took any account of her."

"Everyone knows that story. But we can't very well pretend to be slop girls. And why would we be locked up like this?"

"Very true." Brother Absalom's face lit up as a brilliant idea came to him. "People who have gone mad are confined, are they not?"

Kaia's eyes went wide. "Of course! How very clever of you. Do you think it will work?"

"I think it will have to work, my child. They're coming. Shall we go mad?"

Kaia clutched at his arm. "How, how?"

The door handle rattled.

"Open up in there," a rough voice commanded.

Brother Absalom scrambled for inspiration. "Laugh!"

"What?"

"Don't speak a word, just laugh. Play the fool."

"All right, that's good, I'll laugh," Kaia said shakily. "But what about you?"

"I can't find a key," someone on the other side of the door said. "Break it down."

Just as the wood panel splintered and the door gave way, Brother Absalom of the Worshipful Brotherhood of Milo the Mild began to bark.

"Where the devil is that infernal noise coming from?" Eben snarled.

He was not in good humor. For four hours they had stumbled through unknown terrain in the dark and prowled the fetid back alleys of a town some three miles along the coast. Few denizens of the place were abroad at that hour, and those who staggered through the streets were probably not the most upstanding citizens. Eben had not been able to determine whether or not they had come upon a civilized people, who would welcome them and provide assistance.

One thing he had learned: the men must be accomplished seamen. The ships that lay at anchor in the harbor were well equipped and maintained, strong and fast. Probably, the men were fishermen. Perhaps the larger vessels carried pilgrims to the Holy Land. These people might be explorers, long-distance traders. Or pirates.

"I believe it is coming from our ship, my lord," Jocco said.

Only eight of the ten crewmen who set out with Eben, Jocco, and Merlin had returned with them. Two had last been spotted climbing through the window of a brothel, and would likely not be seen for some time, if ever again.

Although the crew of the *Apostle* had rallied behind him in the worst hours of the raging tempest, Eben doubted he could count on their cooperation for long. Men who chose the lonely and dangerous life of the sea would not long delay the gratification of their needs in the numerous brothels and taverns of the port, and the best Eben could hope for was to buy their loyalty until he could find friends and allies amongst the populace. Since he carried little coin with him, it would not be long before they deserted en masse.

"I think we had better find some vantage point where we can see what's going on down there." Eben led the party to a wooded bluff overlooking the inlet where the *Apostle* lay concealed.

A most peculiar cackling noise interspersed with short bursts of frenzied yapping floated up from the ship. Something giggled, something yapped.

"My God, the bastard bit me!" someone howled.

"Hee haw! Hee haw! Hee haw haw haw!"

"Hold her. Look out, she's going for your ballocks!"

"Aaarrrgh!"

"Wheeeeee!"

"Woofwoofwoofwoofwoof."

NAME: _____

ADDRESS: _____

_____

_____

TELEPHONE: _____

E-MAIL: _____

_____ I want to pay by credit card.

__ Visa   __ MasterCard   __ Discover

Account Number: _____

Expiration date: _____

SIGNATURE: _____

*Send this form, along with $2.00 shipping
and handling for your FREE books, to:*

Love Spell Romance Book Club
20 Academy Street
Norwalk, CT 06850-4032

*Or fax (must include credit card
information!) to: 610.995.9274.
You can also sign up on the Web
at www.dorchesterpub.com.*

Eben glanced around to make sure Merlin was still with them in human form. The magician held up his hands. "Don't look at me."

"Quick, she's getting away," someone shouted. "After her."

"He's foaming at the mouth!"

"Owooooo!"

"My God, it's a werewolf! Let's get out of here."

Only the faintest blush of the new dawn hovered over the sea, but there was light enough for Eben to see two small figures scramble off the ship and face off against at least a dozen ruffians. The two appeared to be unarmed but were somehow holding their ground. The attackers would rush forward. One figure, the smaller of the two, would erupt into demented laughter and jump about like a beetle in an apple and wave its arms like a windmill in a high gale; the other crouched and snapped and snarled. The attackers would reel back, confer, regroup, and charge again.

"Sweet Jesus," Eben shouted. "Kaia!"

Merlin hadn't bothered to effect his transformation out of sight as he generally preferred to do, and was already bounding down the hill like a hound from hell, leaving terrified crewmen shaking in their boots. Eben and Jocco were close behind.

"Honor and the Dominion!" Eben bellowed out the ancient war cry as he drew his sword and charged. The sailors of the *Apostle*, inflamed by the sheer drama of the moment and always up for a good brawl, echoed the cry, rushed down the hill, and waded into the fray.

It would have been an equal fight if a band of horsemen hadn't thundered onto the scene. When Eben and his men turned to face that threat, the ruffians made their move. Poor Brother Absalom found himself pinned beneath an enormous brute of a man, who couldn't possibly have bathed since the midwife wiped him down straight out of the womb; a rough sack was thrust over Absalom's head and his hands tied behind his back.

"Run, Kaia, run!" Absalom shouted.

Kaia didn't just run, she flew.

The leader of the troop swung around and went after her with the harsh cry of the chase. She couldn't possibly have outrun him, but she didn't falter. Even when, at full gallop, he leaned down and hauled her up across his saddle, her long, slim legs were still pumping at full speed.

"No!" Eben shouted, but it was too late. Horse, rider, and his little Kaia disappeared over the crest of a dune, with the black hound in flat-out pursuit.

The battle was winding down. The ruffians—those who were not sliced or skewered—had dragged poor Absalom away. Jocco lay bleeding from a dagger wound to the shoulder. The sailors were bearing their wounded back to the ship.

Eben Dhion would never forgive himself, but he could not allow himself to dwell on the horror of Kaia's abduction until he had taken command of the situation and seen to the safety of his men. He knew that another attack could be expected at any moment.

By the rising of the sun they had hastily buried three men, tended to the wounded, plundered the *Apostle* for what weapons and stores they could carry on their backs, and hiked into a mountainous wilderness to find some place of concealment.

They set up camp in a small, dry cave far up a boulder-strewn ravine, and concealed the opening with piles of dry brush and a tangle of thorns. They were safe, for the moment.

The men wolfed down what dried meat and fruit they had been able to salvage and dropped into exhausted sleep. With the resiliency and stubbornness of the young, Jocco suffered Eben to clean and stitch up his wound without so much as a peep, but was too weak to take anything but a few sips of watered-down wine.

Eben too was exhausted and hungry, but far too keyed up to sleep. He filled a pouch with chunks of hard yellow cheese and dried fruits, filled his flask with cold, clear water from a nearby stream, and went in search of a quiet spot where he could review the events of the past twelve hours and consider his options.

Sprawled on a narrow grassy ledge high on the cliff above the cave, Eben gazed out over a rough, rocky landscape, largely devoid of the green pastures and fields that signaled a people who relied primarily on farming for their sustenance. His earlier surmise that they lived by the sea was correct. In the distance he could see the town they had explored last night. A few of the large vessels had put out to sea, smaller fishing boats plied the waters closer to shore, and two sleek coasters appeared to be patrolling the rocky coast, no doubt in search of the crew of the *Apostle*.

Where in this hostile land was little Kaia Kurinon? Why had Brother Absalom been barking? Had Merlin been able to keep up the pursuit? What powers could the sorcerer bring to bear to keep them safe?

And what had brought him, Eben, to this godforsaken island? The storm, certainly, but some destiny Eben did not yet understand. He was certain of it. If he survived whatever challenge lay ahead, he knew he would depart this place with his head held high, because he had finally secured his place in the world by his own hand and not merely been born to it.

Eben could not hold his head high this fair morn. Because of his unforgivable negligence, hubris, and small-mindedness, he had left Kaia and the monk with no possible way to defend themselves, locked them away with no avenue of escape. He could not imagine how they had gotten away, let alone held off a dozen vicious cutthroats.

"Hiyo, you down there, what—"

Eben was on his feet with dagger in hand before the voice could even complete the sentence. He pressed back under a rocky overhang, straining to hear how many there were above him. Small stones clattered into the ravine as someone scrambled down to stop slightly above him and to the left.

"Mister?" A small round face peered down. "Are you hurt, mister?"

Eben waited him out. It sounded like a child, but there might be others; it could be a trap.

"Is he dead?" a small voice whispered.

"I don't think so," the first voice said. "I saw him moving."

"I could run and get Papa."

"Be quiet, Zelana. I got to think."

"You always get to do the thinking."

"That's because I'm a boy and you're a girl."

"That's not fair," the child Eben could now identify as Zelana complained. "When I grow up I want to do the thinking."

"I'm doing it now, so be quiet. And what I think is this fellow is just waiting to see what we're going to do. Isn't that right, mister?" the boy challenged.

Eben stepped out from beneath the overhang and looked up.

A pair of curious blue eyes looked back.

"It is, son," Eben said with a smile. "Are you alone?"

"I got my sister here."

Another pair of blue eyes appeared. "He got me here."

"I just said that," the boy argued.

"Oh. I'm sorry, Tavos."

Eben held out his knife so they could see him slipping it back into the sheath. "Look, I'm putting my knife away. I'm going to climb up there. I won't hurt you. I have some food. We can eat and talk."

A few minutes later, the three were seated companionably on a flat-topped boulder, dangling their feet over the fifty-foot drop and munching on cheese and dates. The little girl was about four years old, her brother closer to eight. Their ma had sent them out to pick the sweet yellow bunchberries that grew in sheltered places along the cliffs, but they hadn't found very many. They decided to eat them so they wouldn't have to bother carrying them home. Their ma was probably going to be right angry.

Tavos—that was how the boy had introduced himself—

watched Eben warily. Finally he said, "Are you one of them? The ones they're looking for?"

Eben shrugged. "That would depend. Who are 'they' and who are 'the ones'?"

"Bad men," Zelana informed him around a mouthful of cheese.

Eben smiled down at her. "Then I'm not one of them. I try to be a good man."

"I know," she replied. "I can tell."

Tavos was not to be put off so easily. "The soldiers are looking for outlaws."

"Bad men," little Zelana said.

Tavos sighed in exasperation. "Zelana, you just said that. You're always saying things twice. Why do you do that?"

She shrugged. "I don't know. Anyhow, I was *talking* about the soldiers. They're bad men."

"Are they?" Eben inquired carefully.

"Pa don't like them; he says—"

"Let me tell," Tavos interrupted.

"Yes, Tavos, you tell me." This was important information, and Eben knew he was more likely to get a coherent explanation from the boy. "What is this place? Who is your lord? Start at the beginning."

Tavos did. Ataxi was indeed an island. Most everyone made his living from the sea. Once upon a time—Eben interpreted that, in the boy's mind, it meant any time before he had been born—strangers started coming to the island. Some of them just wanted to buy and sell things, but there were some pirates too. They made friends with the king—

he was dead now—and he told them to come back with a lot of gold and he'd sell them the fungus.

Eben went very still. "Fungus?"

"You know, the fungus. From the moths."

Eben did know. No mere aphrodisiac, the fungus was rumored to give a man the generative equipment and stamina of a young bull. So long as he continued to use it. Once he stopped or it was withheld from him, his parts returned to their normal size and he was left impotent. Addictive as the seed of the poppy, a man would do anything, pay anything to obtain it.

Tavos informed Eben that his pa said the fungus was worth even more than gold, but no good would ever come of it because it made men act like animals and they'd go mad if they didn't have any to eat. Tavos himself wouldn't eat it because he heard it tasted awful.

"And Pa says it's bad for you," Zelana chimed in.

"I just said that, Zelana," Tavos snapped.

"No, you didn't. You said Pa said no good would ever come of it. That's different."

"It's the same thing," Tavos retorted.

"Is not."

Eben popped a date into the little girl's mouth to put an end to the dispute. "You're both right. It is very bad for you, and no good can ever come of it."

"How do you know about the fungus if you never been here before?" Tavos demanded.

"A pirate once came to my island—it is called the Dominion—and tried to steal some gold from me so he could come back here and buy the fungus."

"What happened to him?" Zelana piped up.

"The king had him hung."

"He must have been a very bad man," she said darkly.

"He was. His name was Najja Kek."

"Najja Kek? Everyone knows about him," Tavos exclaimed. "He never came back here, but his friend did. He's the high lord now."

"He's mean," Zelana observed. "The high lord."

"Everyone hates him," Tavos said. "He keeps all the fungus in the palace, and if you want some you have to do everything he tells you to."

For a moment Eben felt nothing. Then the hatred he had nurtured for fifteen years slowly bloomed again like a black rose that has finally found the sun.

"What is your lord's name, Tavos?" he asked quietly. But he already knew.

"Ranulph Gyp."

"He's mean," Zelana reminded them.

Eben looked out over the sea to the east, where the Dominion floated in the azure waters of the Southern Ocean.

Ranulph Gyp. The man who had seized the hall of the Ninth House when Eben was but fourteen. His hall. The man who had tried to take from him everything he held dear. And now he had Kaia Kurinon in his foul grasp.

No, it had been no mere storm that cast Eben Dhion upon the shores of the island of Ataxi but destiny itself. The time had come to finish what had been left undone, to reclaim the honor that was rightly his, to bring him to the full measure of his manhood.

Chapter Twenty-two

It didn't require much convincing to persuade Tavos and Zelana to lead him to their father. Tavos leaped at the prospect of unexpected adventure, and Zelana would have followed Eben to the ends of the earth after only an hour's acquaintance.

Their pa was not so easily won over as his trusting offspring. Amin Samil greeted the arrival of the stranger on his doorstep with deep suspicion. He sat with arms folded and eyes narrowed as Eben briefly told his tale. His wife, Bera, who was no less susceptible to Eben's charm than any other woman, believed his every word at once.

Of course, Eben omitted any mention of talking dogs, magic spells, or wizards who lived backward in time. It would only have confused the issue. What he needed, he told Samil, was information about Ranulph Gyp: how he came to be lord of this land and wherein lay his power and support.

Eben knew he was taking a chance—the man might very well betray him—but he was a good judge of character, and Amin Samil had about him the air of an honest and upright man. It was evident from the outset that he detested Ranulph Gyp.

After the children were safely tucked away in bed, Samil briefly told his tale.

Gyp had come to Ataxi thirteen years earlier. He represented himself as a business partner of Najja Kek and assured the then lord that Kek would be arriving any day with gold enough to purchase the existing supply of fungus; in partnership they would handle the export of the fungus throughout the known world. Kek, of course, never returned, having met his just reward at the end of a rope at the order of Lord Eben's own king. But by the time the news reached Ataxi, Gyp had charmed his way into the inner circle of the court, seduced the High Lord's daughter, and exercised great influence over the old man himself.

Samil broke a stick over his knee and tossed the pieces into the hearth. "'Devil Dust' we call it. That fungus is the worst thing ever happened to this land, I'll tell you. No plague the Good Lord Himself sent down on Pharaoh was bad as Devil Dust. A man's a man, content with the parts he's born with, learns what a woman's for, does his best to please her. Then along comes the snake, like in the Garden, tells him he can be so much more. He can make his woman fall down and worship him. Only the snake doesn't tell him he has to eat the fungus every single day of his life. So the poor bastard's got to keep on buying if he wants to keep on swiving. And the devil that owns the Devil Dust is the devil that owns the man."

"A tool of power indeed," Eben observed.

"It is that, my lord. More than half the men of this land are dependent on it—their women as well—and Gyp is not slow to withhold it when he doles out punishment or needs to force a man to do his will. I would see it and him damned to eternity."

Eben stared into the fire with a frown. "Have there been no attempts to overthrow him? What about the other lords of the land?"

"There have been a few revolts, quickly subdued. As for the lords, there are few in the craven lot who don't use the stuff. Who would voluntarily give up his manhood for the sake of his honor?"

"A real man, that's who," Bera declared. "Maybe once we got rid of the devil, someone could find a way to destroy the moths so no one could ever wield such power again."

"And leave half our men impotent?" said Samil.

"Someone could invent a medicine to reverse the curse."

"That would take magic, not medicine." Samil snorted.

Eben rose and stretched. "Perhaps you will take some air with me, sir, before I return to the cave."

"It's too far for you to return in the dark tonight, my lord," Bera exclaimed. "I'll just make up a bed for you by the hearth while you two talk your man talk outside."

"It seems to me," Eben said as he and Samil wandered down the road a bit, "that we have an enemy in common and reason enough between us to see him brought low. I have my debt to settle with Gyp, and your people need to be rid of this tyranny. If you have no leader of your own, I should be honored to act the part. I serve my king in defense of my own land and have the experience to lead, but I am without support here."

"The sailors of the *Apostle*?"

"Brawlers, with no training and no loyalty. I cannot depend on them. Other than that, I have only my fourteen-year-old squire, who is presently laid up with a bad knife wound to the shoulder, the Lady Kurinon, an old monk, and a, um, traveler we met upon the road. The last three are currently in Gyp's hands.

"Have you allies in your cause?" he continued. "We will not need many. The first order of business is to lay hands on the existing supply of the fungus and any documents that may exist relating to its manufacture. Therein lies the foundation of Gyp's power. Then we must take Gyp himself and anyone else who knows the secrets of the fungus. We need only gain entrance to the palace. I think all this will be more easily achieved through guile rather than major confrontation. I do not need soldiers so much as I need guides and spies."

"There are many who would welcome the fall of Ranulph Gyp," Samil said. "He holds no love for this land. He buys loyalty with that damnable fungus. Sane, upstanding people earn their living from the sea and legitimate trade, as we have always done. We get no benefit from the wealth the fungus brings; it goes into a few pockets only. Nor would good men have it so. Give me two days and I can have at least fifty men at your disposal. I think perhaps you have been brought to these shores for this reason."

"When I first saw this island on the horizon, I knew I had been brought here for some purpose," Eben said. "If in so doing I help you unseat a tyrant, then, as a friend of mine would say, 'It is written.' For you and your people as well as for myself."

* * *

In the morning Eben returned to an enthusiastic reception at the cave with a goodly supply of dried meat, cheese, and day-old bread. Samil allowed Tavos to accompany him—much to the distress of little Zelana, who sobbed pitifully at being left behind—to help carry the food and a keg of new ale.

Eben managed a few hours' sleep and returned to the town after dark to reconnoiter. As it happened, he discovered the missing sailors asleep in a hog pen. When they returned to the cave, the report they gave of men with shafts as long as their forearms came as no surprise to Eben, but excited wild speculation among their comrades. When Tavos let slip that the fungus could provide similar benefits to any man for a few coins, a near riot ensued.

Despite Amin's dire warnings concerning the fungus and Eben's attempts to maintain order, in the end the ten sailors of the *Apostle* opted for libido over common sense—not particularly surprising in a group of men who spent most of their lives at sea—and headed for the town, there to procure the miraculous potion that would make of them sexual gods—and dependent upon it for the rest of their lives.

Neither Eben nor Amin accounted their defection much of a loss, as the call had already gone out for loyal men to meet at the Odd Man Inn outside the capital in two days' time.

They departed that morning for the capital city, Amin Samil astride a sturdy roan, Jocco and Tavos perched atop a gentle mare, with Eben bringing up the rear on a huge black gelding. They kept a slow pace, stopping often so that Jocco would not tire.

Over the course of the five-hour ride Eben had ample time to contemplate the coming confrontation with Ranulph Gyp. Little had been heard of the man for more than a decade. He had left the Dominion in search of Najja Kek's fabled "fungus" with only the vaguest idea of where the island was to be found. Evidently, his own need for the substance had proved motivation enough. Occasional rumors surfaced that he had taken over some of Najja Kek's pirating business, but no one in the Dominion would have believed that the craven lout could ever attain such wealth and power. It was the measure of the man that he had done so not through good effort, talent, and fair means, but by what amounted to the purchase of men's bodies and souls.

And what of Kaia? Eben reflected miserably that he might just as well have handed her over to Gyp himself. What had possessed him to think her safe locked in the cabin with no avenue of escape should hostile forces come upon the ship? That she and Brother Absalom had managed to fend off their attackers as long as they had was a miracle. Now she was in the clutches of a man whose perversions knew no bounds, and it was Eben's own fault. And God help her if Gyp should discover she was a member of the royal family of the Dominion.

For the moment Eben could do nothing but place his faith in four things to keep her safe: her own intelligence, Brother Absalom's absolute loyalty, Merlin's powers, limited though they might be, and Almighty God.

Chapter Twenty-three

"Let's see what you have brought me today, Thrys."

Ranulph Gyp, former armiger of the Twenty-seventh House of the Dominion, traitor to king and country, exile, coward, sometime pirate, and High Lord of Ataxi, settled back against the velvet cushion of his silver-studded ebony chair and regarded the prisoners before him through jaded eyes.

"You found them aboard the vessel?"

"Yes, sire. The *Apostle*. They were locked in a cabin below deck."

Gyp summoned a servant to fill his cup.

"Strange. And where are the rest of the crew?"

Thrys shifted uncomfortably. "Three are dead. My men will have the rest in custody by evening, sire."

"Hmmm. Not a particularly successful engagement, was it, Thrys?"

"No, sire," the soldier mumbled.

"You bring me a girl and an old man, both of whom appear to be insane. You bring me a dog. No coin, no plate, no jewels. You have no idea who these people are, where they came from, or where they are going."

He sipped his ale. "So you really bring me nothing, wouldn't you agree, Thrys?"

Thrys knew better than to try to make excuses. At the

best of times, Lord Gyp was not a reasonable man; over the years, drink and debauchery had taken their toll. He enjoyed neither the respect nor the loyalty of his men. Yet he held them in thrall: Gyp alone knew the secret of making the most potent aphrodisiac the world had ever known. Once a man partook of it, he became more of a man than he could ever have dreamed. Without it, he was no man at all.

"As you say, sire. But we have reason to believe that at least one of the others on board is a nobleman from the Dominion."

Gyp leaned forward. "Indeed? His name?"

Thrys hastened to capitalize on his lord's sudden interest. "We don't know his name, but one of the crew understood him to be an armiger of one of the noble Houses."

Gyp's hard eyes settled on the two prisoners. "I am Ranulph Gyp. Late of the Dominion. Who are you? Who is this man Thrys speaks of?"

Kaia realized immediately that she could be in no greater danger than she faced at the hands of Ranulph Gyp, the devil who had seized the hall of the Ninth House when Eben's father fell ill. This man had plotted to kill Eben and take his place as armiger. He had trafficked with notorious pirates and slavers. For his crimes, he had been exiled forever from the Dominion, and little had been heard of him for over ten years. He would harbor a deep and abiding hatred of the royal family, and most especially of Eben Dhion.

Kaia fought down her rising panic. Brother Absalom knew the tale; everyone in the Dominion did. She prayed that he would be quick enough to recognize the danger and keep the truth of her identity and Eben's from Ranulph Gyp.

"Arf arf," barked Brother Absalom. His tongue lolled from his mouth and he began to pant.

Kaia clapped her hands together, danced a little jig around him, and giggled madly. Thank God, he understood; they would keep up the masquerade.

"As you can see, my lord, they are quite mad," Thrys offered.

Gyp frowned. "So it would appear. Come here, girl."

Kaia thought her knees would give way beneath her. Dressed as she was in rude peasant clothing with her hair in a tangle and her face streaked with dirt, she certainly didn't fit anyone's image of a noblewoman of royal blood, but with Gyp's piercing gaze on her, she ventured forward with her heart in her throat.

"Closer. Let's have a look at you." Gyp took her chin in his hand and turned her head this way and that. He ordered her to turn around, looked her up and down.

"Strange," he mused. "You remind me of someone, I can't think who. Are you from the Dominion?"

Kaia shook her head vehemently. "Yeth, thir."

"Yes you are from the Dominion?"

Kaia nodded vigorously. "No, thir."

Gyp glared at her. "Either you are from the Dominion or you are not."

She bobbed a little curtsy. "That ith correct, your worthip."

"This is getting us nowhere," Gyp snarled. "Obviously the girl is an idiot. Bring me the other, the dog," he ordered.

Brother Absalom and the black hound trotted forward.

"Good heavens," Gyp muttered. "Thrys, get rid of the dog."

"Woof," said Brother Absalom and moved to follow Thrys.

"Not *that* dog," Gyp shouted. He pointed at the hound. "*That* dog."

The hound grinned.

Everyone froze.

Gyp's eyes swiveled from the hound to Absalom and back again.

"Thrys," said he, "did that dog just smile?"

Thrys was no fool. He wasn't about to commit himself one way or the other. If he answered yes, Lord Gyp would think him mad. If he said no, it would appear he thought Lord Gyp was mad.

Kaia threw her arms wide. "Here, doggie, doggie, doggie," she crooned.

Brother Absalom trotted over and butted his head against her shoulder, begging to be petted. The hound twined about her legs in an ecstasy of doggie worship.

"Good doggies, good doggies."

"Get them out of here," Gyp ordered through clenched teeth. "Have them cleaned up. Put the girl in some womanly clothing; witless or not, she's a pretty little thing and I'll have her tonight. Then bring them to my chamber. There's something strange going on here. Mad or not, these are no common travelers. Get rid of that mangy cur; toss it into the moat. And, Thrys, I want the rest of them in chains in this hall by midnight. Understood?"

Thrys understood the threat all too well. He turned

smartly, summoned three burly guards, and herded Kaia and Brother Absalom out of the great hall.

The large hound eyed the sovereign of Ataxi for a long moment. *Mangy cur?* He pattered up the steps of the dais, lifted a leg, and piddled all over a pair of gleaming black boots.

Eben would come for her. Kaia knew she must somehow survive until he found his way to this dreadful place. She had no idea how long she and Brother Absalom could keep up their mad charade, but she did not think it could be very long. Gyp would see through it soon enough.

"He is not at all as I had imagined," Brother Absalom whispered to Kaia while the guards were otherwise occupied in flirting with the two young girls who were drawing buckets of water from the well behind the bathing shed. "He is far, far worse."

Kaia had only been six or seven when Ranulph Gyp had been sent into exile, but she must have seen him at some time in her early life. She searched her memory for some image of him, but could find none. He was described in the tales of the Ninth House as having been a tall, fair-haired, handsome man of uncertain temperament—by turns charming, arrogant, and cruel. He carried himself nobly enough, but at heart he was a coward, and in the end he became nothing more than a tool in the hands of a man far craftier and even greedier than he: the infamous pirate, Najja Kek.

There was nothing charming about the man Kaia had just seen. He was still handsome enough, but his mouth had the dissatisfied cast of a man who now possessed all the wealth and power he had ever dreamed of and discovered that there was no lasting joy to be found in it. She could feel his seething anger, his undying hatred.

No one had ever frightened her more in her life.

Of course, Kaia and the monk were not accorded the luxury of hot water and a tub. As prisoners they had to make do with pouring buckets of freezing water over themselves, but it felt wonderful to wash away the salt and grime of the long sea journey. Brother Absalom had to make do with his old clothes, but a frightened young woman brought Kaia a gown of pale green linen.

"I'm so sorry," the girl whispered as she helped Kaia lace up the sides.

"Sorry?" Kaia did not like the sound of that at all.

"You know. Him. Don't worry. It might hurt, but it doesn't take long and then he sends you away."

With that cryptic bit of information, the girl scurried away.

"Well, that's certainly comforting," Kaia grumbled as she emerged from the bathing shed to rejoin Brother Absalom, who was running back and forth fetching sticks for the laughing guards.

"Really, this is most undignified," he muttered out of the corner of his mouth. "I should have been a canary; all I would have to do is cheep."

"Perhaps next time," said Kaia.

"A jest. Very good. We must keep our spirits up," he said.

The guards escorted them across the great hall, where

tables were being set up for the noonday meal, and up a broad staircase. Thrys rapped at the door leading to the king's private chambers. It swung open to reveal even more guards, who escorted them through another door into a private reception room draped in brilliant silks. Through an arch could be seen an enormous bed hung with black silk. Three identical cats with long, silken white fur lay sprawled over a gold coverlet.

"Go."

Gyp waved away the guards and strolled forward to inspect the prisoners. "Much better," he said as he circled around Kaia. "Excellent, in fact. I find I'm quite looking forward to our time together this evening."

He plucked at the dull green linen of her sleeve. "This won't do at all. Black velvet, I think, would be the thing, and one of those fine silk shifts beneath, to match those beautiful eyes." Quite as though he were taking the measure of a horse he had in mind to purchase, Gyp began a minute inspection of Kaia's person. It was all she could do not to jerk away as he ran his fingers through her long hair, squeezed each breast, ran the flat of his hand down the small of her back and over her buttocks. He forced her head back to check her teeth and sniff her breath.

"You'll do," he decided. "I suppose it would be too much to hope that you are a virgin. You must have seen at least sixteen summers. Let us have a look." With that, he reached down to drag the skirts of Kaia's gown up to her waist.

Brother Absalom, who had been forced to witness the

appalling scene in silence, could bear it no longer. Somehow he must distract the fiend from his evident intent to explore the body of Lady Kaia more intimately.

Kaia too had had enough and was just preparing to ram her knee into Gyp's groin when the howl of a deranged beast rent the air and Brother Absalom lunged past them and sprinted through the wide arched doorway that led to Gyp's bedchamber. The three white cats leaped from the golden coverlet as one and met the charge screeching and scratching.

The melee brought guards pouring into the chamber. The cats, besieged on every side and heedless of who might be friend and who foe, left few unscathed as they clawed their way up legs, arms, and torsos and leaped from shoulder to shoulder and head to head in a frantic bid to escape the chaos.

While Gyp bellowed oaths and orders, Brother Absalom dragged Kaia to safety behind a door. He reached beneath his tunic and pulled out a leather pouch. With shaking fingers he sorted through three smaller pouches and thrust one into Kaia's hand.

"You must find a way to put a few grains of this herb in his wine, my lady," he said. "Use it sparingly, for I carry very little with me when I travel. It will serve to incapacitate him for a few hours. Later we must add it to whatever ale, wine, or food we can find in the palace."

"Where are the girl and the old man?" Gyp shouted.

"You carry poison with you?" Kaia whispered in amazement.

"Of course not, child," Brother Absalom replied with a frown. "I heal, I do not harm. But one must be prepared for all contingencies. The world is not always so benign a place as one would wish. The Lord, of course, will help us if He is so inclined. In the meantime we must help ourselves. Job, an unlucky fellow if ever there was one, said, 'In me is my help.' So say I."

"Find them," bellowed Gyp.

Brother Absalom patted Kaia's hand. "Fear not, child."

Kaia was, in all honesty, less fearful than she was furious. Had Ranulph Gyp thrown her to the floor and ravished her, she could not have felt more defiled and debased than she had as he poked and prodded her like some dumb beast at a market fair. She would see him dead or herself die in the attempt.

"Come now, my lady, we must go on as we began," Absalom said, and then stuck his head around the edge of the door. "Woof?"

"Everyone. Out!" Gyp bellowed. Scratched, bleeding guards trooped from the room.

"Come out from there, you crazy old man." Gyp seized Brother Absalom by the hair and shook him until the old man's teeth rattled.

Kaia suppressed the impulse to launch herself at Gyp in defense of the terrified monk. Instead she took advantage of Gyp's distracted fury and sidled toward the table beside his chair. Clutching the small leather pouch in the fold of her skirt, she took a small pinch of a golden brown powder and stirred it into Gyp's wine cup with her finger, then added some to the silver decanter beside it. She had just thrust the pouch into the pocket of her gown when Gyp let go of Brother Absalom with a final foul oath. The poor monk sank to the floor like a poked pudding.

"Poor doggie, doggie, doggie," Kaia cried. She rushed across the room, dropped down beside Brother Absalom, and began stroking the dazed monk.

"Mother of God," Gyp swore as he threw himself into his chair and drained his cup. "This is a madhouse." He poured more wine from the decanter and rested his head against the tall back of his chair.

Kaia helped a shaken Brother Absalom to his feet. He gave her hand a little pat to assure her he was unharmed. "The wine?" he whispered out of the side of his mouth. She squeezed his hand and nodded.

"Come here, girl," Gyp ordered. "I'm not finished with you."

As she ventured forward, Kaia could only hope that Gyp would be feeling the effects of Brother Absalom's powder sooner rather than later.

"As I was saying, I prefer my companions to be considerably younger. I trust you have wit enough to at least play the virgin for me."

Kaia giggled. "Yeth, thir." She dropped to her knees, folded her hands in prayer, and gazed up at the coffered ceiling with a look of devotion that would have done Mother Superior proud.

"Not *pray* to the Virgin for me, you fool, *play* the virgin."

"Oh. What thall we play then? I know. You hide and I'll theek. No, I could hide and you could theek. Both hide? But then who seekth? Both theek—"

"Not now, not now" Gyp said irritably. "I have been asking myself where I have seen you before. Of course, I can't be expected to remember every woman I've had. A few stand out—the ones who have been particularly adept at providing me with my special pleasures—but in general a pretty face such as yours leaves no impression. No, I think it must be a relative of yours. A sister; your mother perhaps."

Kaia tittered and preened, but she was beginning to tremble. If he pursued this train of thought it might very well lead him back to . . .

"The Dominion," he said thoughtfully. "I understand at least one passenger aboard your ship is a nobleman from the Dominion. Perhaps that is where I should begin. Let me think."

"No, no, no, no, no."

Kaia's head snapped around. Brother Absalom was shaking a bony finger at Ranulph Gyp.

"Wrong, wrong, wrong. You must guess again."

Kaia's mouth dropped open.

Ranulph Gyp's eyebrows shot up. "So you are not mad after all?"

"Ah, now that is an excellent question," Brother Absalom exclaimed. "What, after all, is madness? If a man barks on a Thursday and by the Sabbath is cheeping like a canary, on which day can he be said to be mad?"

Kaia wondered if Brother Absalom truly had gone mad.

Gyp steepled his fingers and tried to take the measure of the man before him.

The monk swept a low bow. "Allow me to introduce myself, good sir. I am Absalom. This poor witless child is my granddaughter. We took passage aboard the *Apostle* for the Western Isles—would I had chosen the *Sea Maiden*, a

177

sturdier craft I now realize—and arrived in your fair land quite by accident after a storm at sea."

"What business have you in the Western Isles? And why were you going about barking like a dog?"

"A dog is a noble beast, my lord," Brother Absalom explained. "There is a great deal of wisdom in the bark."

By now Kaia realized the monk had merely exchanged one masquerade for another. She suspected he had simply tired of chasing sticks, but it was a clever ploy nonetheless. For the moment, at least, Gyp's attention had been diverted from thoughts of the Dominion.

She laughed delightedly. "Woof woof, Grandpapa, woof woof."

He gave her an indulgent smile and turned back to Gyp. "Now you must guess again or you will lose your turn," Absalom warned him.

"I ask again, what business have you in the Western Isles?"

Absalom leaned toward him and said in a confidential whisper, "The stones, my lord." Here he paused, looked to the left, looked to the right. "Few know the secret. Even fewer will live to tell of it."

"What the devil are you talking about?" Gyp demanded.

"We go to the stones," whispered Brother Absalom. "We shall fly like birds and feast on doodles and pizzapie."

Kaia took her cue and flapped her arms wildly about. "Bzzzzzz."

"No, my dear," Absalom said kindly, "birds do not buzz. Bees buzz. It is entirely possible we shall find that birds in the future buzz, but birds as we now know them do not."

"Enough!" Gyp snapped. "It seems you are mad after all. I don't suppose you have the wits to tell me anything more about this nobleman from the Dominion."

"Of course I do. I am full of wits," the monk said indignantly. "He is not."

"He is not what?"

"Of noble birth. I know all my subjects, each and every one. The man is an impostor."

Gyp's mouth gaped open. "You believe you are the king of the Dominion?"

Absalom bristled. "It is not a matter of conjecture, sir. Do you not see that I am every inch a king? I am a dog of impeccable pedigree."

"Thrys!"

Thrys rushed into the room. "Yes, my lord?"

"Get them out of my sight. Their idiocy is making me ill."

"Oooh," Kaia cooed, "ith my thweet lord thick?"

Gyp gave her a strange look, blanched, gagged, and rushed from the room.

"It appears your lord has been taken ill," Brother Absalom observed as Thrys and three guards escorted them from the room. "Something he ate, I should imagine. Come along, child. This gentleman will show us to our chamber."

The chamber turned out to be a small, windowless storeroom beneath the kitchens filled with sacks of beans, grains, and nuts. Brother Absalom observed that it was really quite pleasant if one considered that their original destination had been the dungeon.

179

"A nice young man, that Thrys," Brother Absalom observed, "allowing us to get a bite to eat in the kitchens as we passed through. Such a fine opportunity to spice up the ale and soup with my little powder amidst all the hustle and bustle. I thought it worked rather well. Quickly, too."

"It certainly did," replied Kaia from the comfortable spot she had made for herself amongst some sacks of flour in the corner. "Thrys certainly couldn't wait to get rid of us. He looked quite sick—it was quite fortuitous indeed that he was unable to take the time to lock us in the dungeon. Now if he would just forget where he put us."

"Poor lad. I doubt he'll be giving us much thought for quite some time. In any event, I don't believe that would be such a good idea. It could be days before anyone happens upon us."

"Surely Merlin is about somewhere," said Kaia. "He's sure to find us soon, don't you think?"

A gentle snore was her only answer.

Kaia shivered. She could still feel the foul shadow of Gyp's touch and see the cold lust in his eyes. They were safe for the moment, but if Eben and Merlin did not come for them soon, she and Brother Absalom would have to come up with some clever scheme to get away from this dreadful place.

Of course, they wouldn't be in this terrible predicament if someone—Lord Eben Dhion by name—hadn't locked them away in the cabin aboard the *Apostle* in the first place.

She really must have a word with Lord Eben about that.

Chapter Twenty-four

"I assure you they are quite safe."

Merlin gnawed the last chunk of greasy meat from the mutton bone and reached for the cracked tankard.

"How did you get them out of there?" Eben said. "Where are they now?"

"I didn't." Merlin took a healthy swallow of the dark sweet ale, wiped his mouth on his sleeve, and settled back.

"What? You mean they're still in the palace?" Eben exclaimed. "They cannot possibly be safe in that fiend's lair."

"Gyp believes they escaped from the palace while the guards were ill. He is out scouring the countryside for them. Where better to hide them than under his very nose?" Merlin replied.

"So you locked them in. They're not going to be too happy with you."

Merlin shrugged. "I expect not; no happier than they are with you for locking them up on the ship. A guard named Thrys was the one who actually shot the bolt. Lady Kaia and Brother Absalom believe he has forgotten where he put them. That herb they slipped into the food and drink was remarkably effective. Half the palace has come down with a disgusting loosening of the bowels. Nasty." Merlin shuddered, then smiled fondly. "They make quite a clever pair when it comes to the point."

Tavos lay curled up sound asleep on a bench in the corner of the public drinking room of the Odd Man Inn. Eben had taken a room above stairs for Jocco, who was still weak from loss of blood. The long ride had left him exhausted, though he would have died before admitting it. Eben had to order him to bed.

Amin Samil had shown himself to be a man of few words. Now he eyed the tall man across from him with skepticism. "I wonder that you, a stranger, were able to move about the palace without exciting suspicion."

"It is a gift, I must admit," replied Merlin with due modesty. "I find that people are inclined to see what they expect to see, not necessarily what is there in front of them. A great scholar once said, 'Just because you do not see the cat does not mean he is not there.'"

Eben laughed. "Or dog, as the case may be."

Amin looked from one grinning man to the other. This was not the first time he suspected that this enterprise was not exactly what it seemed. Eben and this Merlin were not in the least surprised that this Brother Absalom fellow, who was presently locked in a storeroom with the lady, should have a hand in bringing the entire court, the palace staff, and the garrison down with a bout of intestinal distress the like of which had not been seen in the capital in a generation.

Then there had been the black hound. Amin could have sworn it wore a wide grin on its face when it bounded up to Lord Eben as they dismounted in the courtyard of the inn on the outskirts of the city. It had since disappeared, grin and all.

Eben was not entirely pleased with Merlin at the moment. "You know, you could make this whole thing easier for all of us," he observed.

"I thought I had explained all that to you aboard the *Apostle*. I find myself severely limited on this leg of my journey. I cannot even play the role of Cupid this time around. I do so enjoy wielding my little bow and arrow. Alas, the lovers in this farce will have to find their way to one another without my help. As for the events of the present moment, I stand by to guide and advise only."

"You know the outcome, I know you do."

"Well, of course I do. I cannot help but doing so, having already—"

Eben lunged across the table, toppling candles and sending dishes and cups crashing to the floor, and seized the wizard by his long white beard. "We are not here for your amusement, old man," he snarled. "You may only be passing through, but we are living real lives, the only ones we will ever live. Use us as your playthings at your peril. If any harm comes to Lady Kaia, I will hold you personally responsible, and I will hunt you down when and wherever you are."

It was, Amin Samil thought, the oddest speech he had ever heard.

Chapter Twenty-five

"Honor and the Dominion!" Kaia howled as she launched herself at the sinister figure framed in the open doorway of the storeroom.

"Begone, fiend from hell!" shrieked Brother Absalom and sank his teeth into the intruder's leg.

The enemy kicked out but got himself tangled up in his long cloak. He went down like a tall tree toppling before a fierce wind. "Ooof," he grunted as a lithe figure dropped onto his back and began to beat him about the head.

"Look out! There's another one!" Absalom shouted as he sprang at the new threat, sending the shadowy figure reeling back into the dim passage.

"Sweet Mother of God," the man muttered as he wrestled the frenzied monk to the floor, grabbed hold of an ear, and twisted hard.

"Ouch! That hurts," Brother Absalom yelped.

"Not nearly enough, if you ask me," growled Eben Dhion.

"Lord Eben? Oh, my. Kaia, my dear, I think we may have misjudged the situation. If you would just ceasing pummeling Merlin, we might be able to sort things out."

By then the wizard had managed to heave the little demon off his back. He pounced, and pinned her to the floor. "Never in all my days," he wheezed, "have I been treated with such marked disrespect. I should turn you into a toad, you dreadful child."

Kaia glared up at him. "You could have knocked."

Eben helped a shaken Brother Absalom to his feet. "Now that we've made enough noise to raise the dead, I suggest we get out of here."

"This way." Holding the torch before him, Merlin led the little party down a long flight of crumbling stone steps into the cold, dank warren of rooms and twisting passages beneath the palace.

"How do you know where you're going?" inquired Brother Absalom as he pattered along behind the wizard.

"I don't. I'm following my nose. I expect I'll know when we get there."

"What I want to know," came Kaia's voice from the darkness, "is how you knew where we were."

"I put you there," Merlin replied. "Or rather, I made sure you stayed put there."

Kaia stopped dead in her tracks. "You locked us in? For all that time?"

"Look at it more in the light of locking other people out, my dear. As it happened, the man Thrys was far too indisposed to come back for you—well done, by the way, Brother Absalom—but Gyp had men tearing the palace apart from top to bottom. It wasn't likely they would bother looking into rooms that were locked from the outside."

"Keep moving," Eben said from behind Kaia.

"We didn't even have a chamber pot," she complained.

Merlin and Brother Absalom moved on. The light of

the torch dimmed as they rounded a corner into another passageway.

From the moment she'd seen Eben ride up to the Inn of the Bishop's Bastard, Kaia's emotions had veered from one extreme to another and teetered upon every sentiment in between.

One moment she was elated: He was a knight right out of Camelot questing for his lost lady love. He had experienced a stunning revelation: There existed but one woman in all the world for him, the incomparable Lady Kaia. He had been on the verge of offering for her hand and, upon discovering her supposed abduction, had set out to slay the dastardly villain who dared take his beloved Kaia from him.

At other moments she harbored dark suspicions: He had set out to find her only because Jibril had ordered him to do so, not because he cared one whit for her. He had come in search of her only out of a sense of duty: the armiger of one noble House honoring his covenant with another. He had not come for her at all but for Morgana, or he had happened upon Commander Ankuli at the inn and thought it would be pleasant to ride along with him since they were headed in the same direction.

Finally, she was furious with him: He had interjected himself into her great adventure—*her* adventure. He had undermined her, brought her to the point where she began to doubt herself.

That was the worst of it: the way a man would whittle away at a woman's resolve, criticize, belabor, and belittle her until she was no longer sure she had made the right choice, or that she was capable of making any choice at all.

And yet, and yet. In Eben's anger over what he perceived to be her recklessness, was there not something of concern for her well-being, her safety? Had he not come for her, into the lair of his greatest enemy? Had he not torn himself from her on the beach because he would not dishonor her? Had he not gentled her in the cabin when the storm raged above them?

The cabin. Oh, yes, there was that little matter of the ship's cabin to be dealt with.

"My problem," snapped Kaia out of the darkness, "is you."

Eben propelled her forward; they could not afford to fall too far behind lest they lose sight of Merlin's torch. "I see. No doubt you are about to tell me why."

"You. Locked us. Into. The cabin."

If Kaia had expected yet another of Eben's sermons on the need to restrain herself from yielding to every imprudent impulse that came into her head, she was mistaken.

"Kaia, I am sorry for that," said he.

"Sorry?" Eben was apologizing?

"I totally misjudged the element of danger. It was dark. The *Apostle* was well concealed; the three men I left on guard seemed the most reliable of the lot. Obviously, our lanterns were spotted as we rowed up the inlet, though the hour was late. I never anticipated an attack, not before dawn."

"Then why lock us in?" Kaia demanded. "Brother Absalom and I are not so stupid as to wander off in the middle of the night, whatever you may think of us."

"I know that, Kaia."

"Then why?"

"I locked you in to protect you from the guards."

"Oh."

"That crew had been without women for almost two weeks. Do you understand?"

Kaia suddenly felt very foolish. "Yes. I hadn't even considered that. I just thought—"

Eben steered her around the corner; ahead they could see the tall figure of the wizard and the shorter shadow of Brother Absalom pattering along close behind. "I know what you thought."

"I'm sorry, Eben," Kaia said humbly. "You were right."

"Only in that respect. I left you vulnerable and, in the event, put you in the greatest possible danger. If not for your quick thinking, it could have ended very badly indeed, and I would have it on my conscience for the rest of my life."

"It was Brother Absalom's idea to pretend madness," Kaia said. "The credit must go to him."

"I will never allow such a thing to happen again, Kaia. I swear it to you upon my honor."

They had by now caught up to Merlin and the monk at the bottom of a flight of stairs that led up to a small iron door.

"Well, well," Brother Absalom said to Merlin, "your nose has served us well, sir."

Eben motioned the others back, eased open the creaking door, and slipped out. A few minutes later he was back. "We've come out near the main city gate. There's some sort of festival going on. I think we can make our way through the crowd without drawing attention."

As it turned out, most of the revelers were so deep in their cups that they wouldn't have noticed the entire

Saracen army raping and pillaging its way through the city streets, and probably wouldn't have much cared if they had.

Once outside the city wall, they made their way along the moonlit road to the place where Amin, Jocco, and Tavos were waiting with the horses. There, Eben, Merlin, and Amin stepped aside to confer as to the best course of action.

"Gyp isn't going to give up looking for Kaia and the monk," said Eben. "It will not be safe to lodge them in an inn. We must take them back to the cave. Amin, what is the likelihood of soldiers venturing that far into the wilderness?"

"Very slight, my lord," Amin replied. "For generations tales of evil spirits, werewolves, ghouls, and the like have discouraged even the most courageous from venturing into the area."

"I am surprised your clan continues to dwell there."

Amin smiled a crooked smile. "Who do you think has spread these tales about?"

Eben clapped him on the back and laughed heartily. "A fine strategy indeed, my friend."

"I will return to the city and see what is to be learned," Merlin said. "I shall need a guide. Perhaps Amin will consent to accompany me."

In the end, it was decided that Eben would escort Kaia, Brother Absalom, Jocco, and Tavos back to the cave, while Merlin and Amin would return to the city. On hearing this, Tavos threw himself at his father, pleading to be allowed to go with them.

Amin frowned down at the boy, who had the look of a starving puppy hoping for the last scrap of fat. "This is serious business, son. You will have to rein in your natural exuberance. You must stay close and keep quiet."

When Tavos swore an oath on the grave of every relative he had ever known, it was decided he should accompany Merlin and his father into the city.

"When I have seen the others settled," Eben said to Merlin, "I will meet you three at the Odd Man Inn. Let us say, two nights hence. We shall decide then how best to deal with Gyp."

"And I will have had time to gather allies in our cause," Amin said.

"I will go with you, my lord, when you return to the palace." Kaia had overheard Eben's words as she returned from refreshing herself at a small stream across the road. Being excluded from the discussion did not sit well with her, but she had chosen not to make a fuss in front of the others.

Eben did not even bother looking her way as he began tightening the girth on the little mare. "You will not."

"Oh, no, no, no, my dear," Brother Absalom exclaimed from the other side of the clearing. "That would be most unwise. I believe Lord Gyp had some special, er, activities planned for you. We must keep you well away from him."

"Plans? What plans had Gyp for Lady Kaia?" Eben said quietly.

"Well, um, you know, my lord," Brother Absalom hedged. *"Plans."* He didn't wish to be indelicate.

Eben turned back to the mare. Had it been daylight and a man chanced to see the stone-cold look in Eben Dhion's eyes, he would have run for his life. "Lady Kaia will return with us to the cave and remain there," he said flatly.

"He seemed particularly interested in Lady Kaia's identity," the monk continued, relieved that Lord Eben seemed to have caught his meaning. He would not have been at all comfortable having to be any more explicit about Ranulph Gyp's evident lust for Lady Kaia. "First he was certain he had seen her before, but then he decided she reminded him of someone from his past, from the Dominion. If he had thought on it much longer, I believe he might very well have come to the conclusion that she is a member of the royal family."

"Eben, I should like a word with you," Kaia said.

"There is nothing to discuss. Jocco and Brother Absalom, you will double up on the roan." He held out a hand to Kaia and assisted her into the saddle.

"On the contrary, we have a great deal to discuss," she said evenly as he made a final adjustment of her stirrups.

Eben swung up onto the gelding. "Do you think so?"

Kaia ignored the sarcasm of his reply. "Yes. I do think so."

As they moved out onto the ribbon of moonlit road, Eben reflected that he had one more reason to look forward to the coming confrontation with Lord Ranulph Gyp.

The fiend had dared to think of defiling Kaia Kurinon.

Chapter Twenty-six

About four hours into the ride Brother Absalom called out that Jocco seemed to be unwell. Eben called a halt. He lifted his listless squire down and laid him with care on the ground. Brother Absalom and Kaia hovered anxiously over them.

"Fever." Eben could not have said anything more alarming than that single word.

Kaia knelt down and touched her hand to Jocco's hot brow. "We must find a healer immediately."

"We have at least an hour's ride ahead of us," Eben pointed out. "I do not recall that we pass much in the way of habitation between here and the cave. We will have to stop at Amin's cottage. If we leave the main road and follow this valley along, it cannot be far. Surely his wife will take us in. I will have to reopen the wound. This time I'll take no chances; it will have to be cauterized."

"I have some expertise in the use of herbs," Brother Absalom said. "I was often called upon at the monastery to tend to minor wounds."

Eben looked grim. "I fear this is not minor. But we must use what means we have."

Jocco was by now nearly insensible. Eben took him up on the gelding with him and cradled him as they picked their way along the rough path that led up into a narrow valley. As the moon had set some time ago and they had only the faint light of the stars to see by, they nearly missed the cottage altogether.

A small face appeared at a crack in the door even before Brother Absalom lifted his hand to knock. "I heard horses," little Zelana said. "I thought Pa and Tavos were here. Mama," she called into the darkness of the cottage, "Lord Eben and the others have come."

"Good lady," Brother Absalom hastened to assure her in his gentle way, "we have just left your husband and boy in good health in the capital. We must throw ourselves on your goodness. Lord Eben's squire has taken a serious fever. His wound must be reopened; we require herbs and, if you would grant us leave, a bed for him."

Within minutes Jocco was laid upon the only bed in the cottage and Brother Absalom and Bera were busily conferring as to the best poultice for the squire's wound. Zelana kept getting underfoot until Kaia lifted her into her lap to keep her out of the way.

"But I want to help," Zelana objected.

"I have an idea of how you can help," Kaia said. "Let us think of all the good things in the world such as warm sunshine and newborn kittens and the smell of rosemary. The goodness of those things will fill this room and wrap themselves around Squire Jocco and help make him well again. What will you think about?"

Zelana concentrated. "Mama and Papa. Yellow bunch-berries. Angel."

"An angel?"

Bera smiled over at them. "Zelana has a special friend that no one else can see but her. Angel."

"Then Angel, by all means," Kaia said gravely.

"And Lord Eben," Zelana added.

Eben looked up for a moment from the close work of removing the stitches from Jocco's shoulder and smiled.

"Yes," Kaia murmured to herself, "Lord Eben."

The sun was full up by the time everything that could be done for Jocco had been done. He slept peacefully with Zelana curled up beside him—"to keep my good thoughts close to him," she had informed everyone. Brother Absalom snoozed in a corner, Bera in a straight hard chair. Kaia left off adjusting the fur coverlet around Jocco's shoulders and followed Eben out into the sweet morning air.

"His fever is already abated," Kaia said.

Eben stretched his aching muscles. "He's strong; he'll live."

"He will live because of you, Eben," Kaia said softly.

"And Bera and Brother Absalom and Zelana's good thoughts." He laughed. "And you. That was a clever idea of yours. Who knows but that the power of a positive thought is as great a magic as Brother Absalom's poultices and prayers?"

Kaia settled down on a log, extracted a wide-toothed comb from a pocket of her under-tunic, and began combing her long pale hair, carefully loosening the many little tangles. Eben watched her. She looked tired and rumpled and sweet in the dappled light of the cottage yard. The hunger for her awakened in him, as he now knew it would for the rest of his life whenever he looked at her. Perhaps when he got her back to Suriana he would . . .

"Lord Eben," Zelana cried as she popped out of the cottage. "He's awake."

Jocco was indeed awake, and when Eben and Brother Absalom had satisfied themselves that the boy was on the mend, Eben said it was time to continue on to the cave, where they would collect what few belongings they had left there and return to the cottage. He would then go on to the capital to meet Merlin, Amin, and Tavos.

Brother Absalom balked, claiming he had not yet exhausted the catalog of scriptural references appropriate to Jocco's situation, and one never knew if some unforeseen happening might require a shift of focus. In the end, Eben and Kaia set off alone after a midday meal—bread, mutton stewed with beans and onions, and the sweet juice of a red fruit native to the island—leading the roan that would serve as a packhorse on their return that evening.

"Eben," Kaia said as they made their way down the valley to the main road, "I really must have a word with you—"

"Not now, Kaia," Eben growled. "Cannot we just share a pleasant ride without contention?"

"How do you know I intend to be contrary?" she demanded.

Eben looked at her, lifted a brow, and rode on.

He was right, Kaia reflected. It was far too pleasant a morning to dwell on the ugly likes of Ranulph Gyp, or on the near future in which she now knew she must make the decision of her life. Each day the certainty that her destiny lay within the Circle of Standing Stones weakened just a little. She would shore up her flagging resolve with bracing little reminders of the reasons she had set out with Brother Absalom in the first place. But the truth of the matter was that those reasons did not carry nearly the weight they had only three weeks ago.

For one thing, she knew she need only practice diligently to master her skills at reading and writing. Eben had assured her that she would not have to return to her father's hall, to the bullying and threats of beatings if she defied him in the slightest thing. She would never fly, of course, but perhaps she would be able to study how bees and flying beetles, birds and bats managed it; she would have a "profession." Anyhow, Brother Absalom maintained that if God had intended men to fly He would have provided them with wings as He had His angels.

Kaia glanced sideways at the tall, powerful man riding beside her. Gone were the golden curls of his boyhood. They had darkened as he grew into manhood, but the deep amber and pale gold highlights that shone in sunlight and flame held the memory of them. His hair fell in gleaming waves over his shoulders and framed the strong, sculptured lines of his forehead, cheekbones, nose, and chin. Eben Dhion: the Golden One. One of the most desired men in the kingdom, who could choose the woman he wanted to take to his bed any day or night; and choose his wife when the time came from the most beautiful noblewomen in the land.

"We'd best dismount and lead the horses," Eben announced, rousing Kaia from her reverie.

The ravine was indeed treacherous ground for the horses, strewn with rock and debris from centuries of flash floods and the crumbling black cliffs to either side. It was this very inaccessibility that had prompted Eben to scout it on the morning of the attack on the *Apostle* for a safe place to hide from possible pursuit. The cave was not entirely unknown, however, as evidenced by the cold fire pit and piles of dry wood heaped in a far corner.

A faint echo of distant thunder heralded a coming storm just as they reached the debris slide that allowed access to the cave high above the floor of the ravine. They paused to allow the horses to drink their fill from the stream before they led them up the slope and into the cave. Eben threaded a long rope through their bridles and wound it several times around a thick slab of stone that must have fallen from the roof centuries before.

Kaia could hardly conceal her weariness. She and Eben had slept little the night before as they watched over Jocco, taking turns bathing his flushed face and preventing him from injuring his shoulder further in his troubled sleep. Even Eben did not move about the cave with his usual energy as he built up a good fire against the chill of the coming storm.

"We should rest," he told Kaia. "The storm will move through quickly, and there will be daylight enough to return to the cottage."

Kaia searched through the items they had stripped from the *Apostle*, found a rough blanket, and spread it out on the cave floor. The sailors who had gone in search of the Promised Land of incomparable masculinity had devoured all the provisions and finished off the keg of ale Amin had provided, but they had overlooked Eben's wine flask. He took it down to the stream to mix the wine with a little water so as to have enough to share with Kaia, and took the opportunity to wash away two days' worth of dirt and sweat.

The storm broke over the ravine with a violence that sent the horses into a panic. If Eben had not secured them well, they would have posed a very real danger in the confines of the cave. They calmed when the crackling of lightning and booming thunder moved inland, leaving only the sound of heavy rain that battered the cliffs and cascaded into the ravine below.

An ominous sound drew Eben and Kaia to the mouth of the cave, a rumbling much like the earthquakes that occasionally shook the Dominion. A moment later, a wall of water plowed through the ravine, pushing small boulders, tree limbs, even a few small struggling animals before it, rising up the cliffs on either bank until it was barely ten feet below where they stood.

"We will have to stay the night here," Eben decided.

The significance of their situation was not lost on either of them. They were probably in for a very long night.

"Wine?"

"How kind of you. Almonds?"

"Not at the moment, I thank you. Later perhaps."

"Would you be kind enough to build up the fire? It has really become quite chilly."

"It would be my pleasure, my lady."

Kaia cleared her throat. "They will realize we are delayed by the storm."

"No doubt."

"I would not wish Brother Absalom to think . . ."

"I'm certain he will understand."

"Yes."

"Yes."

Having said everything there was to say under the circumstances with the exception, of course, of what was really on their minds, they lapsed into silence. In the shadowed corner the horses shifted and snorted. Outside, the waters rushed and the rain poured down.

"I expect we should get some sleep."

"I agree absolutely; we should get some sleep."

Kaia arranged herself on the blanket. Eben spread a cloak on the ground at the far side of the fire.

"You are warm enough, my lady?"

If she were any warmer, Kaia thought, she'd melt.

"You are comfortable enough, are you, my lord?"

If he got any harder he was going to explode.

"I bid you good night then."

"Good night."

Kaia settled onto her side with her back to the flames and drowsily watched the firelight dancing over the cold stone walls of the cave. Soon she slept, but lightly. Eben set aside his sword belt and pulled off his boots. He immediately abandoned the idea of sleeping on his stomach as impracticable, given his present state of arousal. Eventually he too slipped into a kind of half sleep, but the adamant demands of his body woke him again and again, until he gave it up and lay staring up at the ceiling in the dying light of the fire.

Not even as a young man in the full throes of unrelenting sexual appetite had Eben Dhion felt so desperately the need to thrust himself into a woman as he did at this moment. Perhaps any reasonably attractive woman would have done for that simple act. But beyond need lay something he had never before encountered: the hunger for one woman and one woman only. The need to claim her for himself alone, to pleasure her, to pour his seed into her sweet warmth, and his soul into her safekeeping.

That woman slept not five paces away. She could not know it, but only the shield of his honor now kept him from assuaging the need, the hunger.

Eben considered whether he had the willpower to look but not touch. Yes, he did, he decided. Well, probably he did. How was he to know if he didn't put it to the test?

With hands clasped firmly behind his back, he gazed down at Kaia, who was sprawled in the abandon of sleep on her back with one arm flung out to the side and her long hair spread like a spray of new wheat over the deep blue wool of the blanket.

She could not know he was standing over her, but suddenly her eyes opened, and for a long moment she looked up at him with a dark, unfathomable expression.

Then came Eben Dhion's undoing.

In a motion so simple, so graceful, so enticingly female, she opened her arms and summoned him to her.

Before he even knew he had done it, he was covering her, taking her mouth with the urgency of a man fearing that some emissary out of deepest hell would snatch it away at any moment. Her soft moans against his lips, the whispered sound of his name, the feel of her fingers in his hair to hold him to her, summoned forth the timeless impulse in a man to possess a woman, to command surrender. He slipped his hands beneath her tunic to cradle her firm, smooth buttocks and raised her up against him so that she would know his hardness and the strength of his need for her.

"Eben, say my name," she whispered when he was at last able to raise his head. He looked down at her black, slumberous eyes and swollen lips.

"Kaia," he murmured against the delicate hollow of her throat.

"Kaia, Kaia," he groaned when they had torn one another's clothes off and he could at last feel her warm skin along every inch of his body.

He tasted the sweetness of her breasts, explored her

with his fingers and tongue. "Kaia, my little one. Let me . . . please, Kaia, please."

"Yes. Yes."

He settled her beneath him and hooked his arms under her knees to position her for his entry. "Oh, God, forgive me," he begged when he could no longer bear the careful probing of her tight passage and thrust himself hard and fully into her.

"Yes, yield," he whispered as she softened beneath him. "Feel me deep inside you, Kaia, moving against you.

"Beautiful Kaia," he groaned as she convulsed beneath him with soft cries of release.

And when he abandoned himself to his own release, it was her name on his lips.

"Kaia. Mine."

Long after his powerful body had stopped shaking and he had fallen into exhausted sleep sprawled atop her with his face buried against her neck, Kaia was still running her hand gently over the hard-muscled planes of his shoulders and back, glorying in the weight of him and the power that wrapped about her.

"Yours."

Deep in the night, when the stream below no longer raged and the rain was but a faint patter on the slick rocks of the canyon, they embraced again, face to face, her leg thrown over his hip; moving languorously against one another until they shared the slow, sweet release gazing deep into one another's eyes.

"Eben. Mine."

"Yours."

Chapter Twenty-seven

There had been no words of love, no talk of a future together, Kaia reflected as she washed away the evidence of her lost virginity. The stream rose higher on the banks this morning, but flowed gently enough for her to wade out into a small pool until she was up to her knees in the frigid water.

Eben had asked her gently if he had hurt her, and she was able to answer truthfully that it had not been all that bad.

"When Gyp touched me I wanted to die," she said. "I have never felt so soiled in my life. But with you, Eben—"

"He touched you," Eben said.

"Yes, he touched me. Oh, but not that way, Eben, not the way you're thinking. I would have died before I'd lie with him."

"He touched you."

She leaned against his chest. "It was as though he was considering a cut of meat. I felt so—"

"He touched you. He is a dead man. I will kill him with my bare hands."

Eben seemed to have forgotten she was there at all, so consumed was he with thoughts of his own injured manhood.

"It is I who was wronged," Kaia snapped. "I think I should do the killing, if killing is to be done."

"He touched you," was all Eben replied. He did not speak of the matter again. In fact, he did not speak at all.

In the cold light of morning, Kaia wasn't sure how she herself felt about their lovemaking. In the heat of passion she had chanted, "I love you, I love you" over and over again in her mind, but now that she had felt the overwhelming power of lust, she realized how easily the one might be confused with the other.

She had always thought that she loved Eben Dhion, but had it been the fantasy of love a young girl might hold in her heart? Was their encounter last night merely the lust of a young woman who yearned for the beautiful man other women desired, and took satisfaction in having lain with him when others could only dream of doing so?

"We need to be under way. It is an hour's ride to the cottage, and then a further five hours for me to reach the capital," Eben informed her.

"You will confront Gyp," Kaia said as they mounted the horses at the mouth of the ravine.

"Yes."

"Alone."

"Yes."

"Eben, Ranulph Gyp knows there is a nobleman from the Dominion on this island. I saw his eyes when he learned of it. He is consumed with hatred, nearly mad with it, I think. If he learns that nobleman is you, he really will go mad. You cannot face him alone."

"I will deal with this in my own way, Kaia," Eben replied harshly. "You would do well to stay out of it."

"Stay out of it?" Kaia demanded.

"This is between me and Gyp alone. I never expected to have the chance to gain revenge for the wrongs he did to my House, my sister, myself. Until a few weeks ago, I did not even know for sure that the man still lived. But fate has seen fit to bring me to this place where I may finally prove myself a man and worthy of the High Seat of my House."

"You, you, you!" Kaia shouted at him. "You think only of yourself. You are not the only one wronged. I am wronged. The people of this island are wronged. They have suffered grievously under Ranulph Gyp. He has unmanned half the men; they might as well be slaves when he holds the key to their virility in his hands. He makes fools of them, and their women too. He takes pleasure in rape and inflicting pain on young girls who cannot defend themselves. He would have done the same to me had Brother Absalom not had the foresight to carry noxious herbs with him for his own protection while on the road."

Kaia brought her mare to a halt with a quick, hard pull at the reins. "Do you think killing Ranulph Gyp makes you a better man than you already are, Eben? What of the past will it change? Does it bring any more honor to the Ninth House than you have already bestowed upon it with your stewardship and good management? Have your vengeance, by all means, but allow others theirs as well. Allow me mine. How much finer a man you will leave this place if you will let go of your personal vendetta and lead these people toward freedom—and yes, allow them, not you, to determine how Ranulph Gyp is to be punished."

Eben said not a word. He spurred the gelding forward, leaving Kaia in his dust.

* * *

Against his better judgment, Brother Absalom assisted Jocco out of bed and into the cottage yard, where he saw him settled comfortably on a log that served as a crude bench. Zelana stationed herself at the squire's feet like an elfin sentinel to make sure no bad thoughts got close to him.

"I'm certain no ill has come to them," Brother Absalom assured Jocco for the tenth time. "They could not possibly have traveled through such a storm. I expect they'll be here any minute."

Jocco, who had no need of such reassurance, replied for the tenth time that Lord Eben knew what he was about and had probably spent an uneventful night safe and dry in the cave. Lady Kaia would have been in the best of hands

Brother Absalom paced about the cottage yard three or four times and said he would just walk a short way down the valley road to see if they were in sight. Jocco's reminder that Lord Eben and Lady Kaia might very well have spent the night together alone and without a chaperon occasioned some anxiety in the old monk. He was not so naive that he had not seen the strong attraction between them, despite their constant bickering. A brief meditation on the subject of lust might be in order. The General Epistle of James seemed appropriate.

"'Blessed is the man that endureth temptation: for when he is tried he shall receive the crown of life, which the Lord hath promised to those that love Him. But every man is tempted, when he is drawn away of his own lust, and enticed. Then when lust hath conceived, it bringeth forth sin: and sin, when it is finished, bringeth forth death.'"

Brother Absalom plopped down on a tree trunk and gave some serious thought to the matter. The apostles seemed ever to be ranting on about sins of the flesh, whereas the patriarchs of the Hebrews seemed to go cheerfully about their lusting with precious little interest or interference from the Lord.

The old monk prayed, as was appropriate, that Lord Eben and Lady Kaia had managed to behave themselves. However, the thought did flit through his mind that there could be no stronger motivation than love to convince Lady Kaia to stay behind. If a lustful act should happen to lead her to the realization of that love, then it might very well be less a sin than an instrument of the Almighty for good purpose. Having satisfied himself that such was the case, Brother Absalom marveled that He did, indeed, work in miraculous ways.

Shading his eyes, Brother Absalom scanned the horizon. With a joyful cry he leaped and ran to greet his lost sheep.

"Jocco is very much improved," he reported as he pattered alongside Eben's horse. "He insisted on leaving his bed this morning, despite all our protestations, but it does not seem to have done him any harm."

Eben could see that for himself as he and Kaia trotted into the cottage yard. The color was back in the squire's face, and little Zelana was stuffing a large chunk of dark bread dripping with honey into his mouth.

Bera bustled about laying out cheeses and fresh-baked bunchberry tarts for the hungry travelers. "Those floods have been the death of more than one foolish man," she said.

"Floods?" squeaked Brother Absalom, whose greatest fear for Lady Kaia and Lord Eben had been that they might contract a slight chill from being caught out in the rain.

After Eben unloaded the horses and he and Kaia piled their few belongings from the *Apostle* in an open-sided shed behind the cottage, Jocco was permitted to lead the horses to pasture about a quarter mile up the valley. Zelana happily assumed the role of guide, although Jocco could see the sward of green with his own eyes.

In less than an hour, Eben was preparing to depart. Jocco, indignant at being left behind, marshaled every argument he could think of to convince Eben to let him accompany him, to no avail.

"But, my lord—"

"I'll have no more arguments, Squire. There is much to do before we leave this place. You will be of no help if you cannot handle a sword."

Kaia had no intention of being left behind.

"I'm going with you," she declared.

Eben gave her a flat stare. "We have been over this before, my lady. You will remain here. Is that understood?"

"No, it is not understood," she retorted. "If you think you can simply throw out orders and expect me to scurry to obey, you are sorely mistaken. I will say what I have to say. Preferably in private, but if you will have it so, then here before the others." She planted her hands on her hips. "Which will it be, my lord?"

The issue was resolved by the rapid retreat of Brother Absalom, Jocco, and Bera from the yard. Little Zelana, who'd looked on with the unfeigned interest of the very young at the antics of their elders, had to be picked up by her mother and borne away, protesting loudly.

Eben folded his arms across his chest. "Well? What is it you wish to say to me?"

"It may have slipped your mind that I am a princess of the Second House."

"Believe me, my lady, it is not something I am likely to forget."

"I will not be ordered about."

"I see."

"Do you?"

"Indeed I do, my lady. As you say, you are a princess and cousin to my liege. I am bound by my honor to see to your protection by whatever measures I deem necessary. It is my solemn duty. I have deemed it necessary to order you about."

"Save your sarcasm for a more appropriate occasion, my lord."

"You might do the same with your imperious posturing, my lady."

A long, strained silence settled between them. When Kaia could bear it no longer, she said quietly, "This is absurd. Why can't you see that I could help you, Eben? I could distract him, make him lower his guard—"

"Listen to me, Kaia," Eben said harshly. "He hates me, but I am only one man. You are Ahriman's niece, the man who sent Gyp into exile. You are Jibril's cousin. Do you have any idea what kind of power he will wield against the royal family, against the Dominion, if you fall into his hands?"

"Of course I do, but he would not dare harm me: I am

far too valuable to him. But you, Eben—you he would kill without a qualm."

"Kaia," he said more gently, "I must settle with Gyp once and for all. It is something I must do myself. My honor demands it."

"Did you not hear anything I said upon the road?"

"Yes, I heard. And yes, I now see that the honor of others is at stake here as well. You must trust me to do what is right."

Kaia was stung. "Women too possess honor," she said hotly. "We do not always need men to act for us. You of all people should know that, Eben. When Gyp seized your hall, Syrah fought for the honor of your House as well as any man. And she prevailed."

Eben turned his back on her and walked away. "That was different."

"It was—"

Eben swung up into the saddle and took up the reins. "No. That is my last word on the subject, Kaia."

Brother Absalom, Jocco, Bera, and Zelana ventured out from the cottage to bid farewell to Lord Eben, now that the discord appeared to be over.

Kaia stood apart, watching him move off down the valley with the white mare and the roan tethered behind. She was torn between tears and iron-hot anger. And although she quailed at the thought of ever again finding herself the object of Gyp's close scrutiny, she could not and would not allow Eben to face that devil alone.

And she would most certainly not allow Lord Eben Dhion to have the last word.

* * *

He'd managed to get in the last word, but Eben wasn't congratulating himself overmuch as he made his way toward the capital. Kaia meant well, but she really had no idea just how evil was the man they were dealing with. Eben could not and would not allow Kaia Kurinon to go anywhere near Ranulph Gyp ever again. She had tried to put a brave face on it in the cave, but Eben knew she must have been terrified when confronted by Gyp at the palace. If Brother Absalom had not had his herbs with him, Ranulph Gyp would have had Kaia—*his* Kaia—would have violated and defiled her with his polluted touch, invaded her sweet body with his obscene shaft. Eben closed his eyes against the unbearable image; banished the very thought lest he come apart.

Kaia belonged to him now; she would always belong to him. In that first embrace last night he had experienced the most powerful surge of lust and the most explosive release of his life. He had gloried in her womanly surrender, triumphed as she abandoned herself to her own wild release in his arms.

In that second slow, sweet embrace, it was he who had surrendered, body and soul. He had fallen in love, once and for all, with the grubby little urchin, the mischievous prankster, the maddening mouse chaser, the giggling drunkard in the garden, the madcap adolescent, the irresponsible runaway, the beautiful woman in the firelight as the heavens opened up and the floods raged below.

No force and no one in the universe were going to take Kaia Kurinon away from him.

And that was Eben Dhion's very last word on the subject.

Chapter Twenty-eight

"Did he say where he was going?"

Eben was surprised when he arrived at the Odd Man Inn to find only Amin and Tavos waiting for him.

"Nay, my lord," Amin answered. "He said only that he had business elsewhere. It was very strange. One moment he was there and the next moment he was gone."

Merlin's disappearance, when added to Eben's chaotic thoughts about the harsh words that had passed between him and Kaia, put him in the foulest possible temper. He had intended to consult with the wizard as to the best way to gain access to the upper floors of the palace, and was seriously annoyed to find that the man had taken himself off on some capricious errand of his own.

"I asked Merlin how he'd find us," Tavos piped up, "and do you know what he told me? He said he would just follow his nose. That didn't make much sense," he added with a frown. "I told him that my nose is always pointing in the same direction I'm going. I don't see how it can go off in one direction while the rest of me is trying to go the other way."

"And what had he to say to that?" Eben inquired.

"He said I really must read a book called *Through the Looking-Glass* someday. But I don't know how to read," Tavos added wistfully.

"This Merlin," Amin said carefully; "how come you to know him, my lord?"

"Pa thinks he's strange," Tavos declared.

Eben looked at Amin over the rim of his mug. He suspected that the man was far more perceptive than his stolid demeanor suggested.

"He travels with Brother Absalom to the Western Isles," Eben replied.

"Also an unusual man," Amin observed.

Eben shrugged, hoping to put an end to the inquiry. "They have interests in common, I understand."

"And the hound? Does it too share their interests?"

"What hound?" Tavos demanded, looking from one man to the other.

Eben and Amin held one another's eyes for a long moment.

"I will try to explain another time, my friend. When we have finished with this business," said Eben.

Amin nodded and emptied his mug.

"I wish you would tell me what you're talking about," Tavos complained.

"Tavos, your mother sent along some bunchberry tarts. Why don't you go fetch them from my saddlebag," Eben suggested.

"Don't say anything until I get back," Tavos yelled as he bolted out the door.

"A good lad," Eben laughed.

Amin smiled. "And a good son."

Eben sobered. "I'm going into the palace tonight, Amin. I intend to take Gyp down."

"You cannot go alone, my lord. Gyp surrounds himself

with men over whom he wields the power to give or with-hold the fungus. They will guard him well. I have already insinuated men into the palace in the guise of servants. One important thing we have learned is that Gyp keeps his most valuable papers in a small iron chest beneath his bed. I suspect that documents relating to the making of the fungus must be in that chest. But I do not know how we can gain access to his bedchamber."

"I will have done with this once and for all," Eben said stubbornly. "I myself will get into that chamber. As Merlin is not here—"

"Fortunately, he is," said the wizard himself.

"And where have you been, old man?" Eben demanded as Merlin settled onto the chair Tavos had vacated.

"Hither and yon, hither and yon."

"Well, that narrows it down," Eben remarked dryly.

"If you will know," Merlin said with dignity, "I have been nosing about the palace."

"That nose again," Amin murmured into his ale.

"Gyp seems particularly obsessed with Lady Kaia," Merlin reported. "I expect he now has a fairly good idea of who she is, or at the very least her lineage. He is furious that she has escaped him—I'm afraid poor Thrys is going to pay dearly for his indisposition—and is leading the search for her himself. He rode out early this morning to inspect the *Apostle* and track down the crew."

Eben looked over at Amin. "Is there any likelihood he would think she might be found in the area where you live?"

"He would pass close to our valley if he travels the main road. I suppose he might send a scouting party up

213

my way, although I think it unlikely. Outsiders rarely bother with us."

Eben slammed his fist down onto the scarred table. "Sweet Jesus! We must get them out of there. We cannot take any chances. Is even the cave safe enough, Amin?"

"It is, my lord," Amin replied with absolute conviction. "Someone must go back."

Amin was on his feet. "Bera and Zelana may also be in danger. They must all be taken to the cave. I will leave immediately."

"I think my, er, special skills may be required in the event Gyp and his men show up," Merlin said.

Eben raised a brow. "Canine skills, I presume, since you claim to have few others at your disposal at the moment."

Merlin smiled. "Just so."

Eben ran his fingers through his hair. "Yes, you must go. Tavos," he said to the boy, who had just rushed in with the cloth-wrapped package of bunchberry tarts, "you will be going home with your father at once."

Tavos gazed up at his father's grim countenance with wide eyes. "Pa?"

"I will explain later, son. Come, you must help me with the horses."

Merlin summoned a serving girl to bring him wine.

"I suppose you will take the opportunity of Gyp's absence with his most loyal troops to set a trap for him in his own lair. It is a dangerous undertaking on your own, Lord Eben. If you should be taken, we must know where you are."

"I will not be taken," snapped Eben.

"I believe that at this juncture Brother Absalom would

dip into his bottomless well of pertinent scripture and inform you that 'Pride goeth before destruction, and an haughty spirit before a fall.' Proverbs 16:18, I believe."

"Please," Eben said wearily, "don't you start."

"You cannot go alone," Merlin said, serious now. "Take the boy; he can act as go-between."

"It is far too dangerous—"

"Young boys," Merlin interrupted, "are, in my experience, of far greater value in a crisis than grown men. They are as slippery as eels, fast on their feet, and particularly adept at finding good hiding places. Tavos is a bright lad; he will do well for you and can be relied upon not to lose his head."

"Perhaps you're right," Eben said. "Let us use the storage room as a place to meet. Amin already has a few men inside the palace. When he returns he will station others outside to raise a distracting disturbance should one be necessary. I really need only find the documents to begin. Without them, Gyp has no power. I will, however, personally relish a few private moments with him for my own purposes. Lady Kaia has convinced me that his ultimate fate must lie in the hands of the people he has so grievously wronged."

"A wise young woman," Merlin opined.

"Yes," Eben said quietly. "A wise young woman indeed."

Tavos started leaping up and down and tearing around the stable yard with joy when informed that he would go with Lord Eben.

"Are we going to scale the walls? Are there cannibal fish in the moat? Will I get to see the king?"

"You will," Eben told him sternly, "do exactly as I say. A

good squire follows his lord's orders to the letter, without question and without complaint."

"Squire?" Tavos barely breathed. "I'm to be your squire? Just like Jocco?"

Eben smiled down at the boy's glowing face. "Aye, and you must begin by conducting yourself with the dignity of your new station. Control yourself, listen, and learn."

Tavos threw back his shoulders, lifted his chin, and tried to assume the dignity of his new station. "I will not fail you, my lord."

"You are disturbed in your mind, Lord Eben," Merlin observed as he and Eben returned to the inn.

Eben shrugged.

Merlin sipped his wine. "Lady Kaia?"

Eben folded his arms across his chest and glared down at his boots. "We had words. She may show flashes of wisdom, but she does not learn; she is as reckless as ever."

Merlin smiled. "How is that?"

"She declared she would be at my side when I meet with Gyp to settle old accounts. I told her she would stay where she was and that was my final word on the subject. She did not take it well."

Eben looked so disgruntled that Merlin could not resist teasing just a little. "'And Ruth said, entreat me not to leave thee, or to return from following after thee; for whither thou goest, I will go.' Ruth 1:16."

"That will be enough," Eben growled.

"Is loyalty in a woman to be despised?"

"Gyp is the most dangerous kind of man: a coward. He

cannot stand up to men, so he takes his pleasure by hurting women. Kaia wouldn't stand a chance against him."

As someone who, just a few days earlier, had been flattened and pummeled by Lady Kaia Kurinon, Merlin wasn't quite so sure about that.

"I am a worm!" Brother Absalom wailed. "'I am a worm, and no man: a reproach of men, and despised of the people. All they that see me laugh me to scorn; they shoot out the lip, they shake the head . . .'"

Merlin glared down at the supine figure in the dust. "How long has he been going on like this?"

"Since early this morning, sir, when we discovered Lady Kaia was gone," Jocco replied. "He blames himself for her disappearance, although I don't see how anyone could have guessed her plans. She gave no sign that she intended to leave."

"Woe, woe, woe!"

"This is intolerable," Merlin snapped. "Help me get him up, Amin." Between the two of them they managed to haul the keening monk to his feet.

"Be still, you blithering idiot," Merlin shouted directly in Brother Absalom's face. "Here, Amin, take the cord at his waist and wind it several times about his head. Yes, between his teeth. Good. You, fool, will remain gagged until you regain your wits. If you ever had any in the first place," added Merlin in disgust. He pushed the astounded monk down on the log bench by the cottage door and brushed the dust from his hands.

"All right, Squire, let us have the story."

Jocco launched into his tale, although there wasn't all that much to tell. Since the cottage was small and there was only the one bed, it had been decided that Bera and the child would occupy it as usual and that Kaia, Jocco, and Brother Absalom would sleep outside. Sometime in the night Lady Kaia had taken a horse from the stable and ridden away.

Merlin frowned at the squire. "You did not wake?"

"Bera insisted I take a potion for sleep," Jocco admitted.

"And the monk?"

"He sleeps like the dead."

"It looks as though Lady Kaia had the last word after all, Lord Eben," Merlin said to himself with a smile.

This time it was Jocco who would not be left behind.

Merlin rubbed his hands over his face. "I'm getting too old for this," he groaned.

"Getting too young," Brother Absalom reminded him.

"If," Merlin said between clenched teeth, "you say one more word on the subject, it will be your last. Do you understand me, monk?"

Brother Absalom realized he had almost let the cat out of the bag—well, the wizard out of the bag really—apologized, and meekly followed Bera and Zelana down the road. Amin would see them to the cave and follow Merlin and Jocco to the capital as quickly as possible.

"How will you find Lady Kaia?" Amin inquired.

"I shall follow my nose, of course," Merlin replied.

"Like a hound on the scent of the fox?"

"Exactly."

Amin nodded. "Somehow I thought you'd say that."

Chapter Twenty-nine

Being out and about in the world all on her own had been Kaia Kurinon's fondest dream for as long as she could remember. There would be no one to tell her to go east if she wished to go west, that she must set off at dawn when she preferred to travel by the light of the moon. No one to order her onto the timid palfrey when she longed to mount the fiery stallion.

At one critical moment the night before, Kaia would have been delighted to leave the decision to someone else as to whether to take the east fork in the road or the west. She had also discovered that there was much to be said for traveling in daylight; the moon, especially a waning moon, had done little to help guide her way. And her choice of mount—a particularly feisty young stallion—had landed her twice upon her bottom.

Still, Kaia could take satisfaction in the fact that she had arrived in the capital city without serious mishap. As she had no idea of the location of the inn where Eben was to meet up with the others, the only logical place for her to go was the palace itself. She was certain she could find the alley where they had emerged from the underground passage. She would make her way to the storeroom and wait there; one of them was bound to come along sooner or later.

There was one matter she must take care of immediately. She could not very well go around dressed in the gown of embroidered green linen Gyp had ordered for her without attracting notice. Just outside the city gate she waylaid a young woman of about her own age and size and offered to exchange her gown for the girl's homespun and some coin. Both went away well satisfied with the transaction, although the young woman gloated all the way home that she had come off far better than the yellow-haired stranger. In all her days she had never dreamed of owning such a gown.

Kaia stabled the horse for a few coins and asked the way to a marketplace, where she purchased three meat pies, cheese, a jug of water, a rush torch, and a flint. She had no trouble finding the iron door to the labyrinth, and breathed a sigh of relief when she had closed it behind her.

As the darkness enveloped her, her courage began to waver. Even with the torch she might never find her way through the labyrinth to the storeroom. It was not so much a matter of taking the wrong turn as taking any turn at all, as she hadn't the slightest idea in which direction the palace lay. Once she set out, there would be no turning back. As daunting as the prospect was, she was not ready to give up. She would never forgive herself if Eben had need of her and she was not there to help him. But if she set out, she must at least make sure she could return to this spot if she became hopelessly lost.

A labyrinth: In the ancient legend had not Ariadne marked her way through the labyrinth of the Minotaur to rescue her lover? Kaia would do the same. She managed to light the rude torch, and set about tearing strips of cloth from the hem of her shift. These she tore into tiny pieces.

With a fervent "Hail Mary" she ventured into the darkness and let drop the first bit of cloth. Only ten or so paces from the steps she noticed an almond on the path, then another and another. Someone had been there before her and marked out a route. Of course, it might not take her where she needed to go, but it seemed a good sign, so she followed along trying to keep up her courage.

Ten, perhaps fifteen minutes later, the trail of almonds ended abruptly. Kaia peered around a corner and nearly screamed with relief when she saw four doors, two on either side of the passage. One of them must surely be the storeroom where Thrys had confined her and Brother Absalom.

The two on the left were locked. The first on the right was empty. That left door number four. Kaia held her breath as she eased it open with exquisite care.

Two huge eyes, fiery red in the torchlight, stared out at her. Kaia only managed to fight back a scream of pure terror.

"Tavos?"

"My lady?"

"Oh, Tavos! Thank God it's you. You nearly scared me to death."

"Come in quickly, my lady." Tavos tugged her into the stuffy room and set about piling up heavy sacks of grain and rice against the door. "Do you have any food? I'm powerful hungry."

"Yes. In the satchel. Where is Lord Eben?"

Tavos took an enormous bite of meat pie. "He went into the palace. I'm to wait for him here. If there's trouble I'm to follow the almonds back to the door and go to the inn for Pa and Merlin and the others."

Kaia drank some water; she was still far too shaken to eat anything. "But how will you know if he's in trouble?"

"Every once in a while I sneak up to the great hall. No one seems to take any notice of me. Maybe they think I'm a serving boy. Lord Gyp came back a while ago in a terrible rage. He was out looking for you." Tavos frowned. "You're not supposed to be here, my lady. Lord Eben sent Merlin and my pa to hide you in the cave. I think Lord Eben is going to be real mad when he finds out that you're here and not there."

Kaia sighed. "I expect he will be."

"Why are you here, my lady?"

"I came to help him."

Tavos shook his head. "Really, really mad."

Eben could be easy in his mind on one count at least: Kaia was by now safe in the cave.

Merlin and Amin would have reached the inn by now to rendezvous with the others.

He decided he would just take a few more minutes to observe the comings and goings along the corridor outside Gyp's chamber before returning to the storage room to collect Tavos and return to the inn to make final plans.

He buckled on the guard's sword belt and stuffed his long, dark hair into the man's black felt hat. Everything fit well—he had selected his mark carefully—but the tunic and hose could have done with a thorough laundering. Eben retained his own boots, though they were of dark brown leather rather than black; he must have access to the small knife he carried in the heel of the left boot for emergencies. He would pass inspection if no one looked too closely.

The guard snored peacefully on the floor of the broom closet and would suffer nothing more than a nasty lump on the head and wounded pride when he awoke in a few hours.

Eben opened the door a tiny crack. Ranulph Gyp's voice could be clearly heard a few doors down the hall.

"Take that pig swill away and bring me something decent to drink," Gyp snarled. "Tell Delia I want her tonight. And for the love of God, make sure she's clean this time. Come to think of it, forget Delia. Bring that little dark-haired girl, Fraza; I haven't tried her yet. She's nothing compared to that blond idiot girl, but I'll have that one eventually. She'll have some of my special treatment when I get my hands on her. The rest of you get out. Not you, Thrys."

Eben guessed Thrys would have preferred an interview with the Antichrist than face Lord Gyp in his present frame of mind.

Gyp continued his tirade. "You are a great disappointment to me, Thrys. A ship founders upon our fair shores and I send you out to strip her of her valuables; you bring me a witless girl, a madman, and a dog. I tell you to bring me the rest of the crew and passengers of the *Apostle*; they are nowhere to be found. You are to deliver two prisoners—a girl and an old man—to the dungeon; you lose them."

"My lord, please—"

Gyp interrupted. "I'm in no mood to hear you out, Thrys. One year."

"A y-year, my lord?"

"A year without the fungus will do you a world of good. You will have time to reflect on your failures and rededicate yourself to my service."

"But, my lord, my wife——"

"Will no doubt find her pleasures elsewhere." Gyp dismissed him. "You may go."

As Thrys passed into the corridor, other guards shrank from him in pity and horror. He might have been a leper with a bell about his neck. Except for Gyp's worst enemies, who were deprived of the fungus for years on end—in several cases a lifetime—few had been sentenced to a year without the stuff. Many of those so condemned by the High Lord had gone mad, and a few had thrown themselves upon their swords.

Thrys shuffled away down the long corridor, trailing his hand along the wall for support. When he reached the door of the broom closet, it opened inward as though from his weight. An arm jerked him inside and a hand was clamped firmly over his mouth.

"Silence," a voice whispered, "or you die. Do you understand?"

Thrys nodded vigorously in the darkness.

"Will you be free of this tyrant?" the voice continued.

Thrys nodded again.

"Then hear me, man. And do as I say."

"My lady, listen," Tavos whispered.

Kaia heard it too, the distant clink of metal, the grate of a turning key, the squeak of an ancient ill-fitting door.

Someone was coming along the corridor, trying the door of each storeroom, moving ever closer.

"Do you have a weapon, Tavos?" Kaia said. "I only have my eating knife and this walking staff I used in the tunnels."

"Yes, Pa gave me his knife."

"Climb onto the highest stack of sacks beside the door. I will stand full where he can see me when the door opens. I shall distract his attention, and you leap upon him. If there is only one—I think that must be the case, because I hear no talking—we can subdue him between the two of us. Keep your knife sheathed. God willing, it is a friend. If not and we must shed blood, so be it. Hush now, he comes."

The key turned in the lock. After the briefest pause, a small crack appeared, letting in the faint light of a rush torch. "Boy? Are you there, boy?"

Kaia did not move. Perhaps if she did not answer, the man would pass by.

"Lord Eben sends me," the man said. "Fear not, I am a friend."

The door opened wider. Kaia could see the man's face clearly now. "Thrys?"

The guard pushed the door open and slipped into the room. "My lady, whatever are you doing here? I thought you long gone. Lord Eben sent me to find the boy—"

The boy in question dropped down upon poor Thrys like a stone. The ensuing struggle was brief, cut short by Kaia's cry of alarm as the torch set fire to a sack of nuts. When it had been stamped out, Kaia offered the shaken

Thrys a drink of water and begged him of news of Lord Eben.

Lord Eben, it seemed, was safe. Thrys told her that Eben, dressed now in the garb of one of the High Lord's personal guards, was moving carefully about the palace in search of the place where Gyp kept his greatest treasures and most important documents. The object of his search was the iron chest in which all the information relating to the moths was to be found.

The moths themselves lived on a well-guarded island several miles off the coast, Thrys explained, where grew the hoola bush—their only food. The bushes grew nowhere else in the known world; thus the moths never departed the island. There the larvae were culled and the fungus extracted. But the fungus had to be treated with a secret distillation to give it full potency, and it was that recipe that Gyp alone knew and kept in the iron chest.

"The cleaning maids say there is a chest beside the High Lord's bed that they are not permitted to touch on pain of death," Thrys said. "That must be it. I told Lord Eben so."

"Surely he is not going to try to enter Gyp's private chambers himself?" Kaia cried.

"Oh, no, my lady. He has sent me to instruct the boy Tavos to rally his father and the other men. They must stir up some sort of disturbance both within and outside the walls in exactly two hours' time. Tavos, your father and the man Merlin are to meet him here in this storeroom, and the three of them will take possession of the chest. Gyp will come for it when he realizes the ruse, and will be easily taken."

"Why are you helping us, Thrys?" Kaia asked. "It is possible the fungus will be destroyed forever. You may never have the use of it again."

"I know," Thrys said sadly, "but I am no man, whatever my proportions and skill in love, if I have not the honor of a man. We have allowed ourselves to become slaves to the Devil Dust and whomsoever knows its secret. It is time we free ourselves, whatever the cost."

"You are a brave man," Tavos declared. "A hero."

"No, son, merely a fool."

"Tavos, you must hurry. Go to the inn. Bring Merlin and your father," Kaia said.

"You must come too, my lady. You cannot stay here alone."

"Someone must remain. If Lord Eben is taken before they get here, we must know of it. I will act as go-between."

"I am Lord Eben's squire now," Tavos declared. "It is my sworn duty to protect damsels in distress."

"I am not in distress," Kaia snapped. "Go."

"And I will go above to see how Lord Eben fares," Thrys said.

Alone in the darkness, Kaia brooded. Someone really must do something about this myth of damsels being ever in distress. It certainly suited men, and not a few foolish women, to have it so. A man might be seen to best advantage riding to the rescue of some mewling damsel, and could expect as a reward not only the admiration of his own sex but the sweet favors a grateful damsel might be inclined to grant her hero. In Kaia's opinion, it was a transaction that showed neither the man nor the woman to particular advantage.

One could only hope that the women she would meet in

the far future would have put the myth to rest and learned to look after themselves. If not, perhaps she would take pen in hand—now that she could take pen in hand—and write stories of strong men and strong women who had no need to play such childish games.

Kaia had not long to brood. Thrys was back in a matter of minutes. All was not well above.

"He is taken, my lady! Lord Eben is taken!"

"How, how? Surely he was not so foolish as to confront the beast in his lair?"

"No, my lady. He went to the aid of a damsel in distress!"

"Of course," Kaia muttered.

"Truly, he did. Lord Gyp had ordered little Fraza brought to him for his amusement because you were not available to him. She is but nine, my lady. But she would not suffer him to touch her and bit him upon the arm."

"Dear God. What happened?"

"He struck her, my lady, whereupon she rammmed her little fist in his, er, his, um—"

"Yes, Yes, I understand. Go on."

"She fled past the guards. Gyp was angrier than I have ever seen him. He drew his knife and chased her down the corridor. He seized her by the hair, and God only knows what would have become of her if Lord Eben had not at that moment burst from the closet where he had been hiding. He fought gallantly, my lady—I have never seen the like—but soon was overwhelmed by the guards and dragged into Lord Gyp's chambers. I do not know what has become of him."

"And the girl?" said Kaia.

"She is safe with her mother."

"Thank God for that," Kaia said. "Good for you, little Fraza. You at least are no whimpering damsel. Thrys, we must go to Lord Eben's aid at once. We have not time to wait for Merlin and Amin."

"I am banned from his sight, my lady. I cannot gain entrance to his chambers now."

"No, but I can."

Chapter Thirty

Ranulph Gyp held out his silver-chased goblet for a page to refill.

"Go. Leave the decanter. I do not wish to be disturbed."

"Aye, sir." The door closed softly behind the boy.

Gyp leaned back and studied the man tied firmly to the chair opposite.

"Dhion. I must say I never expected to find the exalted armiger of the Ninth House lurking in my broom closet. I count it as one of life's unexpected little pleasures. How came you there? Oh, of course, you are the mysterious nobleman of the Dominion who sailed aboard the *Apostle*. You are far from home. Perhaps you came looking for me with a pardon from Jibril. But no, like his father he is not a forgiving man. Not that I would want to return to that dreary little island in any case. To think I might have been content with your puny hall when all this awaited me. I am a king in my own right here. I have everything I could ever desire. You may take your meaningless pardon back to Jibril and so inform him."

"Believe me, Gyp," Eben said, "I bear no pardon. It is you and I who have unfinished business."

Gyp rose and strolled around the room. "You can have no quarrel with me, Dhion. Your witless father is no doubt dead by now. You sit the High Seat in your hall. Ahriman rots in hell. Syrah plays the whore in Jibril's bed. It is all in the past now. Let bygones be bygones."

"For some, past wrongs are not so easily forgotten," Eben said.

"Ah, I see the little jester has become quite the man of honor," Gyp said with a sneer. "Does it gall you that it was Syrah who plotted my downfall, Jibril and Zebengo who took Kek? Syrah who begged for mercy on my behalf and had me sent into exile rather than hung? Did she unman you, little Eben?"

Eben fought back the fury that clawed at his gut. He could not afford to let Gyp bait him. He concentrated instead on continuing to twist his left ankle against the rope that bound it to the leg of the chair. If he could free his foot, he might be able to get at the knife in his boot.

"*I* have no doubts as to my manhood," he said evenly.

Gyp was upon him in a flash. "Bastard! Do you imply that I do? I am more a man than you can ever hope to be."

The door opened. "My lord, there is a woman here who claims to have important business with you."

"I said I was not to be disturbed," Gyp shouted. "I have no business with any woman, save she serve me at my pleasure. Detain the wench, whoever she is. I'll deal with her later."

"But, my lord, she says she is—"

"Princess Kaia Ellora Kurinon of the Second House."

Kaia stepped into the room and swept Gyp a graceful curtsy. "At your service, my lord."

It took Gyp a few moments to realize that the regal figure before him was none other than the half-witted girl who had snickered and pranced about this very room a few days before. Clad in an indecently low-cut, close-fitting gown of black velvet, her glorious golden hair bound up with strings of onyx and pearl, she was, every royal inch of her, one of the most beautiful women he had ever seen.

His mouth tightened in anger. He struggled to keep his composure. He did not like being made a fool of. "Not so witless after all, then."

For a brief moment Eben was certain that his brain had been thoroughly scrambled. The composed young woman who regarded Ranulph Gyp with a cool eye and unruffled demeanor could not possibly be his Kaia. Surely she was fifty leagues away, safe in the cave.

"Well then, Your Ladyship, may I welcome you to my humble palace," Gyp said with a mock bow, "and inquire why you honor me with your presence?"

"Why, I thought we had an assignation this evening. I have dressed exactly as you wished. One of your servants was most obliging in finding exactly the right gown. I confess I am partial to black velvet. Does it please you? I should, of course, have preferred my own jewels, but as I am far from home I must make do.

"I find I am quite looking forward to those 'special' pleasures you promised. Oh, but here is Lord Eben. Good evening, Eben, how came you to be here?"

"You know one another?" Gyp asked suspiciously. "Oh, yes, from the *Apostle*. You traveled together, my lady?"

Kaia laughed. "No, indeed we did not, Lord Gyp. The man is quite mad for me. He chased me clear across the Dominion. I cannot seem to shake him off. He cannot accept that our relationship is over. He is really quite tedious. I hope, however, you will not send him away. Perhaps we can find a use for him."

"I have a vague recollection of you, Lady Kaia," Gyp remarked as he handed her a cup of wine. "You could not have been more than five or six when last I saw you. I believe it was at Lord Eben's hall. Tell me, how fares your father? Does he still play the buffoon?"

"My father is well, I thank you," she replied in a steady voice.

"Please, have a seat, my lady. We must become better acquainted."

Kaia smiled slyly. "Oh, I'm sure we shall."

"You were a pretty little thing even then," Gyp continued, reaching down to stroke Kaia's cheek. "Like your sisters. I believe I may have had the eldest—now what was her name?—but then, it was all so long ago it is difficult to remember."

Eben could see the hard lust in Gyp's eyes, hear it in his voice. He wanted to leap at the man, bury his dagger in his throat, watch him suffocate in a flood of his own blood. For the first time, he could see Kaia's fear, although he was sure Gyp was too caught up in reveling in his own power to notice. Her hand trembled ever so slightly as she lifted the cup to her lips.

"It seems the *Apostle* has brought me greater riches than I had first thought," Gyp remarked. "Eben Dhion and the little cousin of Jibril himself. I really must thank Thrys after all. Perhaps I will reduce his sentence: six months without the fungus rather than a year."

He smiled at Kaia. "I can be most generous, my lady, when I am pleased with services rendered. You will soon have occasion to discover it for yourself. Or not if you displease me."

"My lord!" The nervous guard was back again.

"What is it?" Gyp snapped. "Can't you see I am busy here?"

"But, my lord, there is some disturbance in the street. The captain of the guard has had to deploy an entire troop to deal with it."

Gyp slammed his cup onto the desk and strode to the window. "Damn! I'll deal with this. Lady Kurinon, delightful as you are, I find I do not quite trust you. If you lift so much as a finger to assist Lord Dhion, my guards will cut you down where you stand."

"I have no desire to assist Lord Dhion, I assure you. Perhaps we will pass the time reminiscing over old times. Do hurry back, my lord." Kaia arranged herself voluptuously across the foot of Gyp's bed and smiled.

Two burly guards took up positions just outside the door as Gyp stormed out.

For the first time, Kaia looked Eben full in the face. She could no longer mask her fear. "Eben—"

He shook his head ever so slightly to indicate she

233

should remain silent. "I see you choose to play the whore once again, my lady," Eben said loudly, jerking his head toward the small chest that rested on a table beside the bed.

Kaia's eyes went wide as she gaped at him.

"It is no wonder your father confined you to a convent," he continued. He rolled his eyes at her, willing her to understand that she must take the chest and hide it. "You have put me to a good deal of trouble chasing you all over creation. I think I deserve a reward. Perhaps you would deign to share your favors with me when Lord Gyp has done with you. I confess I miss our old times together. Do you recall that time on the battlements?"

Kaia stared at him, wondering at his strange behavior. Then her lips formed a silent "oh" of understanding "Yes, yes, the battlements," she said as she slid off the bed. She placed a hand on the chest and looked to Eben for confirmation that she had understood him correctly. He nodded.

Kaia looked about for a place to hide it, but the possibility that one of the guards would come in to check on them at any moment compelled her to slide it beneath a huge pile of soft red and gold silk pillows at the head of the bed.

"Ah, yes," she said, raising her voice. "Tied together in midair, my legs about you. I must confess I found the danger of our position most exciting. Like this." She moved to Eben, straddled him, and rubbed herself suggestively against him.

"Move away," one of the guards ordered from the doorway. "You heard Lord Gyp. If you attempt to free this man, we must cut you down."

Kaia laughed and stood up, fussing with her skirts so that the guards could not see Eben palm the knife she had left on his lap. "I have no intention of aiding Lord Eben. He means nothing to me. Lord Gyp may do with him as he wishes. Besides, the man is a fool if he thinks I would have him when there are so many desirable men to be found on this island. They are said to be the most virile in the world. Their special endowments are legendary."

The guards grinned. "You have heard aright, my lady," one of them boasted.

"I doubt Lord Eben can measure up—as it were—to the standard I require of my men. Judging from what I know of him, he has not the stamina either. Let us see whether I am correct as to the first matter." She reached down to cup him, once again hiding him from the direct sight of the guards as he cut the last of the ropes that bound him.

"What the hell is going on here?" Gyp demanded from the doorway.

With one swift motion Eben leaped from the chair, spun Kaia around, and hauled her against him, the tip of his dagger at her throat.

Gyp's eyes narrowed. "What do think to achieve by this, Dhion? You are both still my prisoners, and I doubt you would murder King Jibril's sweet little cousin. You value your so-called honor too highly."

Eben shrugged. "It is *her* value you should consider, Gyp. Think of the power you hold in your hands. You can bring Jibril to his knees. Of course, if she is dead she can be of no use to you."

"Please, Lord Gyp," Kaia begged, playing her part. "My cousin will pay handsomely for my return."

"I have no need of Jibril's gold. I have more than I know what to do with."

"Yes, you have the fungus, Gyp," Eben remarked. "I had forgotten. If it should transpire, however, that you lost control of the supply, you might look at the matter differently and Lady Kaia might prove useful indeed."

"The supply is quite safe, I assure you. Give it up, Dhion."

"Is it?" Eben pushed Kaia aside out of danger and stepped back so that Gyp could see the empty place on the table where the chest had rested.

"Where is it?" Gyp shrieked. He drew his sword and lunged at Eben. "Tell me or I'll kill you."

Eben threw himself to the side as Gyp swung wildly. They both went down, but the crazed Gyp was no match for the pent-up fury Eben Dhion had nursed for fifteen years. In the blink of an eye, Eben was straddling him with the point of his knife at his throat.

"You will never touch anything that is mine again, Gyp," he said fiercely.

"Please, Eben," Kaia said. "You will gain nothing by killing him."

Eben ignored her. "I would as soon finish you myself here and now, but I will leave your fate in the hands of the people of this island. You may not find them so forgiving as our late king."

"Hey!" yelled one of the guards, but he was too late to grab the huge black hound as it raced past him. Amin Samil and Jocco followed close behind.

The dog settled onto its haunches and regarded Gyp with a cold eye. "I find you are becoming a boor, my lord," it said.

For long moments the tableau might have been frozen in time: Eben with his dagger at Gyp's throat, the guards too shocked at the sudden turn of events even to blink.

"Oh, I beg your pardon," the hound continued. "Perhaps I should introduce myself properly."

The air shimmered as the black outline of the hound blurred and re-formed into the shape of a tall man in a cloak of deepest midnight blue.

"That's better," said the apparition.

One guard screeched and bolted from the room. The other plummeted into a dead faint.

Gyp could not tear his eyes from the tall man.

"I am Merlin. I see we've missed all the excitement. Lord Eben seems to have things well in hand."

Eben hauled Gyp to his feet.

"Please, don't let him kill me," Gyp blubbered.

"'Cowards die many times before their deaths; the valiant never taste of death but once,'" Merlin proclaimed. "The Bard of Avon wrote those immortal words. Or will write them in a few hundred years," he amended.

"Take him," Eben said, shoving Gyp at Amin.

"Eben," Kaia said softly, shaking now that the danger had passed. She needed the warm shelter of his arms.

For a long moment he stared at her with an unreadable look in his eyes, then strode from the room without a word.

Chapter Thirty-one

Kaia took little interest in the events of the following sennight. Eben virtually ignored her after the confrontation in Gyp's chamber. On the fourth day he disappeared altogether; no one had any idea of where he had gone. She was left only with the sad memory of that last stony look and his silence.

Brother Absalom returned to the capital and took up lodging at the inn near the palace where Eben, Merlin, Jocco, and Kaia were now staying. His joy at the happy outcome was tempered by concern for Kaia's state of mind. He hesitated to intrude upon her private thoughts, but let her know that should she feel the need to confide in him, he would be there for her.

Merlin spent his days at the palace, sitting quietly by as the nobility of Ataxi sorted out the issue of succession, offering advice if requested to do so. Four low-ranking lords were seized as traitors for their complicity in putting Ranulph Gyp on the throne, and the full story of how he had come to hold sole access to the fungus came out.

Rumors ran rampant regarding Merlin's supposed transformation from beast to man, but as the two guards who had witnessed it were now confined to a madhouse and Ranulph Gyp was being held in isolation, there was really no one to substantiate the wild tale.

Amin went off to see for himself that his family was

safe. Jocco and Tavos had become fast friends and went about the city getting into such mischief, as boys of fourteen and eight will when let loose in new and interesting circumstances.

Merlin and Brother Absalom took close counsel together as to what could be done about the fungus. The existing supply could be easily destroyed, of course, and the moths themselves eliminated by the simple introduction of a colony of bats into their habitat. That, however, would leave half the male populace of the island of Ataxi impotent for the rest of their lives. A more benign substitute must be found.

A council of healers was quickly convened to see what could be done. Brother Absalom's concoction of gnats steeped in tulip juice occasioned considerable interest, but everyone agreed that having half the male population of Ataxi copulating with any available female—human or not—was ruled out as being rather extreme, even under these desperate circumstances.

"I don't suppose there's any citrate sildenafil lying about," Merlin inquired when all other possibilities had been exhausted.

"Citrasafil?" someone echoed.

"No. Citrate sildenafil."

"Oh. Well, no. I rather doubt it," Brother Absalom confessed. "What is it?"

"A small blue pellet, enormously popular in a land I once visited."

"Like Dramamine?" Brother Absalom inquired eagerly. "Perhaps if we set our minds to it we could invent it now. What exactly is it?"

"Citrate sildenafil is designated chemically as 1-[[3-(6,7-dihydro-l-methyl-7-oxo-3-propyl-1H-pyrazolo [4,3-d]pyrimidin-5-yl}-4-ethoxypheny]]sulfonyl]-4-methyl] piperazine citrate. It exhibits a solubility of 3.5 mg/ml in water and a molecular weight of 666.7. Would you care to know the inactive ingredients?"

"Er, no, that will not be necessary," Brother Absalom replied, wondering what strange tongue Merlin was speaking. "I feel quite sure we have none about the place."

"I rather thought not," said Merlin with a grin.

A discouraged silence settled upon the assembly.

"I suppose there is always prayer," Brother Absalom ventured finally. "Let me see. 'Ask, and it shall be given you; seek, and ye shall find; knock and it shall be opened.' Matthew 7:7.

"No, that doesn't have quite the right ring to it. Ah! I have it! Matthew 21:22. 'And all things, whatsoever ye shall ask in prayer, believing, ye shall receive.'"

"Yes! That's it!" Merlin shouted, leaping from his chair and pounding poor Brother Absalom so soundly upon the back that the poor man toppled from his stool and had to be assisted back to his feet. "You are a genius, monk!"

"I am?" wheezed Brother Absalom.

"'Believing, ye shall receive!'" Merlin crowed. "Placebo! Right there in Holy Scripture! Gentlemen, we have our substitute. It is called Placebo. Let us adjourn and reconvene in two days' time. By then, Brother Absalom and I will have prepared the potion and tested it in a double-blind clinical trial."

"We will?" inquired Brother Absalom.

"Yes, we will. One unfortunate shall receive a dose of

gnats stewed in tulip juice—fear not, we shall keep him under lock and key—and the other will partake of Placebo. I assure you, the latter is our solution. Come along, monk, we have much work to do."

"Must it taste so bad?" Brother Absalom said, his face all puckered from the tiny sip of noxious brew that bubbled in the cauldron. "Perhaps a tad less centipede oil and a dollop of honey would make it more palatable."

Poor Thrys, who had been drafted as the participant who would receive Placebo, nearly went to his knees as he forced down a goblet of the foul blue brew.

"Why blue?" Brother Absalom inquired of Merlin.

"It seems appropriate." Merlin answered with a smirk.

"I doubt Thrys can be persuaded to take any more of the stuff," the monk opined.

"He'll be back."

And so he was. The following morning found Thrys clamoring for more Placebo, having discovered its efficacy in a night of wild abandon with his grateful spouse.

And thus it was that the men of Ataxi were restored to manly vigor. The moths, larvae, and fungus were destroyed, and Placebo could easily be brewed upon any hearth in the land. The recipe was readily available: a few bitter herbs, five drops of centipede oil, a small cup of a man's own urea, and the absolute conviction that the unpleasant act of swallowing the stuff only added to its efficacy.

If a few of the more perceptive women of Ataxi suspected the ruse, they kept it to themselves, and smiled sweetly each morning as they ladled the miracle potion into a cup and watched their foolish husbands force it down.

* * *

Kaia knew nothing of Gyp's fate, only that he had finally lost all reason and been confined for his own protection. For the first few days she kept to her chamber at the inn; she sat at the window watching the rain wash over the city below or working her way laboriously through Brother Absalom's tattered breviary. When the weather turned fine she would descend the long flights of steep steps that led to the harbor, and browse among the stalls in the huge marketplace near the port.

One day she discovered a stall run by a cheerful young couple. They fashioned lovely combs of silver and polished wood. One in particular caught her fancy: a delicate arc of fragrant sandalwood, cleverly carved with flowers and vines. She bought one for herself and, on impulse, another for Morgana. For her little cousin Oriana she chose a small silver comb embedded with pretty blue stones. For three-year-old Ahriman she selected an exquisitely carved little ketch, and for twelve-year-old Akritos a splendid leather sheath for his eating knife. She would send these tokens home with Eben. She hoped that whenever her friend and cousins looked at them they would remember her with some fondness.

The evenings she spent with Brother Absalom, although she would rather have been alone. He would come tapping at her door, anxious to draw her away from her sad thoughts. She could not very well refuse him. They would play draughts and tables; chess was out of the question, as the little monk got all muddled and could never remember the rules.

Eben returned two days before Merlin, Brother Absalom, Jocco, and Kaia were to board the *Peacock* for the Western Isles. Obviously, he had not spent his time in the most salubrious manner; he was unshaven and reeked of ale. He did not seek out Kaia until the following morning when he waylaid her as she was about to walk down to the port to look over the *Peacock*.

"I would have a word with you before the ship sails."

He might just as well have struck her with his fist, so sharp was the blow to her heart in knowing that he would not try to keep her from sailing on the *Peacock*. With great care she picked up her skirts and started down the first steep flight.

"Of course. Will you be returning to the Dominion soon?" she inquired politely.

He made no reply.

Kaia gave him a quick sidelong glance. The set of his mouth betrayed a barely suppressed anger. When they reached the quay, he took her arm and steered her away from the marketplace and the colorful crowds. Dozens of small craft were drawn up along the shore; fishermen relaxed in the sun, trading stories and jesting as they mended their nets.

It was a lovely morning, but this was no pleasant stroll on a warm summer's day. They walked on and left the last of the boats behind. Soon they were alone with the swooping gulls and the sand crabs that went skittering away at their approach.

Eben's grim silence was starting to get on Kaia's nerves. She stopped abruptly.

"If you have something to say to me, my lord, I wish you would say it and have done. This determined silence of yours is most annoying."

"You may not like what I have to say, my lady."

It was not a promising beginning, but he meant to intimidate her and she would have none of it.

"You have said a great many things to me in the past weeks that I have not liked. I believe I can withstand yet another assault."

"I have said nothing that you did not deserve to hear," Eben replied.

Kaia traced a small circle in the sand with the toe of her boot. "It must be most gratifying to speak your mind with the complete confidence that your listener deserves to hear what you have to say, even if you are incorrect in your assessment of the matter or their character."

"I am in no mood to bandy words with you, Kaia. There is something I must make clear to you."

She folded her hands behind her back and stared out at the last of the fishing boats coming in with the morning's catch.

"You disobeyed me," Eben began. "I gave you a direct order to remain at Amin's cottage while I settled my business with Gyp. Instead, you stole a horse—"

"I borrowed a horse."

"—and rode five hours alone and without protection, at night, through hostile countryside. Somehow, by the grace of God, you managed to navigate the underground passageway without becoming hopelessly lost—"

"I was prepared to leave a trail to find my way back if necessary. I am not a fool."

"That, my lady, is open to question," Eben retorted. "I shall continue. You stumbled onto the storeroom, where you nearly scared an eight-year-old boy to death."

"He seems to have suffered no permanent harm from his ordeal. And might I point out that it was you who left him there in the dark without food or water?"

A gull swooped low, so close that Kaia could hear the rush of its wings. It snatched a sand crab and flew off with the creature waving its little legs helplessly in the air.

Eben too seemed to be moving in for the kill.

"And finally, with no thought for your own safety and with every possibility of compromising the security of your country, you attempted to match wits with a man who would have subjected you to perversions you cannot possibly imagine, and would not hesitate to use you for his personal vengeance and political advantage."

Eben fell silent, no doubt expecting her to try to explain or justify her actions, or, more likely, to confess to the truth of his charge and repent accordingly.

"You have overlooked one thing, my lord."

"And what would that be?"

"You were in danger of your life."

"What has that to do with it?" he snapped.

Kaia stared at him in amazement. "Did you expect me to walk away and let Ranulph Gyp murder you in cold blood?"

"I expected you," he replied through clenched teeth, "to obey me."

Kaia heaved a deep sigh, closed her eyes, and shook her head. "You really are a dolt, Eben Dhion, you really are." With that, she picked up her skirts and started to walk back toward the town.

Eben lunged, grabbed her arm, and spun her around to face him. "He might have killed you," he shouted.

"He *would* have killed *you*," Kaia retorted. "Can you fault me for trying to save your life?"

"You chose to disobey me," he yelled, shaking her hard.

"Yes, I did!" She tore herself from his grasp and stepped back. "I chose to disobey you. I chose to try to save your life. It was my choice to make, and I made it."

For long minutes neither spoke. The wind had picked up, carrying from the town the muffled sounds of a barking dog, a pealing bell.

"I will try to explain," Eben finally said. "Will you hear me out without interrupting me at every turn?"

"Very well." Kaia walked a short distance to a large flat boulder, sat down, and folded her hands in her lap.

Eben paced up and down in front of her. "You were very young at the time Gyp tried to take over my father's hall, and Syrah and I came up with the scheme to hire Obike Zebengo to help us. The tale has been much embroidered. A young girl might think it merely a grand adventure, a romance with a happy ending. And so it was, except for one thing: Gyp was spared. I wanted vengeance. I needed vengeance. It was denied me."

Kaia, who had been listening with considerable charity until that moment, leaped up. "Was your vengeance worth your life?"

"My honor is worth my life," Eben said.

"What of *my* honor? Is it any less important than yours? Was I to sacrifice mine—leave a friend to die—so that you could keep yours?"

"You were not to be involved at all," Eben shouted. "I told you that I would handle Gyp in my own way. But no,

246

you, with your usual reckless disregard for the wishes of others, had to interfere—"

"How dare you! As I recall, you weren't 'handling' things all that well when I walked in. I don't see how I made it any worse."

"I will tell you how you made it worse, Kaia. Until that moment I had only my own life to save, but I was then forced to save yours as well."

Kaia's eyebrows shot up. "Forced?"

Eben threw up his hands in frustration. "That's not what I meant to say and you know it. All you had to do was obey me in the first place."

"Oh. So we're back to your favorite subject: obedience. My obedience, of course. I have done with that subject, sir."

She picked up her skirts and marched away.

Eben stalked after her. "Do you think you are the only one who has to obey orders, to answer to a higher authority?"

Kaia did not look back. "Of course not, but despite what you may think, you are not one of my higher authorities and I do not have to answer to you, Eben Dhion."

"Well, I have to answer to my king, my lady, and it was Jibril who commanded me to keep you from this folly and bring you home."

"I shall be pleased to write to my cousin before I leave and inform him that you did everything in your power to fulfill your commission. If you would prefer that he not think the less of you for having failed, I am sure I can invent some reasonable explanation. Perhaps I drugged you, or Merlin turned you into a toad until we sailed."

Eben surged past her, and now it was she who was talking to his back. "Will that make up for my inexcusable recklessness? My disobedience? My misguided attempt to save your life?"

"That will not be necessary," Eben yelled over his shoulder. "You will not sail on the *Peacock*. I gave my solemn oath to Jibril and your father that I would bring you back, and bring you back I will, although heaven only knows why they want me to. A sane man has no idea how to deal with such a woman."

Eben had reached the edge of the marketplace before he realized that Kaia was no longer behind him. She had stopped some way back, and although he could not see her expression, he saw her erect carriage and the proud lift of her chin. She was simply standing there watching him as the gulls wheeled overhead and the breeze played with wisps of her golden hair and the sea caressed the shore.

His mind in a whirl, he headed for the nearest tavern.

Chapter Thirty-two

Eben did not awaken with a sore head and bloodshot eyes. He was not that fortunate. His head had split right down the middle, and he would not have been able to ascertain the color of his eyes because he could not open them.

"My lord," whispered a timid young voice.

"Don't shout!"

"I am not shouting, my lord."

"Blessed Mother of God." Eben rasped. "Whatever it is you want, take it and get out."

"I require nothing, my lord. I was charged to bring you this potion for your head. And this box."

Eben managed to raise his right eyelid. When the pain subsided, he saw a girl of no more than eight or nine hovering near the door of his small chamber. She held a cup in one hand and cradled a small carved chest in the crook of her other arm.

"Who sent you?" he groaned.

"The lady, my lord."

Eben squeezed his eye shut again and tried to sort through his fractured thoughts for some memory of the night before. A woman. There had been women in the tavern—on his lap, draped over his shoulder, rubbing their breasts against him, whispering in his ear.

"Is there anyone in this bed with me?" he said.

"Don't you know, my lord?" The girl obviously thought him mad.

Eben stretched out an arm and felt around. When his fingers did not encounter warm flesh, he groaned, "Thank you, sweet Jesus."

"I'll . . . I'll just set the cup on the table here beside you, my lord," the girl said.

"Thank you, child. Now go."

When the door had clicked shut behind her, Eben fumbled for the cup. The potion tasted awful, but no worse than he deserved. He dropped back into blessed oblivion, and when next he woke his head was clear and he could recall stumbling back to the inn, alone. Whoever "the lady" was, she had not been one of the half dozen or more harlots who had importuned him in the tavern.

A lady. Kaia.

The girl had set the carved box on a low chest at the foot of the bed. Eben undid the clever little clasp. Inside were two combs, a carved wooden boat, and a leather sheath. Beneath these items he found a sheet of folded paper.

> *Please give the wood comb to Morgana and the silver comb to Oriana. The boate is for Ahriman. The sheet is for Akritos. Tell everone I love them. I thank you. I am sorry I put you too so much truble. I will always think of you as my frend. Kaia*

Eben glanced at the window. The sun was already low on the horizon. When he went to look out he knew what he would see.

The *Peacock* had sailed.

Amin Samil could not say he was particularly surprised to find Lord Eben Dhion knocking at his door at dawn. These Dominians were a strange lot: a runaway princess with a lovesick lord in hot pursuit, a game young squire, and a befuddled old monk. One even appeared to be a hound.

Amin liked them very much.

"A ship, my lord?" he said when Eben explained that the *Peacock* had sailed without him. Amin suspected there was a good deal more to the tale than Lord Eben let on, but he was a man who prided himself on minding his own business and asked no questions.

"I need the fastest ship we can find. I must catch them before . . . well, before they travel farther. I inquired at the port; there is no ship leaving for the Western Isles for a fortnight. I must leave today."

"Today!" Amin exclaimed.

"The matter is urgent."

"But, my lord," Amin said with a frown, "you cannot possibly lose them; they can travel no farther. Nothing lies beyond the Western Isles."

"I wouldn't be too sure about that," Eben murmured.

"My cousin might be persuaded to take you, my lord. He is about to depart with a shipment of fish bile and scorpion oil."

Eben was on his feet. "Let us ask him now."

"Er, my lord, I do not think he will thank us if we rouse him at sunrise."

Eben dropped back onto the log bench and rubbed his hands over his face. "Forgive me, Amin. I need to gather my wits together."

"What you need, my friend, is some sleep. In the morning we will talk to my cousin. I will bring you a blanket."

Eben lay awake for a long while.

I gave my solemn oath to Jibril and your father that I would bring you back, and bring you back I will, although heaven only knows why they want me to. A sane man has no idea how to deal with such a woman.

He might just as well have told her to go.

He might just as well have plunged his own dagger into his heart.

Chapter Thirty-three

Strange, Kaia thought as she gazed at the swath of moon-light riding the sea like a shimmering path to the west, that there could be tranquillity after such pain, such comforting silence when there were no more noisy tears left to shed.

I gave my solemn oath to Jibril and your father that I would bring you back, and bring you back I will, although heaven only knows why they want me to. A sane man has no idea how to deal with such a woman.

He might just as well have pierced her heart with a dagger that day on the beach. He might just as well have said, *I do not want you. Go.*

Now, three days out from Ataxi, Kaia reflected wryly that he must surely approve her obedience to his unstated command: *Go.* She had boarded the *Peacock* early the next morning to travel with her friends to the Western Isles and the Circle of Standing Stones. He would finally be free of her.

But she would never be free of him. There would be men as beautiful as he in that future world, with laughing eyes as deep a blue, but she would have none of them because there had once been Eben Dhion in her life, in her heart.

As for marrying a man of her own choosing, there would be no need to choose at all. There never had been, not since the image of the insouciant El__ first impressed itself on her two-year-old mind; not since the day he tweaked her nose, called her "little one," and promised he would marry her when she grew up.

"Thank goodness the storm has passed," Brother Absalom said as he joined her at the rail. "It was not so bad as the one we endured on the *Apostle*, but I have only a few drops remaining of my ginger syrup. Would I had some pellets of this Dramamine Merlin touts so highly."

"You will soon enough," Kaia reminded him.

"Yes, but then I shan't need them. Whatever this new world may be, I vow I shall never step foot off dry land again as long as I live."

Brother Absalom had been so sweet these past days. He had not sought to lift her spirits as he had at the inn with games and riddles, but his anxious glances and efforts at casual conversation were proof that although he did not know the cause of her sadness, he shared it with her nonetheless.

"I wonder if flying through the air occasions queasiness as well," Kaia said.

"Oh, dear. That hadn't occurred to me. And there isn't likely to be a rail handy if one is traveling inside a metal box high in the air, is there? Just as well, then, that the potion has been invented. Or will be invented," he added with a frown, since he had not yet sorted out the conundrum of something existing before it came into existence.

"I wonder if each of us will find what we seek," Kaia mused.

"Oh, I believe so," the monk replied. "The secret, I think, lies in our understanding of what we truly need. It is not enough to say 'I want to be happy,' or 'I want to be rich.' One man's happiness is another's burden, and having riches in one's pocket is not the same as being rich in friends. Jocco, I think, has the easiest path, because he knows exactly what he must do. Once the healers have repaired his poor mouth, he can begin his studies to become a troubadour."

"And you?"

Brother Absalom pursed his lips as he considered his answer. "I know I want the freedom to investigate the problems of natural philosophy—science, as it is known then—without interference or condemnation, but there are bound to be unexpected consequences. '*Nam et ipsa scientia potestas est*,' you know."

Kaia laughed. "No, I'm afraid I don't know. You must translate for me."

"Oh, I'm sorry, my dear. 'A man of knowledge increaseth strength.'"

"That sounds like a good thing," Kaia observed.

"It can be, I suppose," Brother Absalom replied, "but strength—and I imagine by that is meant power—in the wrong hands can lead to great evil, as we have just seen with Lord Gyp. If there is as much knowledge in the future as Merlin intimates, then there can exist much abuse of the power it gives. We have our black magic and white magic. Perhaps there are such things as black science and white science."

"Will you have some wine with me now that your stomach is somewhat settled?"

"I should be honored, my dear."

They made their way to the poop deck—not so very far, as the *Peacock* was but 125 feet long—where Kaia unlocked the door to the captain's cabin. She did not bother to light the small lantern; the moon provided quite enough light for her to see by as she filled their cups.

"It was very kind of the captain to allow you the use of his cabin," Brother Absalom observed.

"Yes. He is such a kind man. But what of me, Brother Absalom?" she inquired when they had settled down, she on a low stool, he perched at the edge of the narrow bed. "Will I find what I am seeking?"

"Hmmm. Let me recall your words that night at the convent. You said you wanted to read and write. You are making splendid progress in that, so I don't think that need be a priority for you anymore. Then you wanted to learn about bees. Well, I can't imagine that bees will have changed all that much, and people must have their honey, so there should be ample opportunity for you to learn about bees now that you can read. Merlin says people are always flying about from here to there—I can't imagine what they think they will find in one place rather than another—and that the sky is filled with metal boxes, so you'll be able to fly anywhere, anytime you choose. Now, what was the last thing you sought?"

"To choose my own husband."

"Oh, yes. A more difficult proposition. You certainly can do the choosing—women seem to have an inordinate amount of freedom to decide such things for themselves—but the man must agree to be the chosen. If you choose poorly, there is even a remedy. Merlin calls it 'divorce.' I must say I do not like the sound of that transaction at all—what joy can it bring to anyone?—and I seriously doubt the Mother Church looks upon it with favor."

"I will not be seeking a husband."

"Ah."

"I will never marry."

"Ah. Well, I am sorry to hear it, my dear. I had thought you cared deeply for someone." A blind man could not have mistaken Lady Kaia's love for Lord Eben, and his for her.

Kaia rose and went to the window to see the last of the moon settle into the waves of the Western Ocean. "I did, once," she said softly. "But he did not, as you say, want to be chosen. He bade me leave him. And so I have."

"He did? He said that in so many words?" Brother Absalom could not hide his surprise and consternation.

"He said he had no idea how a sane man could deal with such a woman as me."

Not the same thing, not the same thing at all, Brother Absalom thought with relief. "I would think that if he wished you to leave, he would have said so. Sometimes we hear what we expect to hear, or fear most to hear, when that is not what is being said at all."

Kaia turned to look at the old monk. "What else could he be saying?"

"That, I think, you must ask him, my dear."

"It is too late."

"Kaia, you have not traveled so far down this road that you cannot retrace your steps. A wise man—or woman—need not go in search of a treasure he has already found."

Brother Absalom placed a gentle kiss on her forehead.

"Good night, my dear. I do not count myself particularly wise, but I hope you will think on it."

The ship rolled in a gentle swell. "Oh, dear," Brother Absalom groaned and rushed from the cabin clutching the near-empty vial of ginger syrup.

In the darkest hour of the night Kaia awoke. The voice must have spoken in her dream, as there was no one near.

Kaia. Mine.

Chapter Thirty-four

As to it being a place of power, the Circle of Standing Stones was something of a disappointment to Kaia.

True, its situation far out on a windswept headland at the westernmost edge of the westernmost isle of the Western Isles was dramatic enough, and it did describe a rough circle perhaps a hundred paces across. There were stones, some truly enormous, and some were even still standing. So, yes, under the strictest definition it was a circle of standing stones, interesting as old ruins often are.

If there was magical power here, though, Kaia saw no sign of it. Not that she had all that much to compare it with. There were churches, of course, but that wasn't at all the same thing. Her great-grandmother claimed to have seen a vision of Mary Magdalene clinging to St. Polyp's Pillar, but then, great-grandmama steadfastly maintained to her very last breath that she was a virgin, despite having produced eleven sons and three daughters.

And then there was Groaning Martyrs Glen on her father's upland estate. No one had any notion why it was so called. If someone had been martyred there, the incident had been of such little interest to anyone but the martyrs themselves that no record existed of it having occurred at all. The groaning, however, was real enough, as many young couples could attest to, having explored the glen of a summer's eve.

"I had expected something rather more exciting," Brother Absalom said wistfully as he wandered around the inner circle.

Jocco leaped from slab to slab like a young mountain goat and poked into the crevices formed by the jumble of fallen stone. "Someone on the ship told me the old priests painted themselves blue and practiced human sacrifice," he reported with the ghoulish relish particular to the young. "He said the earth is soaked with the blood of a thousand virgins and you can hear their screams when the wind blows from the east."

Kaia plopped down on a weathered slab. "Why is it always girls who were sacrificed in the old stories? Boys are virgins too until . . . well, until they're not. Why didn't they sacrifice boy virgins? You'd think the goddesses would prefer boys."

"You would, wouldn't you? And quite a few gods as well, I suspect," Merlin said with a sly grin.

"For shame!" admonished Brother Absalom.

"Ugh," opined Jocco.

"Human sacrifice is an abomination before God," Brother Absalom exclaimed.

"What about Abraham and Isaac?" Jocco challenged. "God told Abraham to sacrifice his son. That's human sacrifice."

"Hmmm," Brother Absalom mused. "Genesis 22:2. A most problematic passage."

"He even had Isaac all laid out on the altar. He took that knife and—"

"Yes, yes, we all know the story," Brother Absalom said irritably. "But the point is, God rescinded His command. It was a test of Abraham's faith, you see."

"And little Isaac's, I should imagine," said Merlin dryly.

"I trust, Merlin, that you will seek to enlighten these heathens when the time comes and put a stop to it."

"I expect if I try to put a stop to it, I will end up lying where you're sitting right now with a knife at my breast."

"Oh. I hadn't thought of that." Brother Absalom blushed. "Are you a virgin, then, sir?"

Merlin rolled his eyes.

"It is nothing to be ashamed of if you are," Brother Absalom said kindly. "I admit I should like to have had children, but chastity has served me well. I have not found it so very difficult."

"You've lived in a monastery all your life," Jocco pointed out.

"I don't see what that has to do with it," Brother Absalom replied indignantly. "It is simply a matter of willpower."

Jocco grinned. "I'd like to see you try to hang on to your willpower in a brothel."

Brother Absalom glowered at him. "I am beyond temptation."

"Since you are so interested in the subject, Brother Absalom," Merlin interjected, "you might want to investigate a different perspective on the matter when you reach your destination. There are some fascinating treatises on the subject."

Brother Absalom perked up. "Really? What would you recommend?"

Merlin pursed his lips. "Well, you might begin with the two most widely appreciated works on the subject, which are available everywhere. They are called *Playboy* and *Penthouse*. They are even illustrated. Most enlightening."

"*Playboy. Penthouse*," Absalom repeated so that he would not forget. "Thank you. I'm sure I shall find them most enjoyable."

"Oh, you will, you will. Now, I have other matters to discuss with you. I must ask each of you one last time if you have any doubts. The time draws near. The spell must be spoken as the last ray of the sun touches that stone." He pointed to the largest upright slab. "Brother Absalom?"

"I have no doubts."

"Squire Jocco?"

"I want to go."

"Lady Kaia?"

"I am content with my decision."

Merlin rubbed his hands together. "Good, good. Now that we have that out of the way, let us get down to business. As I have explained, we must all speak the spell together. Squire Jocco, have you memorized the spell exactly as I taught it to you?"

"Yes, sir. 'E equals emceesquared.'"

"Lady Kaia?"

"'E equals emceesquared,'" she replied promptly.

"Brother Absalom?"

"Er, yes I believe I have."

"'Believe?' You only believe you have?"

"No. Yes. I mean, I have."

Merlin threw up his hands. "Good heavens, man. We are not speaking here of restoratives and poultices. We are not eradicating fleas or turning perfectly good wool orange. We are about to hurl the three of you into the future. One wrong word could mean catastrophe. I have structured the spell so that you will arrive precisely in time for the evening meal on the twenty-third day of the seventh month in the year one thousand nine hundred and fifty on the doorstep of 112 Mercer Street, in the city of Princeton, in New Jersey, in the United States of America. If you bungle so much as a single vowel, who knows where you will wind up or when?"

"Oh, dear, oh, dear," moaned Brother Absalom. "Perhaps I've taken on too much. I've never performed well under stress. I don't see why we all have to say the spell with you." He pouted. "You're the magician."

Merlin glared at him. "You say it with me because it is you who are doing the traveling. You must speak your desire."

"Why can't we just say, 'We want to go into the future,' rather than 'squareceemem' or whatever it is. I haven't the faintest notion what it means. It doesn't make any sense."

"*You* don't make any sense, old man," Merlin shouted, tearing at his hair.

"I'm sorry," Brother Absalom said humbly. "I can't seem to do anything right."

"That's not true," Kaia cried. "You saved us when the ship was attacked. You protected me from Ranulph Gyp. You were the hero of the day."

"I was, wasn't I?" the little monk said, suddenly shy.

"Be that as it may," said Merlin sternly, "I see we will have to go over it one last time. But first, here are some items you will need." He reached beneath his cloak, extracted a leather satchel, and spread the contents on the stone. "The first thing you must do is find a healer—they are called doctors. Tell him that you come from a remote people in a distant country and have need of inoculations."

"Inoculations?"

Merlin frowned, trying to think how to explain the entirely counterintuitive process of injecting one with a disease which one is seeking to prevent to a man who had no knowledge of the invisible bits of matter called germs or the concept of airborne disease.

"It is a means of preventing many maladies," Merlin said at last. "The doctor will know what is to be done. It is very important that you do this immediately. Your life may depend on it."

"I enjoy perfect health," said Brother Absalom primly.

Merlin closed his eyes and prayed for patience. "I'm sure you do. And you wish to continue to do so, do you not?"

"Of course."

"Then do as I say," snapped Merlin. "Let us continue."

He picked up a thick roll of green paper. "You cannot go about without the means to provide for yourselves. This is all the money you will need until you get settled."

Absalom examined the item. "Will we not need coin?"

"These pieces of paper are worth far more than coin. You must find a building called a bank. Give the paper to the people there; they will hold it for you, and you can ask for any amount when you need it."

"It doesn't seem like a very sound practice to me. Who is to say these people are trustworthy"

Merlin glared at the monk. "Brother Absalom, if you are going to question my every directive, perhaps you should not proceed with this endeavor."

"I apologize. It is just that it is all so new to me."

"Which brings me to my next point. You will have a great deal to learn, and will have free use of any library you choose. You will find more books than ever you dreamed of. You will start out living near one of the finest universities of the time, and Al will be able to direct you to the best teachers. Then—"

"Who is Al?" Jocco interrupted. He had been listening with growing excitement as the first real information about his new life was being revealed.

"Oh, did I forget to mention Al? How remiss of me. Yes, Albert Einstein. The greatest mind of his generation. You will be staying with him. He's an old friend."

"Is he expecting us?" Absalom inquired.

"No, but there is nothing in the universe that would surprise Al. In fact, your sudden appearance on his doorstep may be the most exciting thing to happen to him in years."

"But how are we to explain how we came to be there?"

Merlin laughed. "I shouldn't worry about that. Al will figure it out for himself."

Absalom wasn't entirely convinced. "Are you sure we won't be imposing?"

"Just mention my name. He's in my debt. He'll understand."

It was all just a little too much for Brother Absalom. "The greatest mind of his generation in your debt? How can that be?"

Merlin winked. "Where do you think he got his best ideas?"

Lost in thought, Kaia did not hear Jocco come up behind her. When Merlin had finally completed his little lecture and taken Brother Absalom off for his final rehearsal, she had wandered off along a path that followed the line of the cliffs. She found solitude of great comfort of late, and had enjoyed far too little of it on board the *Peacock*. She could just see the ship at anchor far down the coast to the south.

"You are troubled, my lady? I hope I didn't startle you. I saw you out here all alone, and I thought you might like some company. Of course, if you would rather not . . ."

Kaia smiled at the young squire. "No, stay, Jocco. I should like that. I was just thinking that eight hundred years from now the sun will be setting over the town of Princeton, just as it is this moment here on these cliffs. Nothing will really have changed."

"Oh, no, my lady," Jocco said earnestly, "everything will have changed. Did you not listen to all that Merlin told us? It is going to be splendid. The healer—doctor, I must remember to say doctor—will fix my mouth. I have decided to study to be a troubadour. Merlin says a good troubadour can become as rich as a king. No one will dare laugh at me if I am rich as a king. I will be handsome—as handsome as Lord Eben—and the women will be begging me to kiss them."

"Have you never been kissed, then, Jocco?"

"Of course not," he replied with a shrug. "Who would kiss someone who looks like me?"

"I would, Jocco, and I think there are many others who would. Not all women mistake the outer man for the inner. Here, let me show you."

Jocco stumbled back. "No, my lady," he said, shocked to his very core. "I am repulsive."

Kaia touched his cheek. "You are not repulsive, Jocco. You are beautiful. You will have many kisses in your life. I should be honored to give you the first, if you will allow it."

The perfect bow of her mouth settled on his twisted one for the briefest second, but Jocco knew he would never again taste a kiss so sweet as long as he lived.

When Kaia returned to the center of the Circle of Standing Stones she found Brother Absalom staring about him with an anxious look on his face. "Something is wrong, Lady Kaia. The circle feels different somehow."

"I feel it too," she said. "When we first arrived, I thought how empty and ordinary it seemed, but now—"

"Yes, yes," said Brother Absalom with a shudder. "It is making me quite nervous. Perhaps it's this mist. Let us step away for a moment. I don't like this at all."

Kaia hastened after him as he practically leaped over a stone slab and sprinted toward the shelter of a small copse of trees nearby.

"There, that's better." Brother Absalom exclaimed. "I was beginning to feel quite chilly. Only to be expected in a sea mist—"

"Brother Absalom."

"What is it, my dear?" he inquired as he checked for the hundredth time that the little leather satchel was tied securely to the cord at his waist.

"Look."

"Look at . . . ? Oh. I see. Not sea mist, then."

"I rather think not," Kaia murmured.

The Circle of Standing Stones no longer stood empty. While the land all around basked in the last red glow of the setting sun, a silver mist swirled gently within the perimeter of the ancient stones.

"It would appear Merlin knows whereof he speaks," Brother Absalom observed when he managed to find his voice. "A place of true power. Not that I ever really doubted it, of course. It's simply that I never imagined—"

"It would be so beautiful," Kaia finished for him.

"Yes, God has created beauty all around us. We have only to believe to see it is so. Oh, I see Merlin waving to us. It is time, child. But before we go further I must tell you what joy you have brought into my life. I dreamed of having such a daughter, and God sent you to me. I would not have missed one day, one hour, one minute of my time with you."

Kaia burst into tears and threw her arms about his neck. "Even when I forget to put in all the letters?" she sobbed.

Brother Absalom smiled down at her. "Even then. How can I fault you for that when I cannot get the words of even the simplest spell right? You have been a most apt pupil, my dear.

"Oh, dear, Merlin is looking quite testy. Let us go. But before we do I have one more thing I would like to say—a bit of wisdom, as it were."

"Yes?"

"Kaia, we may fly only in our dreams, but even then we fly. Will you remember the words of an old man?"

"Of course I'll remember. But you make it sound as though we are parting."

Brother Absalom patted her hand as they walked toward the Circle of Standing Stones. "Do you remember what I told you on the ship one night when your spirits were low?"

"You said many things."

"Yes, but one bears repeating, especially at this moment. I said, 'You have not traveled so far down this road that you cannot retrace your steps. A wise man—or woman—has no need to go in search of a treasure he has already found.'"

"Oh. I remember now, but I didn't understand."

"I know, not then. But think on it now, child, quickly, for I believe in your heart you do understand."

"Come, come," Merlin said irritably. "This is no time to dawdle. Stand precisely in the center of the circle and stay there. Don't go wandering off. I don't want one of you in Princeton and another in Outer Mongolia and another in Tierra del Fuego."

"C equals emeesquared," Brother Absalom began, his voice not quite steady.

"Not yet," Merlin shouted. "All four of us must say it together. And it is 'E equals emceesquared,' not 'C equals emeesquared.'"

"Oh, dear," Brother Absalom wailed. "I was feeling so confident and now I'm getting all muddled."

"Well, pull yourself together or you'll end up in the middle of a space war between the Klingons and the Tribbles."

Jocco took hold of Brother Absalom's hand. "Whatever happens, we all go together."

Tears stood out in the old monk's eyes. "Thank you, my son. Farewell, Merlin, farewell! And thank you," he cried.

"My pleasure, sir," said Merlin stepping out of the circle. "Now all together at the count of three. One, two, THREE : 'E equals—'"

"Stop," Kaia cried.

"What is it now?" Merlin groaned.

"I can't."

"What can't you?"

"I can't go."

Merlin's eyebrows snapped clear to his hairline. "You're not going? Now you tell us?"

"Yes, now I tell you," she said softly.

"Would you care to enlighten the rest of us as to the reason for this sudden change of plan?" Merlin growled.

Kaia looked up at Brother Absalom. "A great teacher once told me that one never travels so far down a road that one cannot retrace one's steps. And a wise man has no need to seek the treasure he has already found. My treasure lies here, in this world."

"You are sure, child?" Brother Absalom said.

"I am sure, Brother. Thank you."

"Never in all my days," Merlin was muttering as Kaia kissed first Brother Absalom and then Jocco on the cheek.

"Farewell, my dear friends. God be with you."

"Off with you, off with you." Merlin shooed Kaia from the circle. "Go stand in that little copse over yonder and cover your eyes.

"Now, unless anyone *else* is undergoing a change of heart, may we finally proceed? All together—"

"Wait!" Kaia shouted, running back to the edge of the circle.

Merlin tore at his hair. "I can't stand it."

"The riddle, Brother Absalom," Kaia called. "Nothing! The answer is 'nothing!' Nothing is greater than God. Nothing is more evil than the devil. The poor have nothing. The rich don't want nothing. And if you eat nothing, you will die."

"I had already reasoned that out for myself," the monk announced grandly.

"You did not," Jocco objected. "If you already knew, why didn't you say so before?"

"Enough!" roared Merlin. "You are all driving me mad. Let us get on with it or the moment will pass. "And one and two and THREE!"

Merlin the Magnificent, Brother Absalom of the abbey of the Worshipful Brotherhood of Milo the Mild, and Squire Jocco, late of the company of the Ninth House of the Dominion threw wide their arms.

"E equals emceesquared," they shouted into the infinite reaches of the universe.

Chapter Thirty-five

"Wait!"

Eben Dhion ran as he had never run before. Far up on the barren headland he could see four small figures dwarfed by great slabs of dark, brooding stone, a scene out of some hideous nightmare framed against a sweep of fiery orange and blood-red sky as the sun settled into the Western Ocean.

"No!"

This couldn't be happening. Some maleficent deity was about to reach out from its foul den and snatch his Kaia away from him forever. How could a good and loving God have willed it so? How came that sweet, dusty little urchin who had toddled after him from room to room of his father's hall, upper bailey to lower, cellar to chapel, bake house to barbican, to stand in this abominable place? How could she choose to leave him forever?

How could he have driven her to it?

Too late; he was too late. Even now an eerie mist which seemed to gather into itself all the colors of the dying sun streamed over the headland and swallowed up the figures one by one until only the very top of the tallest slab could be seen, and then even that was gone. The very earth seemed to hum with power, and from the very last rays of the sun an arrow of blinding green shot across the sea and pierced the mist, sending it shooting like a fountain high into the clouds.

Slowly the mist, now a shimmering silver, settled back to earth and drifted out over the cliffs and away.

And the Circle of Standing Stones stood empty once more.

"Good evening, Lord Eben."

Eben leaned back against the cold slab and closed his eyes. "Merlin. I thought you had gone with them. You all disappeared together," he said dully.

Merlin drew his cloak about him and sat down beside Eben. "The eye is easily deceived. No, I had some business with the captain of the *Peacock* down the coast, which took longer than I had anticipated. I am glad to find you still here."

"She's gone."

"Yes."

"Bring her back."

"That is far beyond my powers."

Eben leaped to his feet, fury running like fire through his body. "No, it is not beyond your powers, and you know it. Bring her back, you meddling bastard," he shouted. "What right had you to interfere? What right to send her away from her people, her time? From me?"

"Nay, I did not send her," Merlin replied quietly. "Lady Kaia was granted a rare grace. The grace to choose. She looked deep into her heart and embraced her future by her own will. She has chosen, and I must say she has chosen well."

Eben stormed about the clearing. "Are you dispensing grace now, Merlin? Have your powers so seduced you that you think you stand for God? Your will for His?"

"Had I such power, would I not know my own future? From the sweet oblivion of my own death, I journey back toward my birth, knowing no more of those events that precede this moment than you or the Lady Kaia know of your own futures."

"You will say it is written," Eben said bitterly.

"So it is."

Eben dropped onto a fallen slab and buried his head in his hands. "I don't understand."

Merlin smiled. "I am not sure anyone does." He walked to the far edge of the clearing and saw, in the last vestige of dusk, the billowing sail of a ship heading out to sea.

"There is the *Peacock*. Those who sail tonight look to have a safe journey," he observed. "And speaking of journeys, I believe the time has come for me to continue on with my own. I rather thought that would be the case. This is certainly the right place for it."

Eben heard the swish of silk robes and felt a gentle hand on his bent head.

"You must trust me, son. Lady Kaia chose well. She will find great joy in her life. You may comfort yourself knowing it will be so."

The whisper of silk faded away. Eben looked up to see the great wizard framed against the moon, full round and misty orange as it rose in the eastern sky.

"Arthur," he said.

Merlin turned back. "Arthur?"

"Sooner or later your journey will take you to Arthur,

who is the once and future king. Your name and his will be linked in glory for all time to come."

"Indeed?" mused Merlin. "How could I not know of it?"

Eben almost managed a smile. "Perhaps it was not written that you should."

"Well said, Lord Eben. Thank you for reminding me that I am never so wise as I suppose myself to be."

From somewhere beneath his cloak the wizard drew out a tall conical hat and settled it carefully upon his head. "I always like to look my best when I arrive," he said.

"Farewell, Merlin."

"Farewell, Lord Eben. Know that all blessing and joy will come to dwell in the hall of the Ninth House."

In a searing flash of violet and blue and blinding white, the tall, spare frame of Merlin vanished, and in his place, for the briefest flicker of the eye, a noble black hound grinned at Eben, and then was gone.

Chapter Thirty-six

Eben recognized the rider immediately. No one in the Dominion sat a horse quite like the king.

There may have been a few horsemen whose technical mastery of their mounts equaled his, but Jibril carried about him that ineffable ascendancy that proclaimed his royal ancestry, set him apart from other men, and inspired the deepest respect and loyalty in his people. His white Arabian gelding too bore the bloodline of peerless mounts, as Eben had good reason to know, since the horse had been born and bred on his own estate.

Eben had known, of course, that someone would come looking for him eventually, but that that someone would be Jibril himself could mean only one thing: The king was not pleased and was taking matters into his own hands.

Eben had repeatedly ignored the summonses, signed in Jibril's own hand, to return to the capital. He had finally left the inn where he had holed up and fled to the only spot in the Dominion where no one would dare search him out: the Isle of Lost Souls, said to be haunted by the ghosts of monks gone mad and declared a place of abomination by the Church.

No one except Jibril, of course, who was personally acquainted with the place, having been abducted some years ago by Lady Syrah Dhion and her precocious little brother, Eben, and held on the island for ransom. Eben had taken up residence in Jibril's old cell, and found it quite comfortable, although not furnished quite so well as it had been for the crown prince's short confinement.

The rider had first appeared atop the towering cliffs at the landward end of the causeway that connected the island with the mainland. He reappeared half an hour later, having negotiated the steep switchback trail that led down to the beach, and urged the Arabian into a graceful canter along the shore.

Eben watched as Jibril dismounted, tied his horse to a stunted sourbush, and stood looking out at the island. Waves washed over the causeway, but the tide was receding quickly. It should only be an hour or so until Jibril could make his way out to the island. He settled down with his back against an enormous boulder and seemed to be relaxing in the warmth of the sun that shone down.

For his part, Eben made himself comfortable in a grassy hollow, out of the incessant wind, folded his hands beneath his head, and tried to prepare himself for what would undoubtedly be an uncomfortable confrontation with his old friend.

"What do you want? Go away." Eben hadn't bothered to open his eyes, but he knew Jibril was standing over him.

"Greetings to you too, Lord Eben," Jibril said politely.

"I'm not ready to go back."

"I see." Jibril dropped down beside Eben, plucked a long, succulent spear of grass, and nibbled at it thoughtfully. "What you're saying, then, is that you're not finished sulking. Do I have it aright?"

"I am not sulking."

"Of course, how foolish of me," Jibril exclaimed. "Grown men do not sulk; that is the province of small children. Grown men brood. Yes, that is the better word for it."

Eben turned his head, opened one dark blue eye, and glared at Jibril. "Can't a man take a few days to enjoy some peace and quiet? Reflect on the great mysteries of life?"

"He can," Jibril agreed.

Eben closed the eye. "Then I'm enjoying peace and quiet and reflecting on the great mysteries of life. Or I was until I was so rudely interrupted."

Jibril stretched out on his side a few feet away with his head cradled in his hand, and frowned over at Eben. His friend looked drawn, as though he had not been sleeping well and had been drinking too much wine, to deaden the emotions rather than lift the spirits. He had never seen Eben Dhion so.

"Syrah and Morgana are worried about you."

Eben grunted. "Morgana has good reason to be worried. I'll not soon forget her part in this fiasco."

"She grieves for her friend Kaia. She grieves for you, Eben. She believes she has forever lost your love and respect."

Eben pulled himself up to a sitting position, picked up a small stone, and threw it over the edge of the cliff. "No, that would never happen. But if she is the wiser for it—"

"She is wiser than you, my friend."

Eben's head snapped around. "And just what is that supposed to mean?"

"When Kalan brought Morgana back to Suriana, she was consumed with guilt. Even Syrah could not console her. She wept incessantly—that can really get on a man's nerves, I can tell you—because she could not undo what she had done and could not accept that her life had to go on despite it all. She is calmer now. A friend has come to stay with her at the palace, a remarkably wise young woman, and Morgana is wiser for it."

Eben hurled a stone at a low-flying erne. "Wise young women are as rare as hen's teeth in my experience."

Jibril grinned. "Then I am most fortunate to have discovered such a tooth with my Syrah. Perhaps there are others out there, and you don't recognize them when you see them."

Eben scrambled to his feet. The tightness in his chest was far closer to pain than he cared for Jibril to see. "I'll get some wine."

Jibril leaned back on his elbows and considered how best to persuade Eben to return to Suriana with him. He could, of course, as his king command Eben to do so, but in Eben's present frame of mind Jibril suspected he'd have a fight on his hands.

Getting Eben to return was as much for his own sake as Eben's, Jibril reflected ruefully. The past two weeks had seen an endless parade of tantrums, sulks, hysterics, crying babies, and weeping women. Jibril didn't think he could take another day of it.

Syrah, never at her sunniest when recovering from childbed, had taken the unexpected appearance of twins as a personal affront and hinted darkly that Jibril would not be coming to her bed again anytime soon. His own mother, usually the most placid of souls, had actually spoken a harsh word to a serving girl, upon which the poor child fainted dead away and the dowager queen was seen falling to her knees in the middle of the great hall and gathering the little thing to her breast, weeping with remorse.

Eben returned with a leather flask, some dry bread, and an enormous chunk of cheese on which a green mold was making excellent progress.

"For the love of God," Jibril said, "you're living like a savage." He reached for his knife and began excising the offensive green patches. "No, I misspoke, not a savage. Like a man who just doesn't give a damn anymore."

"I don't give a damn anymore," Eben said softly.

"I can see that. Listen to me, Eben. I don't pretend to understand what went on out there. I only know what you told me in your letter. It all seems so fantastic—Gyp, this Merlin person—but I must believe it because I would never doubt your word. You say Kaia is gone, but you do not say why. Did she tell you why?"

For long minutes Eben did not reply, just stared out over the sea. "I told her to go."

Jibril could not conceal his shock. "You *told* her to go?"

"I was furious with her. She disobeyed my orders and nearly lost her life."

"From what you wrote, she risked her life to save you."

"Yes!" Eben exploded. "How dare she? So young, so lovely . . . to risk dying at the hands of a fiend like Gyp so that I could live? How did she think I would be able to live with that on my conscience? How could she think I would be able to live without her?"

Eben buried his head in his hands. "I didn't know how to tell her. Everything I said came out wrong. I've always known exactly what to say to get what I want. I can be charming and funny and flattering and tell outrageous stories when it serves my purpose—"

Jibril laughed. "I can certainly attest to that. Let's see: You threw Ankuli off the scent with a rousing tale of dromedaries when you and Syrah smuggled me out of the city in a coffin; Obike will never forget the image of Syrah blowing up frogs; Orini still has nightmares about cannibals."

Jibril's effort to lighten the mood fell on deaf ears.

"I can be whoever people want me to be," Eben went on miserably. "But when it came to the point, I couldn't say what I needed to say to Kaia. So I tore into her for disobeying me. I said terrible things to her."

"Sweet Jesus," Jibril said. "What did she say?"

"Nothing," Eben replied dully. "She didn't say anything, just looked at me."

"And?" Jibril prompted.

"I stormed off and drank myself into a stupor. When I woke up the next morning, Merlin and the monk and Jocco were gone. And Kaia with them." He shook his head. "God, I am such an idiot."

"I can't disagree with that."

In the end, Eben knew there was nothing for it but to return to Suriana with Jibril. He couldn't hide out on the Isle of Lost Souls forever. Somehow he would have to get on with his life. He would return to his hall, carry out his duties, see to Morgana's welfare and her future. He would stand as godfather for Jibril's and Syrah's children. He would have to marry one day, continue the line of his ancient House.

It could be done and it was worth the doing. But it would be a life of empty gestures, because Kaia would not be there to share it with him.

They rode hard the first day and took lodging at a modest inn shortly after sunset. The sudden appearance of the king of the Dominion in the public drinking room caused an uproar such as had never been seen before in the place. The cook suffered a minor heart seizure when informed His Majesty would require a meal. She recovered sufficiently to produce a five-course meal that was considerably more elaborate than Jibril was served most days at the palace. She would live out her days basking in the glory of that one meal and telling wildly embellished tales of the king's commendation and largesse.

Throughout the two-day journey Jibril found it difficult to keep his own counsel in the face of Eben's melancholy.

He could have eased his friend's mind with a few words, but he had made promises and he would keep them. In any event, it was not he who could make it right for Eben Dhion. That would be up to someone else.

They parted ways at the western gate of the city, Jibril riding on toward the palace, Eben to the manor the Dhion family had used for generations when on business in the capital.

To Eben's relief, he was spared his first meeting with Morgana, who was living at the palace in his absence. He stabled his horse, called for a bath, ate a light supper, and took his wine flask with him to his bed.

"He was there, of course." Queen Syrah handed the serene little bundle to the nurse and took her other babe to her breast. The woman bustled out with the little princess.

Jibril leaned over, kissed his wife's fair hair, her lovely breast, and lastly the tip of the nose of his newest child, who paid him no heed and went on with her determined sucking.

Jibril smiled down at the pair. "You were correct, as you always are, my love."

Syrah scowled up at him, then smiled. "Don't tease me, Jibril. You knew he'd be there too. How is he?"

"Much as one would expect. He told her to go, you know."

"No!"

"He lost his temper; said one thing when he meant another. Then he stormed off and drank himself into a stupor."

"Why is that always a man's way of coping when things are difficult or he is unhappy?" Syrah wondered.

Jibril ruffled her hair. "Why are tears always a woman's?"

"Hmmph."

"Heaven knows we've had enough tears around here lately," Jibril complained. "I expect our little ones, being female, will howl their way through the christening tomorrow."

"Does he know she's here? You didn't tell him, did you?"

"I didn't tell him. He's in for a shock. I wonder how they'll deal."

"Poor Eben," Syrah sighed. "And poor Kaia."

Jibril's page rapped on the door to the royal bedchamber. "Your bath has been drawn, sire."

Jibril stretched and pulled his tunic over his head. "I for one will be relieved when this whole sorry tale is told and, one can only hope, everyone lives happily ever after."

"As should we all," said his wife.

Chapter Thirty-seven

"Kaia, my dear," said Queen Alya; "I must get some air. It is a madhouse in here. Will you give me your arm and walk with me a while in the upper garden before we go down to chapel?"

Kaia left off tucking in stray wisps of Morgana's unruly hair and bobbed a little curtsy. "Of course, Your Highness."

"Me too, me too, Grandmama," begged three-year-old Prince Ahriman, tugging at the hem of Alya's silver gown.

The dowager queen leaned down and tweaked his nose.

"You, my little monkey, are the worst of the lot. You are to stay here with nurse and try to behave yourself. Come, Kaia."

Queen Syrah's private quarters were indeed a madhouse. One of the tiny princesses had just spit up all over her mother's ivory silk gown; the other was howling at the top of her tiny lungs. Maids rushed to and fro trying to repair the damage and calm both babes. The king strode in demanding to know what the devil was going on in here, and made a strategic retreat when he realized Morgana was still in her shift. Princess Oriana was hopping around in one slipper, while her nurse crawled about on the floor looking for the other.

"These occasions can be so very exhausting," Alya remarked as she and Kaia set off down the long corridor, trailed at a discreet distance by her maid and one of the royal guards. "My husband had the good sense to stay out of the way until the last possible moment. But Jibril seems always to be underfoot."

Princess Oriana flashed past them, a blur of pale rose. "He's here, he's here!" she shouted and bounded down the stairs.

"Good heavens," Alya exclaimed. "I believe the child is running about without her slippers."

Kaia loved the cheerful disorder of the royal household, so very different from the dull pomposity of her father's hall. Of course, King Jibril, Queen Syrah, and the children presented the dignified demeanor expected of the royal family when in public. Even Ahriman and Oriana knew the time and place for proper behavior, and Crown Prince Akritos, at twelve, possessed the same chameleonlike quality of his father, mischievous one moment and appropriately grave the next.

The upper garden lay at the east side of the palace complex and was reserved for the private use of the royal family. It was not nearly so large as the west garden, which had been laid out in the formal manner with radiating pebbled walks, classical statuary, an ancient maze, and an enormous central fountain in the form of dancing dolphins.

"I have always preferred this garden," Alya said as they descended the shallow steps. "It doesn't have the view, of course, but I love the arrangement of the beds; each with a variety of blooms of one color. Isn't that yellow bed lovely?"

Kaia agreed that it was. She was content just to listen as the dowager queen chattered on about this and that: babies, the outrageous price of silk fringe these days, a simply awful poem someone had written in her honor.

"I am, apparently, a beloved vessel floating upon the bosom of my people," she remarked. "Such drivel. Some people should not be allowed to take pen in hand. Vessel indeed. How Ahriman would have laughed."

"But you are beloved, ma'am," Kaia pointed out.

"I am a queen. What else are they to say? Not that I ever wanted to be a queen. But what choice did I have? I was told I was to marry Ahriman; he was told he was to marry me. He was born to be a king; I must be his queen. He had no more choice in the matter than I did."

"I never thought of it that way before," said Kaia.

"That men cannot always choose as they would? I assure you, it is true."

"They certainly have more choices than women," Kaia

grumbled as she helped the queen adjust her shawl against a sudden cool breeze.

Queen Alya laughed. "And so have more opportunity to make mistakes. I think a man's greatest fear is that he will be wrong. Even worse is that he will be *seen* to be wrong. Therefore he must constantly be trying to prove that he is right. It must be terribly exhausting."

"Nonetheless, he at least is free to make the choice in the first place," Kaia pointed out. "I should far prefer to have the choice and live with the consequences: I succeed or I fail. How else am I to learn? And if I do not learn, I am a child always."

"That is very true," the queen said as they strolled back toward the palace. "However, it occurs to me, my dear, that you have been making your own choices all along. In some you have been successful, in others less so. When Konstantin would not allow you to learn to read and write—such a foolish man—you set out to do it yourself; that was a choice. When you learned of this new world, you set off to find it. When a friend was in danger of his life, you chose to risk yours. When the moment came, you chose to remain in the world you know. The world," she added with a twinkle in her eye, "in which you have no choices."

Kaia cast her a sidelong glance. It occurred to her that beneath the mild, breezy, naive demeanor of the dowager queen, there might lurk a very shrewd woman indeed.

"Men do not thank us for making our own choices," Kaia persisted. "If we are right, they will find some way to take the credit for themselves. If we are wrong, it is because we are women and have overreached ourselves."

"You know, my dear, I believe you are much the wiser for your adventure."

"They can be such idiots," Kaia declared.

The queen let out a delighted laugh.

They had reached the bottom of the stairs leading up out of the garden.

"I understand Lord Eben has finally returned," Alya remarked casually.

The last thing Kaia wanted to discuss was Eben Dhion. The last thing she wanted to think about was Eben Dhion.

"Yes, ma'am."

"A very stubborn young man. Jibril had to ride out to that very odd little island everyone says is haunted and order him to return for the christening. Apparently, he was brooding over some matter or other." The queen frowned. "I can't quite recall what it was all about. Something about having made a terrible mistake, I believe."

"Oh."

"So you see," the queen said brightly, "men make mistakes too and must live with the consequences.

"Oh, there you are, Depta," she said to the elderly maid who had joined them once again. "I think I shall just freshen up before I go down to the chapel. I have enjoyed our little discussion, Kaia. I am so glad you chose to join me. I think you will always choose well."

With that, Queen Alya sailed away, leaving Kaia with the suspicion that the dowager queen had finally come to the point.

"Uncle, Uncle!" Princess Oriana dashed along the colonnade and threw herself into Eben's arms. "I'm so glad

285

you've come. Papa said you would. Have you been hiding? I've been looking for you everywhere."

"Well, you have found me now." Eben laughed and lifted his elfin niece high in the air.

She settled against his chest with her arms wrapped firmly around his neck. "I missed you, Uncle."

"I missed you too."

"Then you shouldn't go away," Oriana pointed out. "Then you wouldn't miss me."

Other than his conversation with Jibril on the Isle of Lost Souls, Eben hadn't yet spoken to anyone about the search for Kaia. He had no idea what was common knowledge. Syrah would know the full story, of course. Now that he thought about it, Eben wondered why Jibril hadn't told him what story would be put into circulation to account for Kaia's disappearance.

"I was on some business for your father," he said.

Oriana nodded wisely. "You were looking for Cousin Kaia."

"How do you know about that?"

"Everyone knows about it, Uncle. You didn't find her," she told him.

"No."

Oriana skipped along beside him as they came to the parapet that looked out over the city. He lifted her up but kept his arms firmly around her so she wouldn't fall.

"Do you like my dress? It's pink."

"So I see. And yes, I like it very much."

"I wanted to look like a flower," Oriana explained. "Do you think I look like a flower?"

"You look exactly like a flower."

Oriana grinned and planted a damp little kiss on his cheek. "Good. Papa wanted me to wear an ivory-colored dress like Mama is wearing for the christening. The little dresses the babies are wearing are ivory too. So he thought it would look well for all of us to be dressed the same. Papa doesn't know anything about colors," she confided.

Eben laughed. "You look like a little pink rose. I think I will call you Lady Rose from now on."

"Only when I wear pink," Oriana advised him.

"Only when you wear pink, little flower." Eben's heart contracted; he had almost said "little one."

"That's what Kaia calls me. Little Flower."

It took a moment. "Lady Kaia?" Eben said carefully.

"I love Kaia. I love Morgana, but I love Kaia more. You won't tell Morgana, will you?"

"Um, no, Oriana, I won't tell Morgana."

"Good. I wouldn't want to hurt her feelings."

Eben wondered if he had missed something here.

"Do you know what I think?" Oriana chattered on. "I think Kaia looks like a bee when she wears yellow. She has such pretty yellow hair and big black eyes just like a bee. Except she doesn't have a stinger. So she's a yellow bee and I'm a pink flower."

Eben lifted Oriana from the wall and carried her to a bench beside a blue-tiled pool swirling with red carp. He suspected he might need to be sitting down soon.

"Oriana," he said. "Is Lady Kaia wearing a yellow gown *today*?"

"Uh-huh. I told you, she's the bee and I'm the flower."

Yes, Eben thought, he had certainly missed something here.

"When did Kaia come home?"

"Don't you know? Didn't Papa tell you?"

No, Papa hadn't told him. He would have to speak to Papa about that little omission.

Oriana climbed onto his lap and began to count on her fingers. "Let's see. She came home one, two, five . . . I can't remember, but it was before my birthday.

"Morgana cried and cried when she saw Kaia," Oriana continued. "Papa said he couldn't stand it anymore and made her go to her room, and then told Kaia to go into his study. That means Papa is really mad when he tells you to go into his study.

"Papa told Mama to stay outside, but she went in anyway. I heard Papa yelling at Kaia, and then Mama yelled at Papa. Then it got real quiet for a long time."

Oriana fiddled with the green silk cord at her waist. "I didn't like it when Papa yelled at Kaia. She looked so sad and tired when Uncle Obike brought her home. And then Great-uncle Konstantin came and yelled at her, and Mama and Papa yelled at *him* and Papa called him an a-s-s and told him to go away and not come back until he came to his senses."

Eben closed his eyes and rested his forehead on Oriana's dark curls as she finished her story.

"Then Kaia came out of the study and her eyes were all swollen and red, and Papa and Mama had their arms around her and they took her upstairs to stay in Grandmama's chambers and nobody was allowed to go and see her because she was sick."

Eben started. "Kaia was sick?"

Oriana nodded sadly. "Grandmama said her heart was

broken. I didn't know hearts could break, but Mama told me that when people are really sad they get a big ache in their hearts."

She hopped down from Eben's lap and skipped over to peer down at the carp in the pool. "She's better now."

A young woman holding a pair of pink satin slippers emerged from the colonnade, looked around anxiously, and bustled toward them. "Really, Oriana, you will be the death of me, running around in your bare feet. Your mama is frantic. Come along. It's almost time for the ceremony."

"A moment, nurse," Eben said to the woman. He took the slippers from her and knelt down in front of Oriana.

"Here, give me your left foot. No, that's your right. Left."

"I always get mixed up," Oriana said as she stuck out her little foot.

"Now the right. Yes, that one. Oriana, does Lady Kaia know I'm here today?"

"I think Papa told her."

"You said she is better now?"

"I asked her if her heart was fixed. She said sometimes it takes a long time for the ache to go away."

"Yes," Eben said softly, "sometimes it does."

Oriana peered down at her slippers. "Pink," she said happily.

"Very," Eben confirmed. He took her hand and led her back to her nurse.

"Kaia's slippers are yellow. Yellow is a happy color. I think she's getting happier now. She smiles and laughs. Except . . ."

"Yes?"

"She doesn't smile in her eyes, Uncle."

* * *

Eben finally hunted Jibril down in his study, where he had taken refuge from the storm. He planted his hands on the king's desk and demanded, "Why the devil didn't you tell me?"

Jibril leaned back in his chair and raised a brow. "Would you have come back with me if I had?"

Eben ran a hand through his hair "How the devil do I know?"

"Exactly. Oh, do stop scowling at me and sit down, for heaven's sake. Do you want to hear the story or not?"

Eben threw himself into a chair. "Yes, I want to hear the damn story."

"Better. You'll need something to fortify you." Jibril poured a dark purple wine into two goblets from a silver decanter on his desk and handed one to Eben.

"Obike realized you'd managed to make it aboard the *Apostle* before she sailed. Kalan was to bring Morgana back, but she was too distraught to travel, so Obike rode out to Lord Pakka's estate and arranged for one of his wife's maids to travel with Morgana. There wasn't going to be another sailing for a week, but Pakka had one of his larger fishing vessels take Obike to Evros. Since the *Apostle* never arrived in port, everyone assumed she'd gone down in the storm."

"So Obike came back to Suriana."

"No. He stayed in Evros."

"Why?" said Eben. "If he thought we were lost—"

"He didn't. He stayed in Evros to wait for Kaia." Jibril glanced at Eben to gauge his reaction.

"To wait for Kaia?" Eben asked with a frown.

The door to Jibril's study flew open and little Prince Ahriman tumbled in. "Papa, Mama says you're to come at once." When he caught sight of Eben, he flew across the room and launched himself into his lap. "I got a new tooth, Uncle Eben. Want to see?"

Jibril came around the desk and plucked his son from Eben's lap. "Uncle Eben can see your tooth later. Go tell your mama we'll be there in a few minutes." He deposited a protesting Ahriman outside the study door and resumed his seat.

"Obike was waiting for Kaia?" Eben repeated. "I don't understand."

"An old man in a tavern told him the woman he sought would arrive on the *Peacock* from the Western Isles in a week's time. Obike had no reason to believe him, but the fact that the man even knew Obike was looking for a woman piqued his curiosity and he decided to wait until the *Peacock* made port."

"Kaia."

"Kaia."

After the events of the past few weeks, nothing could surprise Eben. "Let me guess. The man was thin, very tall. He wore a midnight-blue cloak."

"How did you know?" asked Jibril in surprise.

Eben heaved a deep sigh. "You wouldn't believe me if I told you."

Jibril rolled his eyes. "Hell, if I believe that this Absalom and your squire disappeared into thin air, I can believe anything."

291

Once again the door flew open. Syrah stood on the threshold and glowered at the two men. "Now."

She turned on her heel and marched off.

Jibril tossed back the last of his wine and stood up.

"A woman of few words. Thank God."

Chapter Thirty-eight

Any suggestion of disorder, cheerful or not, or impulse toward inappropriate behavior vanished at the threshold of the private chapel that served the royal family of the Dominion. It was not the heavy bronze-cast doors that marked this boundary. It was not the intimation of the divine beyond.

It was Master Sprum.

The ancient Keeper of the Rolls stood like an avenging angel with a sword of fire, reminding those who would enter that the rituals would be observed as they had always been, and woe be upon the one, sovereign or serf, who questioned or objected.

Of course, the little Keeper was stone deaf. For all he knew, the priest could be belting out the latest bawdy ditty heard in a city brothel. But everyone loved him and was on their very best behavior from the moment they entered the chapel.

Lord Eben Dhion and Lady Kaia Kurinon performed their roles in the christening of the royal twins in exemplary fashion. They watched solemnly as each little girl was baptized into the faith. As godfather and godmother respectively, each recited the ancient oath without forgetting a single word. They smiled indulgently when one little fist grabbed hold of the archbishop's nose as he sprinkled the second babe with holy water. They stood, they knelt, they prayed.

Outward conduct, however, is not necessarily a true indicator of what is transpiring in the inner man, or woman.

Lord Eben: *I wonder what she's thinking.*

Lady Kaia: *I wonder what he's thinking.*

I can't believe she's here. I saw her in the Circle of Standing Stones with my own eyes.

He came after me. I saw him running toward the circle.

I wonder why she changed her mind.

I wonder why he changed his mind.

And so it went as the ancient words were spoken and ritual united man, woman, and child; past and future. Finally, a low murmur of approval—more likely relief—swept through the crowd as the archbishop proclaimed the final blessing.

Oriana is right. She looks like a beautiful little bee.

He hasn't looked at me once.

The great doors had been thrown open; people were drifting out of the chapel. Master Sprum beamed.

"Aren't they just the cutest little darlings," a stout woman confided to Kaia.

"I understand you've got some fine new breeding stock, Lord Eben. I might be interested in having a look."

She's moving away. She doesn't want to speak to me.

He doesn't want to speak to me. He's moving away.

* * *

Kaia stomped from one end of the queen's bedchamber to the other and back again. "He didn't look at me once. He's hard and cold and I hate him."

Queen Syrah sighed. "You do not hate him, Kaia."

"He hates me!"

"No, he doesn't hate you. He just doesn't know what to say."

"Eben Dhion has never been at a loss for words in his entire life."

Syrah laughed. "I can't argue with that."

"He hasn't one ounce of forgiveness in his black little soul."

"What has he to forgive you for, for heaven's sake?"

"For leaving."

Syrah prayed for patience. "If I have it aright, he told you to go. Besides, you didn't leave," she pointed out.

The door to Syrah's chamber opened. Jibril took one look at Kaia's furious face and groaned. "Are we never to have a moment's peace in this house again?" The door slammed behind him.

The queen was growing more and more uncomfortable. She had not fed the babes since before the ceremony and her breasts were painfully swollen. Kaia's tantrum was in full steam and looked likely to continue for some time, so she summoned her maid and had her tell the nurse to bring the first babe to her.

"There, that's better," she sighed as she settled back with the child at her breast. "Where were we? Oh yes, I was reminding you that you did not, in fact, travel on with your friends, and therefore Eben can have nothing to reproach you for. And it occurs to me that even if you had, he would have no right to do so. It would have been your choice to make."

"You sound like Queen Alya," Kaia said.

Syrah laughed. "I expect I do. She and I are often of the same opinion, although we come to the point in very different ways. I am direct—Jibril would put it rather more strongly—and the queen slides her point into the conversation without one noticing it until much later."

Kaia smiled. "I think she's very wise, although she wouldn't want anyone to say so."

Syrah kissed the top of the little head snuggled against her. "I doubt that anyone but a very wise woman could have lived with Ahriman Dhion for forty years and not been squashed like a beetle. The man was a force of nature."

Kaia dropped into a chair, her anger spent for the moment. "Eben doesn't understand me at all. I might as well still be five years old, as far as he's concerned."

They sat in silence for some minutes. The queen cooed, Kaia brooded.

"Perhaps," Syrah said at last, "it is you who do not understand him."

"I don't?"

"Kaia, most men will form an opinion of this or that—or someone—and cling to it tenaciously, even in the face of any new evidence to the contrary. They are either too lazy or too fearful of change to do so. If they are wrong about this one thing, then, heaven help them, they may be wrong about others. Chaos! I think Eben settled into an inflexible view of his world earlier than most; he became armiger of our House at seventeen after Papa died.

295

You were a child in his mind at that point. You've grown up, but he doesn't dare let go of that image of you."

"But why?"

"Then he would leave himself open to reacting to you as a man would a woman. He wouldn't know how to handle it."

Syrah couldn't miss Kaia's furious blush. "Oh. I see. Well, that puts a new light on things."

Kaia slid off the bed and went to the tall window to hide her discomfiture. She absently plucked at the thick green velvet of the curtain as she stared out over the formal gardens to the city below. "Just because a man . . . knows . . . a woman, it doesn't mean he'll treat her like one."

The nurse bustled in with Syrah's second babe. Kaia was grateful for the interruption. She was terribly embarrassed, and thought to change the subject as soon as the woman left the room.

"You were saying?" Syrah prompted.

It seemed Kaia was not to be let off easily. "I just think men and women don't look at things the same way," she replied, intentionally vague.

"Lust."

Kaia turned around and stared at the queen.

"You're talking about lust, I imagine," Syrah said bluntly. "Men and women most certainly think differently when it comes to lust. In fact, I'm not sure men think at all when it comes to the subject, or at least they have a terrible time thinking past it. It seems to stop most of them dead in their tracks."

Syrah shifted the babe to her shoulder and patted it gently on the back. Kaia heard a tiny belch.

"I don't understand," Kaia said. But she did. Eben had made passionate love to her as a woman, but it really hadn't changed his understanding of her, or his attitude. The scene on the beach at Ataxi had shown that clearly enough.

"Simply put, Kaia, it is a far shorter journey from lust to love for a woman than it is for a man. She must be patient and wait for him to catch up."

Kaia had to laugh. "Like waiting for a small child?"

"Exactly."

"Why is it that every other woman understands these things and I don't?" Kaia grumbled as she wandered around the beautiful room. Syrah had always favored the colors of her own House over the severe scarlet and black of the First House, and her apartments were decorated in subtle tones of sapphire and sea-green and gold. The blue hangings of the enormous high bed were embroidered with blazing golden suns and silver moons and stars strung along sinuous green vines. Kaia wondered what it would be like to lie beside the man one loved in such a bed, lie beneath him and see beyond his powerful shoulders such a sensual panorama.

"On the contrary, most women don't, and because they will not make the effort, they bring down great unhappiness upon themselves. They carp and complain and whine, and nothing changes."

Syrah laid her sleeping child in a silk-hung cradle and glanced out the window. "Oh, dear," she exclaimed.

Kaia joined her. "Oh, dear God!"

Chapter Thirty-nine

Eben thought his head would split open if Prince Konstantin did not soon cease this outburst of unseemly gratitude for the safe return of his child, the fawning, the maudlin sentiment.

If the prince was to be believed, he had known from the outset that Lord Dhion was the man for the job. If anyone in the kingdom could hunt down his wayward daughter, it was he. Thank heavens Eben had been able to save her from certain violation at the hands of savages, whose predilections were known to one and all to be highly unnatural and an abomination in the eyes of God. Virginity was a woman's greatest treasure, was it not? Kaia would go to her husband with her maidenhood intact and in full flower.

The prince understood that Lord Eben had taken the helm himself when the *Apostle* foundered, and brought her safely to shore. He was to be highly commended for ridding the seas of the Ataxian pirates. Ranulph Gyp had richly deserved his fate. God had certainly designated Eben to serve as His instrument in the matter. True, the crafty Brother Absalom had managed to escape, but he was known to be a practitioner of the black arts, and what could a man do in the face of witchery?

"I didn't," Eben finally managed to interject.

"Didn't what?" said Prince Kurinon.

"Retrieve your daughter. She returned of her own accord."

"Bah," cried Lord Kurinon. "On the face of it only. She knew it was only a matter of time before you caught up with her. She thought to save face."

"Papa!" Kaia rushed into the maze. The sight of her father stalking Eben like a fox after a hare had sent her racing out of Syrah's chamber, down the great staircase, and across the garden to stop her father from making more of an idiot of himself than he usually managed to do. He was not a subtle man, though he considered himself the very soul of tact, and Eben would despise him, and by extension her, for his shameless behavior. Kaia knew very well what he was about.

"Ah, and here is Kaia herself," cried Lord Kurinon. "Lovely, is she not? A bit headstrong, but she is young yet. And, er, untouched, if you catch my meaning. Bow to Lord Eben, Kaia. I have just been telling him how very grateful we are for his kindness these past weeks."

"Come, Papa," Kaia urged. "I am sure you have expressed yourself most eloquently. Let us leave Lord Eben to his private thoughts." She managed to turn her father around and shepherd him back toward the little gate that marked the entrance to the maze.

"I hope you will do us the honor of visiting with us soon," Lord Kurinon threw back over his shoulder. "Kaia would be delighted." He trotted across the garden toward the palace, well pleased with himself.

He left behind him in the maze a silence so uncomfortable that neither Kaia nor Eben could think of a single word to say for some minutes. Eben was the first to speak.

"Oriana thinks you look like a bee." It seemed a safe enough way to begin.

Kaia glanced down at her yellow gown and slippers. "I like bees."

Eben nodded. "So Sister Euphemia said."

"And beetles."

"Preferably inside apples. That was very naughty."

Kaia smiled a tiny mischievous smile.

"But then you always have been," Eben observed. "The night you sewed me to my sheets while I slept was probably your finest moment."

"You shouldn't have put the worms in my bath," she retorted. "Nurse couldn't get me to bathe again for a month."

Eben clasped his hands behind his back and strolled casually around the large semicircle of white pebbles that served as a sort of antechamber to the three aisles leading deep into the maze.

"Your tricks weren't all that bad," he conceded, "but you never could carry off a disguise."

"I thought I a made a very credible nun," she said indignantly.

Eben shrugged. "So-so."

"Enough to fool you!"

"For a few minutes. But you made a terrible Arab woman. You kept groaning."

"I did not. That was Jocco."

"Who was doing the praying up front?"

"Brother Absalom."

Eben wasn't quite sure where this seemingly casual conversation was going. There were questions that needed answering and things that needed saying, but neither of them seemed to be able to bring the conversation around to them.

"I will miss him," said Kaia. "He is such a good man, utterly naive and infinitely wise at the same time."

Eben leaned against the back of the bench and hitched his thumbs into his sword belt. "I can't say I think very well of him. It was he who——"

"Convinced me to stay," Kaia finished for him.

It took a moment for that to sink in. "Indeed?"

Kaia tucked her hands behind her back. "I don't think he ever intended for me to go with him."

"And what arguments did he put forth to convince you?"

Kaia smiled. "No arguments; it is not his way. He simply observed that the wise man has no reason to search out what he has already found."

Eben lifted a brow. "And how does this wise man know that he has found it?"

"Brother Absalom never said. Perhaps it is different for each man. One man may reason it out. Another may simply look into his heart. One thing I do know: No one else can tell him, he must learn it for himself. Or herself," Kaia added with a sad little smile.

He could not account for it, but Eben was growing irritable. "I don't think there is much mystery to it. I can think of at least two other reasons you stayed behind," he said.

Kaia could not fail to hear the hint of sarcasm in his voice. He was about to say something she would not like, and this time she had no intention of letting him have at her the way he had at the beach at Omino.

"Whatever it is you are about to say, I don't want to hear it," she snapped as she marched past him toward the garden.

Eben planted himself in front of the gate. "Oh, no, you don't. You can't run away every time something doesn't suit you."

"Move out of my way, Lord Dhion." She had never been so haughty.

"You will not pass, my lady." It would take Jibril's army to move him from the spot.

Kaia eyed him carefully. "Very well."

Eben should have known better than to relax his stance even for a moment.

Kaia whirled around and plunged into the maze.

"Oh, hell, here we go again." he snarled and went after her.

The Dominion maze was considered one of the most difficult to navigate in the known world. Gardeners were always being dispatched to retrieve the hopelessly lost. If a guest did not appear for the evening meal and could not be located in the palace itself, most likely he would be found hours later, sheepish and hungry, somewhere in the maze.

However, if you were a princess and your cousins were princes and princesses and you grew up playing in the palace gardens, you knew every inch of the maze and could lead a merry chase.

"This is exactly what I mean," Eben shouted from a blind alley to Kaia's left. "Women are always changing their minds. Go, stay, go, stay. You probably decided it with a toss of the dice."

"That just shows what you know about it," she shouted back.

A long silence followed as Eben found his way back to the main aisle, while Kaia took a shortcut and tiptoed up behind him.

"Dear God, you drive me crazy, Kaia. Just stop, will you, and we can talk about this."

"Boo!"

Eben spun around and went for her. She danced out of his reach and darted away, laughing.

Eben stopped and listened. He heard a muffled giggle. She was close by, he was sure.

"I'm not going to play this silly game with you, Kaia. I just spent weeks trailing after you from one end of the world to the other. We are adults now and must be done with games. When you've had your fun, I'll be on the bench by the gate."

"How do you intend to do that, Lord Arrogance?" a voice whispered from the other side of the hedge. She could not have been more than three paces from him, but it would probably take an hour for him to reach the spot, and by then, of course, she could have been anywhere.

"It so happens," said he, "that I know how to find my way out of a maze. The eyes may deceive, but the hand will not."

"Oh." He did know, she thought, disappointed. All he had to do was trail his hand along the hedge and eventually he would find the way out.

"If you're going to stay in here and brood, brood on this, Kaia: It is my opinion that you chose to stay behind precisely because I told you to go."

Jennie Klassel

Kaia wandered out of the maze half an hour later. She had needed the time to get her thoughts together. She perched on the lip of a small fountain in which a grinning little cherub was relieving himself on a lily pad, and eyed Eben, who was sprawled at his ease on the bench by the gate.

"Are we going to talk now, or are we going to play games?" Eben inquired.

"Talk."

"Good. You may begin."

Kaia bristled. "Why must I be first? Because you tell me so?"

"Kaia, please," Eben groaned.

"Oh, all right.

"Eben," she said at last. "When you look at me, what do you see?"

"A bee," he answered promptly.

"Now who is playing games?" She glowered at him. "Be serious."

"I see Kaia. What do you see when you look at me?"

"I see Eben."

"Well," said Eben with a smile, "now we're getting somewhere. Next question."

Kaia smoothed out a crease in her gown. "Do you see a woman?" She didn't dare look at him.

"I see a woman."

"And when you made love to me, were you making love to a woman?"

Eben laughed. "I can honestly say I harbored not a single doubt."

Kaia got up and started pacing around the little cherub

304

and his lily pad. "I gave myself to you freely, of my own choice."

"You did," he said softly.

"You would not have taken me if I had not chosen to give myself to you."

Eben stretched out his long legs and watched her moving about the clearing, wondering where she was going with this. "You know I would not. It would probably have killed me, but I would have stopped."

"Not twelve hours later I made another choice. Gyp was about to kill you. I chose to try to stop him. Was I a woman then, a woman making a choice of her own free will?"

Eben surged to his feet. "It's not at all the same thing," he snapped. "You had no right to put yourself in such danger."

"It is exactly the same thing," she cried. "I had every right to make that choice!"

"You had no idea how dangerous Gyp could be," Eben stormed. "He would have used you in the most loathsome ways for his pleasure, then dangled you before Jibril like a worm upon a hook."

"Yes, he would have. And yes, I may have made a poor job of it. But can't you see? I was the only one who could gain access to his bedchamber. I was the only one who could distract him until Merlin and the others arrived. I could not let you die, so I chose to do what I could. Would you not have done the same for me?"

Eben's jaw was clenched so tight that he could barely get the words out. "You know I would."

"On the beach you berated me, called me a fool, called me a child for it. I may have been a foolish young girl when I left the convent, Eben, but when we made love I was a woman, and when I went to your aid, I was a woman. And when I chose to step out of the circle, I made the choice as a woman. I am not a child, Eben. You must take me as a woman or not at all."

Eben held out a hand. "Come to me, Kaia."

She shook her head. "No, Eben. You must come to me."

"As you will, my lady," he said softly.

And then his arms were around her.

"Kaia, Kaia. You have to understand what happened at Ataxi. From the moment I saw that island I knew I had been brought there for some higher purpose. When I learned that Ranulph Gyp ruled, I thought that purpose was to wreak vengeance upon him for past wrongs. Ranulph Gyp tried to take from me everything I ever cared about. He seized our hall. He murdered my great-uncle, tried to rape Syrah. He would have killed me, stolen my patrimony. For his crimes King Ahriman sent him into exile, and I was left with the festering anger any man, even a boy of fourteen, would feel at being so wronged and having no recourse to act."

"Why, then, did you not just kill him and have done?"

"When I learned what he had done to the people of Ataxi, made fools of the men, enslaved them, I saw that I could help overthrow him. I will not say that I abjured my own need for vengeance altogether, but I would have left the place a lesser man if I had not done what I could to free those people from their oppression. Your words upon the road were not lost on me."

"You did what you had to do and you did it well," Kaia said.

"Yes, I believe I did."

Kaia gently freed herself from his embrace. "As did I. Why can you not see that?"

Eben followed her to the bench and then moved to settle her on his lap, tucking her head beneath his chin.

"I can now, but at the time all I could see was that he was still trying to take what was mine—you, my Kaia—and that you made it possible for him to do so by entering his lair. I had not yet sorted out all that anger when we argued on the beach that day. I said all the wrong things. I let you believe I wanted to be done with you, when all I really wanted was to hold you fast and safe forever."

"I didn't go," Kaia said against his neck.

"Why did you stay, Kaia?"

"You promised to marry me."

"I did?" asked Eben in surprise. "When did I do that?"

"You were fourteen. I was three. You promised to marry me when we grew up. A promise is a promise."

"So it is," he murmured against the soft braid of her hair. "Will you marry me, little Kaia?"

"I will marry you, my lord."

A gentle purple dusk crept through the city of Suriana. It settled over the palace gardens. It drifted through the great maze where so many had lost their way.

Kaia brushed her lips against Eben's neck. "When you look at me, what do you see? Do you see a woman?"

"Let me think. Hmmm. No, I'm sorry."

She leaped from his lap and confronted him, hands on hips. "Just what do you see?" she demanded.

Eben leaned back and smiled at the glowering figure in the growing dark. "I told you, I see a bee."

"I am not a bee."

"A beautiful yellow bee in yellow bee slippers with beautiful black bee eyes."

The bee threw up her hands in disgust and marched away.

"Lady Kaia."

"Bzzzz?" said she.

"Run."

"Whyyy?" she teased, backing away toward the maze.

Eben stalked toward her. "I have found I rather like chasing you."

"Should I allow you catch me, sir?"

"That, my lady, must be your own choice."

Laughing, Lady Kaia Kurinon whirled around and she ran.